BEAUTY
AND THE
SCALPEL

PETER RALPH

Typesetting and layout by WorkingType Design

Prologue

New York 1990

For nearly a year, the judge had encouraged and harangued the warring parties to settle a bitter medical malpractice suit.

Uncompromising lawyers haggled over minor points, then argued and bitched over jury selection. Countless depositions had been taken from nurses, doctors, receptionists, anesthesiologists, psychiatrists, other expert witnesses and even the operating room cleaning team. At midday on the second day of the trial, after the opening addresses, the parties were finally talking compromise. The judge expressed his relief, directed the parties to be genuine in their attempts to settle and stayed the trial until the following day.

Counsel for Dr. Jack Donahue, appointed by his medical indemnity insurers told him that he wouldn't be needed in the settlement negotiations.

"Trust me, Jack. We're going to beat out the best deal that we can."

Donahue glanced around and saw a nurse wheel Valerie Fielding from the courtroom. There was no point in her attending the negotiations as she could barely put two words together. Donahue didn't lack compassion, but it wasn't his fault. Since that terrible day, one thought had haunted him. Would death have been better than living as a vegetable for the rest of her life?

Donahue waited a few minutes before making his way out of the courtroom and into the corridor. He watched as half a dozen lawyers for the plaintiff, followed by his lawyers and respective counsel for the hospital, anesthesiologist and the nurses filed into an adjoining meeting room. Why the insurers for the anesthesiologist and hospital had let it get this far was beyond Donahue, and he couldn't understand why they hadn't settled earlier.

Valerie Fielding, an exotic dancer and the nineteen-year-old mother of a three-year-old girl, had approached her local doctor about breast augmentation. The doctor had been at college with Donahue, and knowing that he had just completed his plastic surgery training, referred Valerie to him. The procedure was simple, and Donahue had performed it many times under the watchful eyes of more senior, experienced surgeons. The operation at the Manhattan Cosmetic Hospital had gone smoothly, and Donahue had checked Valerie in recovery before rushing off to watch the Giants play the Eagles at Giants Stadium.

Donahue had just sat down at the football game with his friends when his cell phone rang, and a panicked anesthesiologist informed him that he had had to give Valerie chest compressions and atropine to sustain her life after her heartbeat became very low. Donahue cursed the anesthesiologist, watched two more plays and then drove back to the hospital. An ambulance with lights flashing and sirens blaring nearly collided with him at the entrance. It was carrying Valerie Fielding to Manhattan General Hospital; where she would remain in a coma for two months before gradually coming out of it severely brain damaged. Barely able to speak she could no longer walk, feed or bathe herself and was incapable of looking after her young daughter. Sadly, Valerie's state of awareness was just enough for her to understand the tragedy that had befallen her and she was chronically depressed.

The media had savaged Donahue, and *The New York Tribune's* editorial headlined the disaster, *Doctor Leaves Teenage Mother in Coma* and gone on to say:

Plastic surgeon, Dr. Jack Donahue, has performed a breast augmentation that has left his patient severely brain damaged and fighting for her life. Dr. Donahue has just commenced practice and at twenty-nine, is one of, if not, the youngest plastic surgeon in the country. While the circumstances are still being investigated, one question that needs answering is, how does someone so young become board certified? Plastic surgeons take their patients' lives in their hands every day, and Dr. Donahue only completed college a mere seven years ago. Since then, Dr. Donahue had to prove his competence in general and plastic surgery to his peers before attaining certification. One doctor, who declined to be named said, "Dr. Donahue is a brilliant surgeon, but he tends to be brash, impatient and overconfident."

Brashness, impatience, and overconfidence are generally associated with youth, and perhaps board certification should be contingent on a level of experience and maturity as well as surgical skills.

Talk-back Jocks jumped on the bandwagon labeling Dr. Donahue the boy surgeon, and many callers said they wouldn't trust a surgeon that young.

Donahue had fumed when the media besmirched his reputation. His lawyers agreed that many of the comments were defamatory, but they cautioned him against taking any action that would keep his name in the public eye. Donahue had no gripe with being described as brash, impatient and overconfident, but the claims about his purported inexperience infuriated him. Last Christmas while most of America enjoyed a short break, he, along with two 'know-it-all' professors had dissected forty cadavers and prepared a groundbreaking peer-reviewed article for *Lancet*. He had been furious when his name appeared last in the article, because it had been his surgical skills – his alone – that had resulted in the breakthroughs. Yes, he was brash, but there was a unique magic in his long, slim fingers. He wasn't outrageous enough to say it, but he had no doubt that he was without peer. To his few friends, he would say, "I am to plastic surgery what Michael Jordan was to basketball."

Donahue had been raised by his mother from the age of thirteen after his parents had gone through an acrimonious divorce. His father had been a brilliant investor and the family had lived an indulgent lifestyle until they were brought back to earth by the 1973/74 stock market crash. The previously happy marriage became punctuated with fights over money, and when the bank foreclosed on their luxurious apartment in Carnegie Hill, Manhattan, it was the straw that broke the union. His father, the man he had idolized, turned to alcohol and became a drunken bum.

Young Jack Donahue had lived a privileged life, been spoiled and never wanted for anything. Before exams, his father would hire a team of private tutors ensuring Jack finished near the top of his class. He had always been led to believe that when the time came, he'd have his choice of Ivy League colleges. When his father walked out, his mother had just enough money to buy a small house in Brookville, Queens. Jack was dragged out of private school and sent to a public school. With one exception, his friends avoided him and didn't return his calls. He despised the father he'd never see again, resented his mother, and felt a deep sense of shame.

The culture change was enormous, and Jack sulked and wallowed in self-pity for six months. He swore at his mother, threw tantrums and was a constant pain in the ass. He was smart but lazy. As time went by, he realized that the luxuries of private school and tuition were gone forever. Slowly it dawned on him that the only way he could re-attain his previous lifestyle was through education. After this, he knuckled down and pushed himself through high school, college and surgical training on scholarships, government grants, his mother working as a cleaner, and mortgaging the house in Queens.

The wealth he perceived as stolen from him by his parents and the adversity that followed drove him relentlessly. His two goals were to be the best plastic surgeon in the world and to be filthy rich. He believed that he'd already achieved his first goal, and was being impeded from accomplishing the second by something for which he bore no responsibility.

Since that fateful day with Valerie Fielding, referrals from other doctors had dried up, and responses to his advertisements were non-existent. Only the reconstructive surgery that he was performing for two large hospitals enabled him to keep his head above water. With the court case and the investigations eating into his time, he was barely making enough to make ends meet.

Lawyers for the opposing sides worked through the night and just before midnight settlement was reached. The following morning, Donahue met his lead counsel, Phillip Shriver, on the steps of the courthouse.

"Jack, you'll be pleased to know it's all over."

"How much did she get?"

"Twenty million."

"Jesus! What's the apportionment?"

"That's unimportant. The important thing is that you can get on with your life."

"You didn't answer my question. How much is my insurer in for?"

"If you must know, fifty percent. The hospital twenty-five, the anesthesiologist twenty-five and the nurses nothing."

"Fifty? Fuck! Didn't you listen to me? I didn't do anything wrong. Nothing! That incompetent anesthesiologist should have been up for eighty percent and the hospital the rest. You sold me out. The media's going to crucify me."

"You don't get it do you, Jack? You're the captain of an Airbus A320, and you've just crashed. Now you want to blame your first officer, Airbus, the flight attendants, anyone but yourself. Do you think the insurers like paying out on your behalf?"

"It's bullshit. I did nothing wrong. Nothing!" Donahue growled through tightly compressed lips.

"It's the law. I've been trying cases like this since before you were born. The next time you go into an operating room think of yourself as an A320 captain and everyone else in there as being reliant on you for their safety. I'm going to ask the court to seal the settlement. Come on, let's not keep the judge waiting."

Jack Donahue was fuming as he took a seat behind his lawyers. Counsel for the plaintiff addressed the judge and then the silver-haired, smooth talking Phillip Shriver took his turn. Donahue heard nothing. Despite the sealed settlement, the media would lay the blame at his feet. It would set him back years, and those surgeons he'd rubbed up the wrong way would tell everyone that he was incompetent. He looked around and saw his only supporter, Vance Morgan, standing at the back of the court. The judge said something and loud applause came from behind Donahue, and he turned to see the plaintiff's family hugging and kissing. Valerie Fielding was still not much more than a vegetable, but fourteen million after fees would buy an awful lot of care. The family's ordeal was far from over, but the financial pressures were gone. The judge thanked the jurors before discharging them. Five minutes later he left the bench, and there was more cheering and back slapping, this time from the plaintiff's lawyers. Anger coursed through Jack Donahue. The bloodsuckers were celebrating their six million dollar fee. He hated them even more than he hated the anesthesiologist and the media.

"Let's go," Shriver said, "it's all over. You can get on with your life now."

"Some life," Donahue replied, "no one in this city is going to be beating my door down for a facelift or nose job."

As they reached the steps, they were joined by Vance Morgan, who looked over at Donahue, and said, "That was a bad beat, buddy."

"Hello, Vance," Shriver said, "can you knock some sense into your friend's head? For the past year, he's been telling me he's the greatest plastic surgeon in the world. Can you bring him back to reality?"

"He is," Morgan replied. "He did everything by the book and still got screwed because you didn't have the guts to try and convince that dumbass jury of the truth."

"You still don't get it, do you?" Shriver said. "The neurologist who operated on Valerie Fielding at Manhattan General was going to testify that her blood pressure plummeted during the implant surgery. According to him, the medication administered to raise her blood pressure triggered the heart attack. He would've buried us."

"That's not Jack's responsibility. It's the anesthesiologist's," Morgan said.

"Really? How do you think the jury would've reacted when they found Jack couldn't drag himself away from the football game to look after his patient?"

"Two plays," Morgan said. "Two plays!"

"Thanks, Vance," Donahue said, wringing his hands. "It wasn't Phillip. He just did what the insurance company instructed. Weak bastards! I don't know what I'm going to do? I'm certainly not going to have any clients here for a long time."

"Come on, buddy, snap out of it," Morgan said. "You're the best. You're young, tall and macho. The ladies love you. You just have to tough it out for a few months."

"You don't have to stay here. What's wrong with the west coast?" Shriver asked.

"It stinks. I like New York. I don't want to go anywhere else."

"I don't know whether you're half as good as what you and Vance claim," Shriver said. "I do know that your presentation is terrible. You come across as a smartass, and even without you saying a word, the jury sensed it. They didn't like you, and if the trial had run its course, I'd hate to think what the punitive damages might have been. You sure wouldn't be my choice for a nose job or brow lift. I'd like to believe you're the best, but you're too full of yourself. Too salesy. I've acted for plastic surgeons who are smooth and laid back. You're too intense and too demanding. You're not selling used cars; you're selling eternal youth. It doesn't figure."

"For Chrissake, Phil," Morgan said, "with friends like you, who needs enemies? I went through college with Jack, and I'm still doing my surgical training. He borders on genius."

Donahue frowned. After he'd been dragged out of private school, Vance Morgan was the one friend who stuck fat. He was a distant relative of the famous and wealthy J P Morgan family. Inseparable at college, they were players and party goers, and no female was safe from them. Vance was Nordic-looking with blonde hair, blue eyes, and a boyish charm. He was still struggling to finish college when Donahue commenced his surgical training. They had drifted apart but maintained some contact over the phone. Donahue's obsession with money intensified after he was board certified while Morgan would probably party for the rest of his life. They were an odd couple.

"Phillip, if it hadn't been for Valerie Fielding, we'd have never met, and my supposed lack of tact would be a non-issue. Let me tell you why. I am the best, and when word got out about my results, clients would've been beating down my door," Donahue said, holding up his hands. "These can work miracles."

"Yeah, yeah," Shriver replied. "Didn't you hear a word I said? Anyhow, you can be sure of one thing. No one's going to be beating down your door in New York. If you're going to have a future, you need to think about the west coast."

"No. I'm not going to California. It's a rat race. GPs and even quacks without any form of qualification call themselves cosmetic surgeons out there."

"It's a great place to party, though," Morgan chipped in.

Shriver shook his head. "I just remembered. Have you ever been to Australia?"

"No. Why do you ask?"

"You want to continue living and working in the Big Apple. My wife calls Sydney, a mini New York. She says it's thriving, and there's a lot of money down there. If you're looking for a fresh start, you could do worse."

"It's the ass end of the world. I wouldn't know anyone. I wouldn't have any clients."

"I'll come down and visit," Morgan said. "I love those Aussie girls."

"You just told me you haven't got any clients here," Shriver said. "You could work in their hospitals for a few years. Build up your contacts and when you're ready, throw up a shingle and start practicing again. You should pay Sydney a visit."

"He's got a point," Morgan said, "and before you go, we'll have a farewell party at my folks' place in the Hamptons. You haven't been there for years."

Beaumont wrestled with Shriver's suggestion for weeks before arranging a ninety-day work visa at The Royal Sydney Hospital. The hospital had organized his accommodation and if he didn't like it down under, it was only three months.

At his farewell party, Donahue had been cornered by Vance's wealthy industrialist father. "Jack, you've declined our invitation to Thanksgiving for God knows how many years. Did we do something to offend you?"

Donahue felt himself start to color. "I'm sorry, Mr. Morgan. That Thanksgiving football game can get pretty rowdy, and I couldn't risk damaging my hands."

"You should have said something. We wouldn't have forced you to play, even though you're a terrific wide receiver." Mr. Morgan laughed.

"I would've felt silly. It was easier to decline."

"Jack, I know how ambitious you are, and I'm not surprised that you wanted to protect your prime assets. I wish Vance was more like you."

"Thanks."

"Some words of advice before you go. I don't know if your mother ever said anything to you, but your father was one of the smartest men I ever met. His problem was greed. He borrowed thirty million on margin, and the stock market started to tank. He could've sold his portfolio, taken a small loss and still been a wealthy man. Instead, he was greedy. He hung on hoping the market would recover."

"I never knew that. It was all so sudden."

"You were too young. Look, you're going to provide a service and your income will depend on the hours you work. You'll be rich, but not as rich as you aspire to be. You'll need to invest wisely or sell a product distinct from your service to achieve your goals. Don't make the mistake of becoming too greedy like your father. Good luck, young man."

BOOK 1

SYDNEY 1992

– THE EARLY YEARS

Chapter 1

The Royal Sydney Hospital comprised two facilities, a large public hospital, and a smaller private hospital within it. It had served Sydney-siders for over sixty years, and while old, it'd had many face-lifts and was fully functional. The public hospital catered to those who couldn't afford private health insurance or highly priced specialists. Dr. Simon Beaumont sat in a small office on the 4th floor looking at the worried face of Mrs. Helena Brown, her husband, Ted, and her seven-year-old son, Timothy.

"Mrs. Brown, we went over this last week," Beaumont said. "You know that Timmy was born with microtia. Unless I operate he'll go through life with a stub rather than a right ear. As I explained to you, I'll remove a little of Timmy's rib cartilage and build a new ear. In six months' time his ears will be a perfect aesthetic match."

"Will he have any hearing in that ear?"

Beaumont sighed. "Mrs. Brown, you're going over old ground. There is nothing I can do about Timmy's middle ear. There'll be no hearing improvement. You told me last time you were here that Timmy was having the surgery."

"Jeez, Helena," her husband said, "the kids at school are torment-ing the hell out of him. We need to let the doctor do his stuff."

Mrs. Brown was thirtyish but looked older. Her face was a sickly white and filled with stress. "Dr. Beaumont, you're very young to be a surgeon. Is it a complex procedure? Have you performed it before?"

Beaumont glanced at his watch. The traffic was building as the evening peak hour approached and the sounds of brakes screeching and impatient car horns could be heard in the background.

"Yes, as I told you, it's an intricate procedure. In the U.S., some plas-tic surgeons do nothing else but specialize in it. Sculpting the ear from the cartilage is a work of art. That said, I have successfully performed the procedure many times. I assure you, Timmy's in the very best of hands," Beaumont said, flexing his long fingers.

Mr. Brown tugged uncomfortably at his collar and tie. He was deeply tanned, and it was obvious that he worked outdoors. "Jeez, Luv, the doc's right. We're just going around in circles. You've gotta decide whether we go ahead or leave Timmy as he is."

"No, Mom," Timmy shouted, "you promised I'd look like the other kids. You promised."

Beaumont glanced at his watch again. "Timmy's booked in for surgery early on Friday afternoon. I have many patients ready to take his place. If you decide not to go ahead, I don't know when it will be possible to reschedule. It could be months."

Still Mrs. Brown persisted. "What about the second operation?"

"We're going over old ground," Beaumont said, his patience starting to wane. "I'll do it in four months. It's simple. I'll incise the ear, and with skin taken from Timmy's bottom, I'll pack the ear with a skin graft. It will grow like a normal ear, and no one will be able to tell the difference from the other ear."

Timmy jumped off his father's knee, crossed his arms and stared defiantly at his mother. "Mom, I want to have the operation. I really want to."

Mrs. Brown frowned. "I hope I'm making the right decision. We'll see you on Friday."

"You have, Mrs. Brown," Beaumont said, standing to let the Browns know the consultation was over.

As they were leaving Beaumont overheard Mrs. Brown say, "Damn Yank. God, what an arrogant, cold fish."

Beaumont smiled. Within two years, he'd be charging ten thousand dollars for performing the same procedure on rich kids.

Beaumont's cell phone rang, and he answered without looking at the screen. "Dr. Simon Beaumont speaking."

"Simon Beaumont," he heard his mom say, not trying to hide the sarcasm. "What type of name is that? What was wrong with Jack Donohue?"

"Jesus, give me a break. You know why I did it. Besides, Jack Donahue sounds more like an FBI agent than a plastic surgeon."

"Hmmph, that's stupid. When are you coming home? I haven't seen you for six months. I'm struggling. I still have the mortgage that paid for your education, you know."

"I'm sending you as much as I can. Once I'm back in private practice, I'll get rid of the damn mortgage."

"Is that how you express your gratitude?"

"Jesus! Get off my back."

"Don't talk to me like that. You didn't answer me. When are you coming home?"

"I'm not going to listen to you whining," Beaumont said under his breath.

"What? What was that you said?"

"I said I'll be home just as soon as I have a bankroll. I don't know how long that's going to take. Right now I'm focused on getting admitted to the Australian Institute of Plastic Surgeons."

"Why? I'm sure you're far more qualified than the yokels down there. They should be glad to have you."

Beaumont grimaced. He guessed he'd inherited his lack of tact from his mother. "It's not a backwater. Some of the world's finest surgeons practice here."

"Rubbish. None of them could hold a candle to you."

It was incredibly difficult to become a plastic surgeon in Australia, and only a tiny number of doctors were accepted for training each year. At first, Beaumont had been concerned, but when he woke up to what was going on, he was pleased. The Institute was controlling the numbers and ensuring that its members earned big bucks. The exact opposite of what was occurring in California. Beaumont had impressed everyone at The Royal Sydney with his surgical skills. Two senior Australian plastic surgeons doing pro bono reconstructive surgery in the private hospital had penned glowing recommendations about his prowess. The elder of the two, silver-haired Brett Golding, was in his mid-fifties and Sydney's king of plastic surgery. He spoke with a plum in his mouth, drove the latest Bentley, and his private practice was in Sydney's exclusive Pitt Street. The Armani-suited Golding was the first choice of the wives and children of Sydney's rich and famous. Beaumont wasn't in a screaming rush to become a member of the Institute. He was still building contacts, and it would be at least a year before he was ready to hang his shingle out.

"I have to go. They're paging me. I have to go to the operating theater. We'll talk soon."

"Theater? What are you talking about?"

"They call the operating room the operating theater down here. I have to go. Goodbye."

As he pressed the end button, he heard his mother say, "God, they sound so backward."

I know why you paid for my education, Mother. You thought I'd be your cash cow. You're going to be disappointed, he thought. Not once during the conversation had he called her mom.

As Beaumont sat in his dingy office behind a small desk, he pondered the events of the past year. After he'd changed his name, it had taken an eternity to get all the other documents changed. His driver's license, passport, certifications and other documents had to be notarized. Perhaps it was because he'd instructed his lawyers to effect the name change in Anchorage. He wasn't worried about his immediate future but was thinking twenty years down the road. By then he expected to be famous and wealthy and didn't want to make it easy for some prying journalist to dig up his past. He was sure that no one would remember Valerie Fielding by then, but it didn't hurt to be cautious.

Beaumont's Qantas flight to Sydney was uneventful until the Aussie pilot was preparing to land the 747. He'd come over the PA and said, "Folks, as a special treat I'm bringing you in via the scenic route. If you look out to the right, you'll see the most spectacular sight in world aviation. Sydney Harbor, Sydney Harbor Bridge, the largest single span bridge in the world, and the eighth wonder of the world, the Sydney Opera House. Welcome to Sydney."

Sydney was everything that Phillip Shriver's wife had said it was. It was big, brash and in your face. The taxi drivers drove like there was no tomorrow, the traffic buzzed and if a driver missed a turn-off he just kept on driving rather than risk slowing down. The girls were sporty, attractive and easy going. The men were forthright and lacked subtlety, but Sydney also had more than its share of conmen.

Within two weeks of arriving, Beaumont had been approached with a "don't miss opportunity" to buy a condominium and later a holiday time-share. Everyone had something to sell. The wealthy were mostly new, self-made and Sydney boasted many multi-billionaires. Kings Cross was the red-light area where blokes could buy anything or get any imaginable sexual act so long as they had money. There was another distinct similarity to New York. Just like the Big Apple's rivalry with Boston, there was intense competition between Sydney and Australia's other big city, Melbourne, six hundred miles to the south. The southern city was home to many old money families, theaters, excellent restaurants, art galleries and hosted many world class sporting events that drew enormous crowds. Melbournians liked to think they were upmarket and a lot classier than their brash northern neighbors.

For Simon Beaumont, Sydney was just a smaller version of New York, and he loved everything about his new home.

Chapter 2

Two nurses ran behind Simon Beaumont as he went in and out of wards checking his post-op patients. The heavy swinging doors invariably swung back in the nurses' faces, but their comfort was the least of Beaumont's concerns. The last patient he saw was a young woman whose hair had been caught in a meat grinder, resulting in shocking facial damage. She would need many more operations. "Can you repair my face?" she pleaded.

You'd be a $40,000 job if I was in private practice, and yes, I'm the only surgeon in the world who can restore you to normality. "I'll do my best," he said.

Beaumont finished his rounds and was waiting for an elevator when he bumped into Brett Golding.

"Simon, how are you coping with this heat wave?"

"Fine, Brett. It sure beats the arctic weather I left behind in New York."

"We need to talk. Let's have coffee in the cafeteria. The noise will afford us some privacy," Golding said.

The cafeteria was buzzing, but there was one free table, overlooking the street with a reserved sign on it. "That's ours," Golding said. As soon as they sat down, a cafeteria attendant took their orders. All the other tables were self-serve. Beaumont momentarily glanced at the older man. He'd had work done. Very good work. A facelift, a forehead or temple lift, and liposuction of the chin and neck. He'd also had Botox in his forehead and fillers in his cheeks. On a good day, he'd pass for forty. The work was subtle, so subtle that only the trained eye of another plastic surgeon would pick it.

"I don't have much time," Golding said. "I want to tell you about our unofficial rules, but before I do, I want to compliment you. You've made a big impression in the nine months you've been here. You're a fine surgeon. I know you got a bum rap in New York."

"Thank you, but I'm not sure I understand."

"You will if you listen, and save your questions until after I'm finished."

"Okay," Beaumont replied, as the cafeteria attendant returned with two lattes.

"Firstly, New South Wales is bigger than Texas, and Sydney's population is greater than most cities in the U.S."

Beaumont sipped his coffee and wondered where the pompous, little man was going with the statistics.

"I mention this because when you're admitted to the Institute later this year, it will result in a doubling of the annual intake."

"You only admit one surgeon a year? Jesus!"

"Please, let me finish. We do this to maintain the highest standards. We want only the crème de la crème. When we admit you, there'll be thirty-seven plastic surgeons in the state. That's ample."

Yes, Beaumont thought, *and you're also protecting your members' incomes from competition. I love it.*

"We know what's happening in California, Florida and to a lesser extent, New York. Anyone with a medical qualification can throw up a shingle and practice plastic surgery. The same thing's starting to occur here. We approached the government seeking to regulate the practice of plastic surgery to only Institute qualified practitioners. They told us we were greedy bastards looking to feather our nests," a red-faced Golding said, wringing his hands. "Well, there's a lot of second-rate surgery being performed here; by non-plastic surgeons. Seeing the bloody government wouldn't help us, we took matters into our own hands."

Beaumont put his hand to his mouth to conceal a smile. Golding's pompous accent had vanished, and he sounded like a Sydney taxi driver.

"As plastic surgeons, we are approached by legal firms asking us to act as expert witnesses. It's quite profitable." Golding winked. "However, this is where the rules come into play. If the defendant is a plastic surgeon, we refuse to help the plaintiff or his lawyers in any way. If the defendant is a dermatologist, ophthalmologist, gynecologist, general practitioner or some other imposter who shouldn't be practicing in our field, we refuse to act as expert witnesses for them. However, we will act for the plaintiffs in actions against them. Do you understand where I'm coming from?"

"Of course."

"Does it present you with any problems?"

After what had happened to him in New York, Beaumont had no objections. He also knew that an affirmative answer would see his application for membership of the Institute rejected. "No," he responded.

As if reading his mind, Golding said, "Most patients, excluding mine, consult with three surgeons before deciding who to use. We don't badmouth each other, and, we say that so long as a plastic surgeon performs the procedure, they'll get an excellent result. If one of us were to breach the unofficial rules, every other surgeon would find fault with his work, and it'd soon become common knowledge."

"They'd be out of business."

"Quite so. I'm glad you understand." Golding smiled, the plum in his mouth having returned.

A slim auburn-haired woman walked past their table, tersely saying, "Hello, Brett."

Golding smirked. "Hello, Debbie." When she was out of earshot, he muttered, "Bitch!"

"Why did you say that?" Beaumont asked.

"She's a psychiatrist from New Zealand who thinks her shit doesn't stink. Every doctor in the hospital has tried to get into her pants, but she won't put out. She's a tease, a dike, or maybe both." Golding said. "I put my hand on her ass in the elevator one day, and she screamed sexual harassment."

"What happened?"

"She didn't pursue it. She knew that if she had, she'd never work in another Australasian hospital."

"You have that much influence?"

"Three phone calls and I would've figuratively fucked her." Golding laughed. "It doesn't pay to get on the wrong side of me."

That's the second warning he's given me Beaumont thought. *I don't like the obnoxious little prick, but I need to tread carefully.* "I can see that."

"Anyhow the bitch was just a hiccup. There's plenty of action in this hospital, but you already know that. You've been very active."

"I wouldn't say that." Beaumont grinned.

"Don't be modest. You'll never match me. I've screwed hundreds of nurses, residents, interns and doctors. It's a smorgasbord of hot flesh – you'll have your fill. There's a very attractive nurse sitting at the third table on the right who hasn't taken her eyes off you. The brunette with olive skin and legs up around her neck. I think she'd like to wrap them around you. Anyhow, I have to fly, but I'm glad we had this little talk," Golding said, getting up. "If you have any problems, please call me. Oh, we never had this conversation."

Beaumont glanced over at the nurse and held his palms out. She came over to the table but didn't sit down. "Did you want me, Dr. Beaumont?"

"I was going to ask you to join me for coffee, but I have surgery in fifteen minutes. How do you know my name?"

"I was your scrub nurse when you operated on that young Aboriginal girl with the deformed eye socket. What you did was nothing short of miraculous."

"I thought I recognized you," Beaumont said. "Sandra, isn't it? No, Sonya."

"I'm flattered that you even remember me, let alone my name." Sonya laughed.

Beaumont glanced at his watch. "I have to rush. I don't expect I'll get away before six-thirty tonight. Would you like to take a ferry ride to Manly for a drink and dinner after I finish? We'll get the sea breeze off the harbor."

"How about I go one better? Why don't I come to your place and cook you dinner? I bet it's been ages since you've had a home cooked meal. You provide the wine."

"Sounds great," Beaumont said, jotting his address and phone number down on a paper napkin and handing it to her.

"Wolseley Road, Point Piper. I'm impressed."

"Don't be, it's the cheapest apartment in the street, but it does have views of the harbor. Shall we say 7:30?"

"That's perfect, Dr. Beaumont."

"Simon, call me Simon, Sonya. I'm looking forward to tonight."

"Me too."

As Beaumont hurried along the corridor, he thought about Vance and their college womanizing days. He was reliving them, and the women were stunning.

Beaumont scrubbed his hands and arms, then pushed open the door to the OR with his hip. A nurse draped a sterile towel over his hands, and he dried them. She then helped him put on a sterile gown before he shoved his hands into a pair of sterile latex gloves.

The mildly sedated patient was supine and covered to his jawline with a sterile sheet. The ink lines Beaumont had drawn around his nose and cheeks in the morning stood out in stark contrast to his pale skin. The anesthesiologist was in position, standing above the patient's head. Danny Carter was a twenty-two-year-old football player who had run into a goal post at full speed, breaking his nose and knocking himself out. The upper part of his nose was twisted, and there was a large hump where the bone had broken. The football club and Danny had not been insured, and he had been waiting for surgery on the public system for nearly two years. It was an ugly break. When Beaumont told Danny what he would look like after surgery, the young man had broken down. Now the anesthesiologist asked Danny to count to ten and by the time he reached five he was with the fairies. Beaumont nodded to a nurse, and Verdi's Rigoletto filled the theater.

"If he'd seen a surgeon at the time, it could've been straightened in less than twenty minutes," Beaumont said to the scrub nurse. "Instead, we're going to be chiseling, filing and resetting for four hours. What a waste of my valuable time."

"Yes, Doctor," the nurse responded as Beaumont made an incision below the nose as a prelude to elevating the skin.

A fourth year resident, Tom Logan, was a little slow in holding the skin back with a retractor. "For Chrissake, Tom," Beaumont snarled. "I haven't got all fucking day. If you're not alert, you might as well piss off.".

Three and a half hours later he closed the incisions in the nostrils with dissolvable sutures and the external incision below Danny's nose with sutures removable in four days. In time, the thin scar would become almost invisible. While his nose was extremely swollen, Beaumont was pleased with his handiwork. It was straight, and the hump was gone. In two months' time when the swelling had subsided, Danny wouldn't know himself.

At precisely 7:30, Sonya knocked on the door of Beaumont's third-floor apartment. She was wearing a sleeveless, yellow cotton dress with matching sandals and carrying a large car cooler. Beaumont mentally undressed her as he took the cooler. "It's heavy. You should've called me."

"It's fine," she said, looking around the living room before focusing on the coffee table. "Why all the law books? Are you studying law?"

"No, it's just a hobby."

"Strange hobby," she said, picking up one of the tomes and glancing at the others. "They're all on medical malpractice. You're not in any trouble, are you?"

"No. I'm curious, that's all."

"Curiosity killed the cat," she said, looking out at the harbor. "God, it's hot. Can we open some windows? Oh, you even have a small balcony. We can eat out there and enjoy the view. Do you know that Wolseley Road is one of the world's ten most expensive streets? Some of the houses are quite grand."

"I knew Point Piper was Sydney's premier location, but I didn't know I was living in a world top ten street," Beaumont said as he carried the cooler out to his kitchenette. "I can cope with the heat, but is it always this humid?"

"I'm afraid so. Especially in the summer. I hope you like lasagna and salad."

"It's one of my favorite meals. I haven't had it since I left New York."

"Good. I just need to heat it. Why don't you put some music on, open up all the windows and pour the wine? I won't be long."

Ten minutes later, they were sitting on the balcony looking at the flickering lights from the boats in the harbor. "This is good. I propose a toast to the chef," Beaumont said, holding up his wine glass.

Sonya giggled as they clinked glasses. "Thank you."

"Jesus," Beaumont gasped as a huge cabin cruiser came into view. "Have a look at the size of that thing."

"I think it's Greg Norman's," Sonya said. "He's in town for a few weeks. It supposedly cost a hundred million, and it uses five hundred liters of fuel an hour. The toys of the super-rich. Can you believe it?"

"I'll own one, one day."

"Are you going to take up golf?" Sonya laughed, but when she looked at Beaumont, his expression was intense.

"I won't need to," he said, through pursed lips.

"I'll get dessert," Sonya said, surprised by Beaumont's sudden mood change.

She returned a few minutes later carrying a tray with two small bowls of vanilla ice cream, a liqueur bottle, a plate of biscuits and two shot glasses. "Frangelico," she said holding up the bottle while passing him a strong espresso. "I hope you like Affogato and biscotti."

Her body was silhouetted against the setting sun and he felt a familiar stirring. "Who doesn't? You're spoiling me."

"You deserve it."

Ten minutes later Beaumont made a pretense of tidying the dessert dishes, but Sonya took them from him. "Would you like a cup of coffee?" she asked.

"I'll stick with the wine. The breeze off the harbor is refreshing."

As she opened the balcony door, Beaumont savored her long, brown, toned legs. He was a connoisseur of females' legs, and Sonya's were enticing.

When she returned, Beaumont asked, "Are you a Sydney girl?"

"Born and bred but let's not talk about me. What did it feel like when you gave that little Aboriginal girl a new face? A new life. You must've felt like God?"

"I don't think in those terms. I'm just lucky I was born with unique skills."

"You're too modest. The hospital staff are in awe of you. You're greatly admired, but also feared."

"Feared?"

"The way you shout and rant at residents and nurses is scary. The residents respect you but don't like you very much."

"I'm not at the hospital to win a popularity contest, and I'm never going to accept second best."

"I know you could practice in Macquarie or Pitt Streets and be earning a fortune. Instead, you're working with the poor. It's noble."

Beaumont was glad darkness had fallen as he fought to stifle a laugh. *So that's the reason Sonya and the other nurses admire me. If only they knew.* "What about Mr. Golding? He does pro bono surgery."

"Piffle," Sonya said, drawing closer. "He takes the simplest cases and does maybe one procedure a week. Then he can boast to his posh clientele that he's helping the poor. Have you seen how he parks his Bentley? There's a chronic shortage of parking spaces, but he takes two, and parks right in the center of them. Woe betide anyone who parks in his spaces. No one respects him. He's everything you're not."

"Woe betide? Who uses language like that? It's Shakespearean."

"You might scoff, but Golding's focus is on status, power, and making as much money as he can. He's real rake too. The pressure he puts on young nurses is disgusting."

Everything I aspire to Beaumont thought. "Let's not talk shop," he said, kissing Sonya's full lips.

The clock radio came on at 5:30 A.M. and Beaumont felt for the warm body next to him. No one was there. He got out of bed, stretched and went out to the kitchenette, fully naked. The car cooler was gone and the dirty dishes from the night before had evaporated. He opened the cupboard where he kept his meager collection of crockery. Sonya had not only washed but packed the dishes away too. Beaumont smiled. The only thing missing from his life was vast wealth, and that was just around the corner.

Chapter 3

It was 7 P.M. on Wednesday, and Beaumont had been operating for thirteen hours with only a thirty-minute break. He mused that if he were a truck driver and the police caught him working those hours he'd lose his license and be heavily fined.

He had started the day operating on a young girl with a cleft lip and palate. Complications had developed and what should have been a two-hour procedure took nearly three.

The second procedure involved a firefighter who had suffered third-degree burns, requiring extensive skin grafts.

The third operation was the most intricate and Beaumont worked with an orthopedic surgeon to reconstruct a young factory worker's lower arm and hand. She had been temporarily distracted, and her hand was crushed between two steel rollers. Luckily, her supervisor had turned the machine off, saving her from far worse injuries. It had been impossible to free her hand, and the machine and rollers were carefully disassembled before she was released. The surgery was complicated and centered on the bones, nerves, and tendons. Unfortunately, there was severe nerve damage. As nurses wheeled her from the theater, Beaumont knew she'd never regain full use of her hand.

Beaumont was drained. The burns victim would still be having skin grafts in three years' time, and the young girl would have many more operations on her hand in fruitless attempts to restore greater usage. He was dying to get away from reconstructive surgery and into private practice where he would operate exclusively on the rich and beautiful.

The coffee in the cafeteria was mediocre but far superior to that in the doctors' lounge. However, the latter was quieter. It was small but comfortable with half a dozen coffee tables surrounded by tatty fabric chairs. There was a large desk and a wall mounted television that was turned off. Two sofas that served as beds were positioned along the walls. A kitchenette with a refrigerator, hot plate, stove, and an instant coffee machine adjoined the lounge.

Beaumont pressed a button and what passed for a macchiato filled a plastic cup. There were a few old, tired looking doctors sitting at tables near the door and Beaumont took the furthest table from them. He knew they weren't plastic surgeons and couldn't help him. He closed his eyes and thought about his first procedure tomorrow morning. Mrs. Masterson had had a mastectomy, and he was replacing her breast using tissue from her lower abdomen. She was more worried about the aesthetics than the seven-hour procedure. Beaumont was confident she'd be stunned by the result.

"Do you mind if I join you?"

Beaumont looked up to see the auburn haired psychiatrist. She gave him a mischievous smile. "There are four free tables, or you could sit with them," Beaumont said, nodding toward the older doctors.

"Wow. So the OR stories about you are true. Can you give me the name of the American charm school that you went to?"

"I'm so sorry I upset you. Pleased sit-down," Beaumont smirked, standing up and bowing.

"Sarcastic and nasty. You've got problems. I can help you."

"I don't need help. Look, I don't want to be rude, but I have little to share with doctors who don't practice a discipline related to my specialty. I know what you do, and I'm not interested."

"Oh, you love being rude, and I'm glad to see you're a man of broad horizons," She laughed derisively. Her brown eyes sparkled, and the freckles on her button nose twitched. "I like to meet as many fellow doctors as I can. It's a learning experience. I've heard about you. Who hasn't? The cosmetic surgeon with the short fuse."

"Plastic surgeon and I practice reconstructive surgery, Dr.–?"

"Debbie Stenson. You're just filling in time here before going out to make a fortune in private practice. Still it figures. Tall, dark and handsome. I mean what else could you have specialized in? I should have guessed. How disappointing, Dr. Beaumont."

"I wish I could say it was a pleasure to meet you, Dr. Stenson?"

"Please call me Debbie."

"Royal Sydney's very own Dr. Phil. An imitation doctor," Beaumont sneered. "Have you thought about a career in television?"

"Touché, Dr. Beaumont. I thought you were just a male model with surgical skills. I'm surprised, but glad to see you have a personality," Debbie said, sipping her coffee and sighing. "I needed that."

As she put her cup down, her beeper sounded. "Emergency," she said. "I'm sorry, I have to go."

"Someone struck down with life-threatening bipolar," Beaumont grinned.

"Oh, you're good," Debbie said, dropping her card on the table. "Call me if any of your patients need my services."

Beaumont flicked her card from hand to hand as she walked away. She had slender, well-shaped legs and was attractive in a feisty, tomboyish sort of way. He liked a challenge, and the thought of bedding her after Golding and the others had failed was appealing.

It was 2 P.M. on Friday and the haunting music of Nino Rota's soundtrack to The Godfather echoed around the operating theater. Beaumont enjoyed intense music and found the greater the intensity, the greater his level of concentration. He couldn't help but admire Mrs. Masterson's reconstructed left breast. It was a work of art. The DIEP flap shaped in the open breast was warm and soft. When he pressed his finger into it, it went from pink to white to pink in two seconds. Finally, he placed a little lubricant on the flap, turned on a small instrument about the size of a pen called a Doppler and put it on the flap. The sound of the artery pulsating emitted from the Doppler. Mrs. Masterson hadn't wanted a silicone or saline implant that would've been far easier. However, she had been concerned about how a breast constructed from her tissue would look. Beaumont had no doubt that when the swelling went down, and she saw what he had sculpted, she would be delighted. In three months' time, he would make a small incision in the breast and construct a nipple from the flap. The final stage would be the creation and tattooing of the areola, and new nipple.

Beaumont took one last look and said, "Perfect. I'll sew her up." The surgery had taken nearly eight hours, and Timmy Brown's ear reconstruction would take at least five hours. It was going to be another long day. Unlike Wednesday, Beaumont wasn't tired. He was ecstatic and in awe of his skill and creativity. Twenty minutes later when the nurses wheeled Mrs. Masterson from the operating theater he gloated in the thought that he'd soon be charging fifteen thousand dollars for the same procedure.

Chapter 4

More than two weeks had elapsed since Beaumont met Debbie Stenson and he'd regularly frequented the doctor's lounge looking for her. Beaumont liked the thought of a challenge. There was something seductive and indefinable about her, which excited him. Though she wasn't as attractive or curvaceous as Sonya or some of the other nurses that he'd bedded. A canceled procedure had freed up his day, and it was only 5:30 when he left the lounge and went back to his nook. She answered her phone on the first ring.

"Debbie, it's Simon Beaumont. I don't know whether you rememb–"

"Plastic boy, and now it's Simon. I feel privileged to be on first name terms with someone so famous. How could anyone forget you? Do you have a problem with a patient? How can I be of assistance?"

"Jesus, and you called me sarcastic. No, I'm not having problems. It's a personal call. I wondered whether you'd like to have dinner with me. There's a new Italian restaurant just opened in George Street. I thought you might like it."

"You did, did you? You've exhausted your supply of nurses and thought you'd move up to doctors. That's nice, but no thanks."

"Why?"

"Ah, there's that American charm again. Did you even consider that I might be married or have a partner?"

"You weren't wearing an engagement or wedding ring, so you're not married. Do you have a partner?"

"Hmmm, very observant but whether I have a partner or not is none of your business. Simon, you're not my type. I'm not into shallow. I like deep and meaningful. I'm sure you know what I mean."

"So you won't have dinner with me?"

"I think I just said that. Was I too subtle for you?"

"Shit! Did you major in cynicism? Can we meet for coffee in the doctor's lounge?"

"You're very persistent. I chair a group counseling session every Friday night. I usually have a snack and a cup of coffee in the cafeteria about six-thirty."

"I'll see you then," he replied. "If you're nice I'll pick up the tab."

"Charming and generous. You must be every girl's dream."

It had just gone six o'clock when Beaumont drove his second-hand Ford out of the packed underground parking garage. He drove past the two vacant spaces signed *Reserved Mr. Brett Golding* where no one dared park. Many specialists in Australia reverted to Mister rather than Doctor and considered the former title to be more prestigious. It was something that Beaumont had no intention of doing.

It was only a four-mile drive to Point Piper, but Beaumont was stuck in bumper-to-bumper peak hour traffic. He wasn't worried, he wasn't operating tomorrow, and his first appointment wasn't until nine. He was relaxed and looking forward to a few extra hours sleep.

He finally made it to his apartment and could hear the phone ringing as he inserted his key in the door. "Congratulations," the pompous voice of Brett Golding echoed down the line. "You were admitted to membership of the Australian Institute of Plastic Surgeons this afternoon. Welcome aboard."

Beaumont smiled. It was far more significant than being board certified in the U.S. or being a member of the American Society of Plastic Surgeons. It was a license to print money. "Thanks, Brett. That's great news."

"I guess this marks the beginning of the end of your time at The Royal Sydney? A word of advice. After you're in practice, do at least one pro bono procedure a week. It's inconvenient and a pain in the ass, but it's good for your image. We don't want to be seen as heartless bastards, do we?" Golding said. "I have another matter that could put a few dollars in your pocket. Are you interested?"

Am I interested? It's going to cost a small fortune to set my surgery up, and I'm broke. Of course, I'm interested. "Depends on what it is."

"One of the city's most prestigious legal firms has asked me to appear as an expert witness for one of their clients in a malpractice case against an ophthalmologist. She's mid-sixties and the

31

ophthalmologist performed a blepharoplasty on all four eyelids. I'm looking at a photo, and there's severe drooping of the lower lids. The lawyers claim that she has permanent ectropion of the lower lids and infection. They claim she can't close her eyes, her corneas are exposed to light twenty-four hours a day and she suffers persistent dryness. More importantly, she's richer than the Queen. You could do very nicely for yourself."

"Two questions. The lawyers have approached you, so why are you asking me? And have you examined her?"

"I've appeared in a dozen cases against ophthalmologists, dermatologists, and other quacks practicing plastic surgery. I've developed a reputation in the courts. Under cross-examination, counsel for the defendants can take up to half a day reviewing my testimony in past cases, and trying to prove bias. Slime bags! I can handle them, but it can be very trying, and the scum are quick to pick up on any inconsistencies in my past testimonies. If you testified, you wouldn't carry that burden. Are you interested?"

Yes, but I'd run the risk of defense counsel finding out about Valerie Fielding and it becoming public before I commenced practice. "Tell me about your examination."

"I never said I examined her," Golding snorted. "I can see from her photos that she's been butchered. That's what happens when ophthalmologists practice plastic surgery. They're greedy, and the paddock on the other side of the fence is always greener. The problem is they don't have the expertise or qualifications to graze in that paddock. If you think it's necessary, you can examine her. The photos tell the story, though. If I were you, I wouldn't waste my time."

*How could a lawyer diagnose ectropion or eye infection and why is Golding taking the lawyer's word at face value? Ophthalmologists aren't quacks, and they're licensed to practice eye surgery. Without an examination, the lawyers might be talking rubbish and touting for a big case."

There was a long pause and Beaumont said, "Brett, are you still there?"

"I told you I had photos. She looks like a fucking bloodhound. Does that diagnosis satisfy you?" Golding shouted. "Where does it say on any ophthalmologist's qualification, license, certification or authority that they can practice plastic surgery? It doesn't! I told you that the firm of lawyers is prestigious, so don't give me that shit about them trying to drum up business. We don't have the problems they have in Cali-fucking-fornia where any prick with a scalpel can practice. We stop 'em before they get a toehold. We all do our bit. If you're not gonna put in, you're gonna wear out your welcome mat. I was just trying to put a few dollars your way."

Beaumont held the phone back from his ear. It was staggering how Golding could go from sounding like Prince Charles to a builder's laborer in the blink of an eye. "I'm sorry if I spoke out of line, Brett. I'm not ungrateful, but I haven't actually hung a shingle out yet. I think you can probably come up with someone with more credibility who'll better serve this lady's interests."

"Quite so. We have many members who'll leap at the opportunity to aid the common cause," Golding replied, the twang having returned to his voice. "You're right, you are comparatively inexperienced. However, in a few years when asked again, you'll be expected to respond in the affirmative."

"Don't worry, I will."

"One last thing. You're going to be looking for financiers, accountants, lawyers, temporary staff, public relations firms and insurance brokers. There's a company with offices near my surgery in Pitt Street, Adamo & Associates. They specialize in acting for doctors. They'll handle all your needs, and save you time and money. Tony Adamo's a good friend of mine. Give him a call. He'll fix you up. We'll talk again, soon."

"Thanks, Brett," Beaumont said, hanging up the phone. *I won't be calling Adamo & Associates. They must have competitors, and I'll be contacting one of them. I don't like or trust Golding, and he already knows too much about me,* he thought.

Chapter 5

The cafeteria was quiet, and Debbie Stenson was sitting at a corner table by herself, surrounded by papers.

"Do you mind if I join you?" Beaumont asked.

"There are thirty free tables, or you could sit with them," Debbie said, nodding toward a table of giggling nurses. "I'm sure you'd be quite a hit."

"What a memory. You're word perfect. I never realized that what I said, would impact you so much."

"Don't flatter yourself. I rarely run across anyone as rude as you, and on the rare occasions I do, it's hard to forget their appalling behavior."

Debbie packed her papers in an overloaded leather briefcase while Beaumont remained standing. "Can we declare a truce," he asked, "I've had a rough day."

"Really? Poor Simon. Why don't you sit down and tell me about it?"

"I will, but first I'm going to get a salad and coffee. What can I get you?"

"The same, thank you. I'll help you carry it."

"I'll get a tray," he responded. "It'll give you a few minutes to get your notes in order."

"Wow! You're quite a catch. I thought you'd send me to fetch it."

"I thought we'd declared a truce."

"Oops. With you, it's hard to remember."

A few minute later Beaumont returned with the salads and two cups of coffee.

"Thank you," Debbie said. "How much do I owe you?"

"Six bucks, but seeing it's our first date, and I want to make a favorable impression, I'll pay."

"Not only charming but a big spender too," Debbie said. "No wonder all the nurses have fallen for you. You were about to tell me about your day."

"I was in OR at 6 A.M. constructing a nipple on the breast of a woman who'd had a mastectomy. Then I operated on a young boy born with webbed feet. The surgery was elaborate and took nearly four hours. There was no time for lunch as I had to remove a tumor from the nose and forehead of a sixteen-year-old girl from New Guinea. I finished by doing skin grafts for a burn patient."

"Soon you won't have any patients like them. You'll be doing face-lifts, nose jobs, tummy tucks, and liposuction. All cosmetic stuff for people who don't need it."

"As a psychiatrist, I thought you'd understand the positives of cosmetic surgery. I've performed breast augmentations for timid, mousy women and the transformation's been amazing. They've gone from quiet to self-assured overnight, and some of them have even become aggressive. Breast augmentation has a tremendous positive impact on many women's self-esteem."

"Rubbish! If it wasn't for the likes of you, and the media, they'd never feel bad about themselves in the first place. Those women would be better off seeing me, than you. I'm sure there's a reason in the plastic surgeon's handbook that'll justify every shallow, cosmetic procedure that you're going to perform."

"How do you know what I'll be doing?"

"It's all over the hospital. You'll be gone within three months and have a private practice in Pitt Street. Bored, wealthy women will pay you a fortune to take ten years off them. What a waste of medical training."

Beaumont had met many doctors who were disdainful of plastic surgery, but never one as forceful as Dr. Debbie Stenson. "I'll still be here. I'll do at least one pro bono procedure a week."

"Ah, the obligatory pro bono procedure," Debbie sneered. "Is that what Brett Golding told you to do? Did he advise you that when it's a poor young girl with a massive tumor like it was today, you make sure your PR people leak it to the media? No wonder his nickname's Gold-digger. He's a rake and a leech."

"I've never heard him called that. He's thought of as the finest plastic surgeon in the country."

"No one's going to call him Gold-digger in front of you. And he's not the finest plastic surgeon, is he? You are. That's right, isn't it? One thing you plastic boys don't suffer from is a lack of ego. You're so up yourself."

"Why do you hate him so much?"

"He groped me, and when I reported him, I nearly lost my job. Bastard!"

"And you're taking it out on me."

"No, I'm not. Have you thought to ask me about my day? The hospital has a funding problem, and I'm going to have to let some of my best people go," Debbie said, then paused. "Sorry, that's unfair. I shouldn't have got angry with you."

"No, you're right. I was insensitive. Tell me about your day," Beaumont said, patting her hand, which she immediately withdrew.

"My first patient was a young mother of three kids less than five. She took out an Apprehended Violence Order against her husband, but the bastard took no notice of it. Three weeks ago he attacked her with a golf club, and she was in here for a week recovering from broken bones, bruises and cuts and abrasions. Physically she's recovered, but mentally she's a wreck. Worse, her husband's out on bail. He breaches an AVO, and the court frees him. She's terrified, and no wonder. Her husband has no respect for, or fear of, the law. He should never have got bail and instead be staring at five years' hard time. The courts are pathetic."

"That's rough."

"It gets worse. My second patient was a ten-year-old girl. Her father's been molesting her for the past four years. He's a religious nutcase who told her that if she said anything, all fire and brimstone would befall her and that she'd go straight to hell. The court nearly got it right with him. He got twelve years, but it should've been twenty. The girl's petrified of men and blames herself for her father being in jail. She's twisted herself in knots and is suicidal which is rare for someone so young. I've spent hours with her, but I'm not getting through. I feel helpless."

"Jesus!"

"This afternoon I saw a sixty-year-old man who was abused by Catholic priests over fifty years ago. He bottled it up all that time, and only came forward when he found out he had cancer. Fifty years of shame through no fault of his own," Debbie said, wiping her eyes. "You don't want to hear any more."

"That's a tough day."

"Oh, I don't know about that," Debbie said, as she regained her composure. "I didn't get any emergency bipolar callouts."

"You even remember my jokes."

"I do."

"Who are you meeting with tonight? What's the agenda?"

"Partners of sex addicts and you don't want to know," Debbie said, pushing her chair back. "Thank you for the salad, and coffee."

"When will I see you again?"

"Call me."

Beaumont left the cafeteria knowing that he had progressed. He was a hunter. She was the prey.

Since Golding told him about Adamo & Associates, Beaumont had spoken to other doctors and done as much research as he could. The business model piqued his curiosity. Cynics said that Adamo bought the doctors on graduation, managed them throughout their careers, and finished by funding their funerals. Beaumont was surprised by the size of the business. They had offices in every state and were virtually without competition.

The one competitor they had in Sydney was Levine & Company, and Beaumont had arranged to see Steve Levine, a former employee of Adamo's, on Monday evening.

Chapter 6

S teve Levine's office was in an old house in Darlinghurst, a little over a mile from central Sydney. Beaumont liked the feel of the suburb and the idea of converting an old Federation house into a surgery. He imagined it having two entrances and two waiting rooms. One for client consultations and the other for postoperative patients. Beaumont knew that postoperative patients, particularly men who'd had cosmetic surgery, wanted total privacy. Brett Golding's surgery had two entrances, but patients still had to take an elevator up twenty-five floors, and there was no privacy from the general public. *Who wants to get in a crowded elevator after a facelift, nose job or a temple lift?* Beaumont thought.

Darlinghurst was also the location of The Paragon, a new, supermodern private hospital designed for the wealthy or those paying the highest level of health insurance. It was similar to those in Beverley Hills. Beaumont had already approached the hospital administrator and had been extended privileged practices to perform his surgery there.

Levine was about 6' with sandy, cropped hair, and a strong, jutting jaw. Beaumont guessed they were a similar age. His office was a tastefully renovated front bedroom, and he directed Beaumont to a recliner adjacent to a small coffee table. There were no papers on his walnut desk, only a desktop computer. After Beaumont had declined an offer of coffee or mineral water, Levine sat down with a pad and pen in hand. "I like to be upfront," he said, "so let me tell you that if Tony Adamo finds out you're talking to me, he'll make you an offer you'll find nearly impossible to refuse. He'll ensure your loans are interest-free for the first and possibly the second years. There'll be no brokerage on your insurance, and he'll waive his standard fees."

"How do you know?"

"I worked for Adamo & Associates for five years. They dominate the medical profession, and they don't like competition. They've broken others before, and now they're trying to break me," Levine grimaced.

"Why are you telling me?"

"I told you. I like to be upfront. Besides, they'll know soon enough that you're going into private practice. If you don't approach them, they'll know you're trying to do everything yourself, or you're seeing me. Either way, they'll want your business."

"I'm one doctor. Are you sure they'd be so determined to win my business?"

"Simon, they're not worried about the size of your practice or what you'll bring to them. They like to crush competition before it threatens them. It's not about you; it's about me."

Beaumont considered the information for a moment. "Steve, do you know Brett Golding?"

"Gold-digger! Sure, do. Tony and he are as thick as thieves. I was about to sign up a young cardiothoracic surgeon when Tony found out and called Gold-digger, and voila, suddenly I'd lost the client."

"What influence would he have on a cardiothoracic surgeon?"

"He's on the board of The Academy of Surgeons. He has influence over every surgeon in the country."

"Is Adamo slinging Golding anything?"

"I don't know, but if he is, he wouldn't pay it directly. They're both too smart for that. Adamo could be waiving his fees, reducing the cost of Gold-digger's medical indemnity insurance, paying him a higher interest rate on his deposits and charging him a lesser rate on his loans. Or if it was a more substantial sum they'd use an incorrectly booked share deal."

"An incorrectly booked share deal?"

"Adamo & Associates make investments for thousands of doctors plus they make proprietary investments. Let's say they've got a profit of half a million on an investment, and they want to kick back someone that amount. They just say they made a mistake in booking the investment and that it should be in the party's name who they want to pay off. Then they backdate documents to evidence it. You can see what I'm up against," Levine sighed.

I want to be in on those type of deals. "So you can't match them?"

"I've been in business for six months. I have about twenty clients, all general practitioners. You can't do deals like that without critical mass. Eventually, I will."

"You've done a great job selling Adamo's services. Why should I use you?"

"They'll take back everything they give you in the first two years, and plenty more over the longer term. In five years, they'll be funding your practice, your investment properties, and your car. You'll be in hock to them for millions. You'll even be dependent on them for patient referrals. The less wealthy of your patients will fund their procedures through Adamo. I don't want to be crude, but you won't be able to take a piss unless Tony Adamo says it's okay. Is that what you want?"

"Why don't you tell me something about yourself, Steve? Why will you be any different to Adamo?"

"I graduated from Sydney University with a double degree in law and business before joining Deloitte as an audit hack. Adamo & Associates was a client, and that's how I got to know Tony. When he offered me a job and a big, fat salary, I couldn't accept fast enough. I know his business backwards, but I work on a different model. I don't want to own you. I want to be your partner. I can do everything that Tony can, except the first two years gratis. Oh, and I've got contacts who can get you into any restaurant, theater or sporting event."

"What's the most important thing I need to do right now?"

"Have you done a budget?"

"No."

"Okay. Work out how much upfront cash you'll need to start your practice and then add twenty-five percent. Then do a budget for the first year. After that, we'll be able to determine how much you'll have to borrow."

"I don't have any security."

"You're a plastic surgeon. You don't need any. You will need life, income, and trauma insurance. The lenders are going to want protection if anything happens to you. I can arrange it."

I don't know whether you'll be arranging anything, Steve. If it wasn't for Golding, I wouldn't even be thinking of signing with you.

"Thanks for seeing me. I need to think a few things over. I'll get back to you in a few days," Beaumont said, getting up from the recliner. "Oh, and Steve, don't ever give me a bone-crushing handshake again. My hands are precious."

After Beaumont got back to his apartment, he pulled out a notepad and started jotting down figures. If he converted an old house, he'd need an office, an injecting room, a reception area, two waiting rooms, furniture, office equipment, surgical instruments, telephones, brochures, paintings, artifacts, and printing and stationery. Then there were the startup fees of lawyers, accountants, power utilities, and the cost of general and medical indemnity insurance. He would need a receptionist and a surgical nurse who could also sell and inject. The hiring of a good surgical nurse would be vital to his success. It was just after midnight when he went to bed, and the figure of a half a million dollars was firmly entrenched in his mind. He was depressed. How was he ever going to pay it back? How was he going to pay the interest? As he closed his eyes, he relaxed. He was worrying over nothing. Half a million was just twenty-five facelifts, the equivalent of one hundred and twenty-five hours in the operating theater. There was nothing to worry about.

Chapter 7

Beaumont arrived at The Royal Sydney at 7 A.M. to complete Mrs. Masterson's breast reconstruction, but she wasn't there. Half an hour later, a nurse informed him that Mrs. Masterson's sister had called to say that Mr. Masterson had been killed in a tragic motor vehicle accident in the Blue Mountains.

The patient for the second procedure was a farmer who'd crushed his right foot under a tractor. Beaumont was working with an orthopedic surgeon, and the surgery was long and arduous. Worse, the other surgeon, who was, at least, ten years older had commandeered the stereo, and the relaxing sound of Strauss permeated the theater. Beaumont's mind intermittently drifted during the procedure to the dinner he was having with Debbie Stenson tonight. Something that would not have occurred had he been listening to Beethoven's 5th or the compositions of Nino Rota. It was mid-afternoon when Beaumont returned to his nook, and a dozen messages were waiting for him. There was one marked urgent from Brett Golding. Yet again, all Golding's messages were urgent.

Golding answered on the second ring. "Simon, I don't know whether this will interest you. Professor Randall Nordstrom from Sydney University and Andrew Houghton, a Melbourne plastic surgeon, are dissecting cadavers over Easter. They're trying to get a better understanding of the subcutaneous musculoaponeurotic system, with the intent of finding a method to lift and firm the face without long incisions and unnecessary skin excision. Anyhow, they're looking for a third surgeon and asked me. Sounds boring, and I'm not going to waste Easter carving up dead bodies. Are you interested?"

Only Golding would be pompous enough to say subcutaneous musculoaponeurotic system rather than SMAS. Easter falls two weeks before I commence my practice and I'm going to need every spare minute, but this is a fantastic opportunity. "Yes, very much. Can you let Professor Nordstrom know that I'm available?"

"He'll get a lot more enthusiasm, attention and concentration from you than he would've from me," Golding chuckled. "It's a win, win, win."

"I'm glad I could help."

"Did you call Tony Adamo?"

"No, I'm arranging everything myself."

There was a long pause before Golding said, "You'll regret it. Don't say I didn't warn you."

"I won't."

Debbie Stenson had an apartment in beautiful, beachside Manly about seventeen minutes by fast ferry from Sydney. The last ferry returned about midnight, so Beaumont opted to drive which took an hour. It was their fourth date, and he didn't know what the night might hold. It had been another hot day, and it was still warm when he parked and made his way up the stairs to Debbie's second-floor apartment. He had been chipping away, and she was no longer as cynical as she'd been when they first met. Her sleeveless black dress and half heels accentuated her slim body and toned legs. "You look stunning," he said.

"Thanks," she said, brushing her lips over his. "It's a balmy night. Let's walk. It's only ten minutes to the restaurant."

As they strolled down to the Esplanade that ran along the fore-shore, Beaumont took Debbie's hand and said, "How was your day?"

She laughed and squeezed his hand. "My you are coming on. That's something you wouldn't have asked four weeks ago. I wasn't going to talk shop tonight, but I have one problem I'd like to bounce off you."

"I'm all ears."

"I had a young man referred to me this morning. He's gay and wants to come out," Debbie said, and then paused. "What's wrong? I felt you flinch. Are you okay? You're not homophobic, are you?"

"Of course not. You're imagining it. Go on."

"Well, his father's a war hero and career soldier who's done three tours of duty in Afghanistan and Iraq. According to his son, his dad makes macho look sissy. You know the type. Tattoos, hard drinking, opens beer bottles with his teeth, brings down towering trees with one blow and has a group of mates just as tough. The son thinks his mom already knows, and she'll be okay, but he's petrified of his dad."

"What did you tell him?"

"I asked him if he'd like me to talk to his dad. He nearly had a seizure."

"Has his dad ever been violent with him?"

"No, but they've never been close. The father's critical of his hair-style, clothes, and friends but that's not unusual. The son thinks his father will go ballistic, and that he'll end up in hospital, and his dad will end up in jail."

"It's a tough one. All I can suggest is that he leaves home. Is he worried about his friends?"

"No, they already know. They're fine."

"How old is he?"

"Nearly eighteen."

"Tell him to leave home. Problem solved."

"If only it was that easy. I'm sorry, I should have asked how you're going, setting up your practice?"

"Fine. I have plenty of help."

"Adamo & Associates?"

"No. Their competition."

"I didn't know they had any."

Manly was a small peninsula, and they turned right into The Corso, the main street, that housed hotels, restaurants, ice cream parlors and retail shops. They walked in silence enjoying the atmosphere. There was a buzz in the air, and young people were lined up at nightspots. As they approached the end of The Corso, they could again see the ocean and the terminal where the ferries docked. Debbie had chosen the restaurant, The Garfish, which was on the foreshore about two hundred yards along from the ferries. It was noisy and crowded, but they only had to wait a few minutes before being shown to their table.

"I know what you're thinking," Debbie said, "but the food is to die for, and the service is great."

"Sorry, can't hear you," Beaumont said, as he scanned the wine list. "I don't know these wines. Would you like to order?"

Debbie didn't take the wine list offered. Instead, she looked at the waiter and said, "A Hunter Valley cab sav, McGuigan's Black Label."

"An excellent choice," the waiter responded. "I'll take your meal orders when I return."

"Simon, I don't want to belabor it, but when I mentioned that the young man I saw this morning was gay, I felt you react. You said you weren't homophobic, so why the change?"

"You're very perceptive. Okay, if you must know, I don't treat gays. It's got nothing to do with homophobia and everything to do with hepatitis and HIV. Surgeons cut themselves. All surgeons do. It's a work hazard. That doesn't mean I have to treat someone who might contaminate me."

"So much for the Hippocratic oath. More like the hypocrite's oath."

"For Chrissake, Debbie. I've heard those smart-ass comments before, usually from people like you who've never picked up a scalpel, or do-gooder surgeons who've taken leave of their senses. That's fine; they can have all my gay patients. That way, they're happy, and I'm happy. Are you satisfied?"

"I'm sorry. I shouldn't have said anything. I didn't want to make you angry. Let's not talk shop anymore. Tell me more about yourself."

"I've told you before. Divorced parents. Very ambitious boy. Studies hard. Class valedictorian in his last year of high school. Flies through college. Completes seven years surgery and plastic surgery training, and voila, here I am. End of story."

"I didn't mean to upset you," Debbie said, placing her hand over his. "Can you tell me why you left New York? In more than one sentence, please."

It's none of your business, Beaumont thought, taking a long sip of wine. "I'll say this for you. You sure know your wines. It's excellent."

"Wait until you taste the barramundi. It's a real experience. I have it whenever I come here."

Three hours later, after two bottles of cab sav, the barramundi and a shared caramel parfait they left the restaurant, feeling satisfied and totally relaxed. The Corso was quiet except for the yelling of young drunks trying to get into the night clubs.

"Are you coming up for coffee?"

"I wouldn't miss it. I might have to stay the night. I don't want to be in the newspapers tomorrow for blowing .05."

"I was going to suggest you stay on the couch."

As Debbie opened her apartment door, Beaumont swung her around and kissed her passionately. She responded eagerly, gasping, "I haven't been with anyone for a long time, and I don't want to be just another conquest. If that's all I am, I'd rather stop now."

That's exactly what you are and a prize conquest at that, he thought. He laughed, picked her up and carried her to the bedroom. "You make me sound like a rake."

"Turn the little sidelight on," she said, "then turn the rest of the lights off. Oh, and open the window."

Five minutes later they lay entangled on top of the sheets, a light breeze coming off the sea providing some relief. "I needed that," he said, sweat dripping from his chest.

"Really? How long's it been? A week, two weeks?"

"Don't you ever let up?"

"I was joking," Debbie said, propping herself up on an elbow. "After seeing and creating so many big boobs, I guess these don't do anything for you."

"They're fine," he said, reaching out and gently fondling her breasts. "I'm not into big boobs. Never have been, but if that's what you want, I'm the best."

"How charming. Do you usually try and make a sale after sex?"

"I'll even give you a discount because we're friends."

"Are we? When you were in New York, you must have performed many breast enhancements. Are you telling me you didn't like your creations?"

"I only did excessively large under duress, and no, only God creates better boobs than me."

"Under duress."

Yes, when I was desperate for the fee. "When the client insisted."

"Would you like it if mine were larger?"

"No. Do you think the chef at The Garfish wants to eat what he's spent all day creating when he gets home? It's the same with me."

"Oh my God, that's terrible. Did all the nurses you seduced purr over romantic lines like that?" Debbie laughed. "You didn't go to the George Clooney School of Charm, did you?"

"All the nurses? You make it sound like half the hospital."

"Yes, I suppose it does. Sorry, was it just every nurse on the fourth floor?"

"That's enough out of you," Beaumont said, pulling Debbie toward him.

Chapter 8

Signing up with Steve Levine had proved opportune, and he was saving Beaumont precious time and money. Levine had found an old house with two front entrances in a beautiful tree lined street. Then he'd haggled with the landlord to throw in the renovations and the first three months' rent free. He'd also shortlisted three receptionists, who were young, attractive and articulate, just as Beaumont had requested. They had chosen Julie Finch; a hazel-eyed brunette whose long hair cascaded over her shoulders. She had been brought up in the country, and perhaps because of this, seemed more friendly and personable than the other two candidates.

Then they had interviewed two applicants for the surgical nurse's job.

"They're both experienced and competent," Beaumont said, "but there's something missing. Once I do the initial consultation, I want to be able to hand the client over to my assistant, knowing that I'm not going to lose the business. They're okay, and the first one, Susan Smithers, has experience injecting. However, until I appoint a practice manager, and that's at least a year away, I need someone to handle that role. It's not an easy ask. Who's our final candidate?"

"Mary Perton. She's older than the other two. Early forties and vastly more experienced. She's just returned from a trip around the world. Before that, she was Evan Sutcliffe's surgical nurse for ten years. He's a plastic surge–"

"I know who he is. Tell me more about her."

"You'll like this. She managed Sutcliffe's practice for a year, but she was such a good surgical nurse, he couldn't do without her in that capacity."

"Did she tell you that?" Beaumont asked.

"Give me some credit. I spoke to Neil Ferguson, a retired surgeon, who operated in two of the hospitals that Sutcliffe does. He told me she was worth her weight in gold. Oh, she's also a trained injector and injected for Sutcliffe."

"Okay. Here's how I want to play it. We know she's a competent surgical nurse and trained injector. We don't need to waste too much time on those facets. When the interview reaches the practice management stage, I want you to butt out. I know what questions to ask and the answers I want to hear. You won't be able to add anything. However, if you listen carefully, it'll help you win the business of other plastic surgeons in the future."

"Jeez, could you be any blunter? I'll get her in," Levine said hitting the intercom. "Kathy, we're ready to see Ms. Perton."

Levine stood up and shook her hand saying, "It's nice to see you again, Mary. This is Dr. Beaumont."

Levine briefly covered Mary's background, surgical experience, and training while Beaumont listened attentively. There were signs of gray in her light brown hair, but her face was wrinkle free. She was a little too solid to be wearing a black pants suit, but in contrast, she had long, delicate fingers that Beaumont liked. There were stubby fingered plastic surgeons, but he'd always thought that if he was a patient, they'd be the type of specialists he'd avoid. She was confident without being assertive. Beaumont was impressed.

"Did you enjoy managing Evan Sutcliffe's practice?" he asked.

"Yes, I'm a people person, and it was interesting meeting patients before their procedures rather than meeting them in the OR."

"Were you still helping Evan in the operating theater?"

"No. He had a busy practice, and I couldn't have handled both roles."

"Let me bounce this off you. I consult with a patient who's considering a facelift. I'm positive and talk about the benefits. I minimize the negatives and allay her fears about surgery. I focus on how good and how many years younger she will look. I know she'll have concerns, and I answer her queries in a truthful but positive manner. At the end of the consultation, I hand her a glossy brochure. It will have before and after pics and truthfully, but superficially, describe the procedure. I then ask if she has any more questions, and she says no. By the time she reaches her car, she's thought of another twenty questions that she wished she'd asked."

"Dr. Beaumont, I've been watching surgeons make sales for over twenty years. I know the process."

"Yes, but if I delegated the second and subsequent consultations to you, how would you handle them?"

She had a friendly smile and perfectly crowned teeth. "Firstly, I would answer her questions truthfully, and then move the conversation to the postoperative phase. I'd tell her that there will be some bruising and swelling, but that the use of painkillers will minimize the pain. I'd advise her to start light walking at nights within two days, and that mild exercise will help with the healing. I'd let her know what drugs and tablets to take and the reasons why. I'm assuming you'll have a second glossy brochure that I'd give to her at the end of the consultation. She'll undoubtedly have more questions as a result of the information I'm providing. I'll answer those questions sincerely. Two questions that Dr. Sutcliffe's patients asked were, *when can I mix in social circles again and will I have almond eyes?* I would respond by saying two weeks and that if she had almond eyes, gravity and time will solve the problem."

"No, no," Beaumont shouted, "no patient of mine will ever have almond eyes. It's old technology. My patients will look young and relaxed, not like they've been dragged through a wind tunnel. You'll never need to talk about almond eyes."

Despite Beaumont's outburst, Mary maintained her composure. "I could've answered your question by saying, I'll never lie, but I'll never lose a client either."

Beaumont leaned back in his chair. "How will you ask the patient for payment?"

"I'll say that the only way we can ensure the hospital booking is if we get two checks, one for the hospital and one for us. Will we be offering finance?"

Beaumont was about to say no when Levine butted in and said, "Definitely. In some instances, you'll have to fill in applications for finance for Dr. Beaumont's patients and get them signed."

"That's fine. I've done it before."

"Mary, in most instances I'll get the Informed Consent signed, but what do you think it should include and when do you think patients should sign it?"

"I'm not a lawyer, but it needs to cover as many specific risks as possible and also be general enough to be all-encompassing. It certainly needs to spell out the risks of brain damage or death and the patient needs to be carefully taken through it. When I was with Dr. Sutcliffe, we arranged for clients to come into our surgery two days before the procedure. That way they only had forty-eight hours to sweat about what they'd just signed. Dr. Sutcliffe used to say that if we gave them any longer, it'd increase the probability of them canceling."

Beaumont frowned. "That's a dangerous practice. Did Evan give his patients a copy of the Informed Consent?"

"She looked confused. "No, he didn't."

"The courts in the U.S. are coming down hard on surgeons who wait until the last minute to have their patients sign Informed Consents. It's important that we allow our patients enough time to make a considered decision. We'll get ours signed seven days before the procedure and provide clients with copies."

"You'll lose some."

"Yes, but I'll also remove the main ground for litigation."

"Can you cope with closing the sale, being in the operating theater with the same client, and then looking after her aftercare?"

"They say variety is the spice of life. Of course I can."

Beaumont smiled. "Welcome aboard, Mary."

Chapter 9

It was late Sunday afternoon when Beaumont's phone rang, and he was surprised to hear Steve Levine's voice. "Simon, are you up for a drink tonight?"

"I'm not a big drinker."

"Well, it's more about sightseeing and making contacts than drinking. I'd like to take you to my club. We can have a meal and a mineral water if you like. Remember, once you're back in practice, you won't have time to scratch yourself."

"What do mean sightseeing?"

"Be daring. I'll show you a Sydney you've never seen before. You might even get to meet some influential people. A-listers! I'll pick you up in thirty minutes."

"Okay, but it can't be a late night."

Steve drove a brand new BMW Z3. "I thought you were a struggling agent," Beaumont said, "but you're driving this."

"You've heard the old saying *fake it until you make it*. I have to look successful. I've got bankers, lenders, lawyers and doctors who I have to impress. If I'd rolled up in an old shit-heap, what would you have thought?"

"That you weren't deep in debt. Where's your club?"

"In the city. It's only a few minutes away. What did you do today?"

"Read law."

"What?"

"It's a hobby."

"Jesus, lucky I rescued you. You're going to enjoy tonight," Steve said, as he swung the Beemer up to the parking garage of a high-rise office building. He swiped a platinum card and the roller door slowly opened. "We're here."

Steve led the way to the elevators and again swiped the card, and the doors opened immediately. He punched level 20, and a few seconds later they got out.

"This isn't what I was expecting," Beaumont said.

"You haven't seen anything yet, Doc." Steve strode toward a platinum door that matched his card and swiped it again. "Welcome to the Level 20 Club."

The floor was polished timber, and the lounge was circular with a large round mahogany table as its centerpiece. The first thing Beaumont noticed was that women wearing slinky low cut gowns outnumbered the men three to one. "You've brought me to a brothel," He grinned.

"For God's sake keep your voice down. It's no brothel," Steve whispered. "Judges, lawyers, politicians, businessmen and anyone who's anyone frequent Level 20. More big deals get done here than in most boardrooms. The joining fee's fifty thousand, then it's twenty-five thousand a year. They knock back more applicants than they accept."

"What about the girls?"

"Some are hostesses; and some are screened volunteers."

"Screened volunteers?" Beaumont smiled smugly.

"It's not funny. Many of these girls are looking for a wealthy boyfriend, or better still, if they strike it lucky, a rich husband. They have to be attractive, articulate and intelligent," Steve said, as a stunning hostess approached them.

"Can I get you something to drink, Steve?"

"Hello, Monica. You're looking alluring tonight. This is my friend, Simon Beaumont, Sydney's finest plastic surgeon. Not that you'll ever need his services."

Beaumont nodded. "It's a pleasure to meet you, Monica."

"The feeling's mutual. What would you boys like to drink?"

"We'll start with the 2009 Yattarna Chardonnay," Steve replied. "You'll enjoy it, Simon. I only drink it when I'm here because half my twenty-five thousand annual subscription is a bar and food tab credit. I'll never get through it, but I can try."

"For a struggling agent, you've sure got some expensive tastes."

"I don't have a choice. It's one of only two places in Sydney where you get to mingle with the movers and shakers."

"Besides the girls and alcohol, what else do you get for your money?"

"There's a library, a smoking room, saunas, masseuses, and a bistro where we're going to enjoy the finest wagyu beef. It's flown in from Tokyo, fresh daily. Let's grab a table."

Beaumont had made eye contact with a blonde whose hair cascaded halfway down her back. "Aren't we going to meet any of the girls?"

Steve laughed as he glanced at the blonde. "Don't worry, they'll come looking for us."

"How do you know?"

"I purposely told Monica you were a plastic surgeon for that reason. Half these gorgeous women think their tits are too small, their asses are too big, their noses are kinked, and they've got crow's feet. They need a psychiatrist, not a plastic surgeon," Steve said. "Forgive the Aussie analogy but in a few minutes, they're gonna be circling us like flies around a piece of shit."

When Beaumont heard psychiatrist he fleetingly thought of Debbie. "Sounds good."

There were plenty of tables in the dimly lit bistro, and soft music was playing in the background. Beaumont found himself relaxing. "Steve, you mentioned another place that the movers and shakers frequent. Is it a club too?"

"Yeah, the Two Hundred Club. Membership is by invitation only. It's very private and no one knows who the members are. It's confined to a select two-hundred. I do know that Tony Adamo and the Police Commissioner are members."

"How do you know about the Police Commissioner?"

"A few years the Commissioner's daughter was dying of a rare form of cancer. Everything they tried here failed, and she was too weak to travel. Tony Adamo found out about it and then found an eminent surgeon in Washington, one of only a handful in the world who'd successfully treated the condition. Don't ask me how, but Tony convinced the surgeon to drop everything and fly to Sydney to operate on the Commissioner's daughter. He saved her, and I heard Tony boasting in the office, that the Commissioner was in his pocket, and that the rest of the Two Hundred Club would have to sit up and take notice. I don't know how much Tony paid, but the rumor was a million plus expenses. You know, before Tony saved his daughter, the Commissioner couldn't stand him. Now they're as thick as thieves."

"Literally?"

"I don't know. What do you think of the wine?"

"It has a nice body."

"Talking of nice bodies," Steve said and stood up, as the blonde and an equally attractive redhead approached the table. "Would you like to join us, ladies?"

"We'd love to," the blonde replied. "I'm Connie, and this is Rebecca. Monica told us you're a plastic surgeon, Simon. Where's your surgery?"

Beaumont felt Steve kick him under the table. "Darlinghurst," he said. "We're about to eat. Can I order something for you?"

"No thanks," Connie replied, patting her non-existent stomach, we have to watch our weight. "I've got a photoshoot in the morning. Don't let us stop you."

"Are you a plastic surgeon too, Steve?" Rebecca asked, leaning forward.

"Even better," Steve replied. "I manage them, and only take on the best as clients. You want something done; I'm your man."

Beaumont coughed and shook his head ever so slightly. "The wine is superb. Can I tempt you, Connie?"

"Too many calories, we'll stick with water, thanks. Can I ask you something?" Connie said, getting to her feet. "Do you think my bum's too big? Is there anything you can do?"

Beaumont felt another kick land on his shin. Connie had a perfect figure. *How can she be so insecure?* he thought. "No, it's fine."

A waitress brought their meals, and Connie said, "We'll let you eat in peace. Can we join you after you've eaten?"

"We're not going anywhere," Steve said.

After the girls had left, Beaumont said, "So you only manage the best plastic surgeons. You're full of bullshit. And where are these influential contacts?"

"Listen to me. I want you to start reading the newspapers' social pages. The husbands of a lot of those women in the social pages will be members here. I can introduce you to them. If they like you, who do you think they'll tell their wives to see? Besides, there are plenty of fiftyish plus men in this club who've had surgery. Jeez, I'd have it myself if you could make me look like Brad Pitt." Steve wiped his mouth with his hand. "I bet you don't get steak like this in New York."

"Yes, it's good," Beaumont replied mechanically. What Steve said made sense. *I never thought I'd end up reading the social pages, though.*

"Can you get yourself home, Simon? I won't have room for you and Rebecca. You can grab a taxi."

"Steve, I told you I couldn't be late, and you said it wouldn't be a problem. I'm operating in the morning," Beaumont lied.

"Yeah, but that was before I got a look at Rebecca's tits. Did you see them when she leaned forward? I'm gonna be bouncing around on them in an hour. They're coming back. Here's how we play it. You say you have to find a taxi. Rebecca told me that Connie has an apartment just a block away. I'm betting she'll offer to let you stay at her place, and find a taxi in the morning. If you're worried about operating in the morning, you can always say no."

"It sounds like a plan," Beaumont smirked, standing as the girls returned.

After five minutes of small talk, Beaumont said, "I hate to spoil the night, but I have to leave. I'm operating in the morning, and have to find a taxi."

As he waited for an elevator, he turned and saw Connie walking toward him. "I'll come down with you," she said. "You're in the wrong part of the city to get a taxi. Even if you're lucky, the drivers hate short trips. When you tell them you're going to Point Piper, they're going to drive off and leave you."

"Where do you live? Do you have a car?"

"No, I don't need one. I have an apartment on the next block,' she said, as the elevator doors opened on the ground level. "Do you mind walking me home? It'll only take two minutes."

She was wearing an unbuttoned beige jacket and Beaumont slipped his arm under it and around her waist. "It'll be my pleasure."

They walked slowly, and Connie plied him with questions. Beaumont knew that one day she would be a plastic surgery junkie. "I've got thick thighs too; I suppose they came with my bum."

She has a perfect body, and yet she sees all these imperfections. She needs to see Debbie. "I think you're exaggerating. If I had time, I'd take a look at them."

"That's kind," she said, as she stopped and kissed him lightly on the lips. "This is my building. Have you seen any taxis since we left the club?"

"No, not one."

"Why don't you stay with me? Then you'll have the time to check out my imperfections and perhaps recommend surgery. You'll find it easier to get a taxi in the morning."

It was six o'clock when he let himself out of Connie's apartment, and the cool morning air on his face felt good. Dawn was breaking, and a weak sun hovered on the horizon. Cars clogged the streets and their exhaust fumes assaulted his senses. It was only three miles to Point Piper and thoughts of a taxi were forgotten as he set off at a brisk pace. His love for Sydney was intensifying.

Chapter 10

After shaving and showering, Beaumont felt refreshed and on top of the world. He had a day of consultations at The Royal Sydney that allowed him to finish early and get home at a reasonable hour. Four more days and he'd finally be back in private practice.

He turned on the television, and the newsreader was talking about an operation that had taken place at The Mercy Hospital to separate Siamese twins conjoined at the head. "Neurosurgeons, pediatricians, orthopedic surgeons and plastic surgeons operated for a mammoth twenty hours to free six-year-olds, Sophia and Josephine Albanese. We spoke to exhausted lead plastic surgeon, Brett Golding, immediately after he came out of the operating theater."

Beaumont turned the volume up and dragged his chair closer to the television.

"Mr. Golding, can you tell us about the surgery and how the twins are faring?" the reporter gushed.

"Well, this was the first of three, possibly four procedures and I must say that it went extremely well," Golding said, wiping his forehead. "The twins are now recovering in ICU. The next twenty-four hours will be critical."

"How many surgeons were involved?"

"Twenty, and might I say the nation's best in their respective fields. The four plastic surgeons who assisted me would have to be the finest team ever assembled."

And you being their leader makes you the finest of all, Brett. Prick!

"It must be incredibly expensive for the parents. Do they have insurance?"

"All the surgeons are providing their services pro bono. You see something like this, and it tears at the heartstrings. The last thing you think about is money."

Bullshit!

"I can see that you're drained. I won't keep you. How lucky are we to have selfless surgeons like Brett Golding in our community? This is Jennifer Lang, signing off from The Mercy Hospital."

Beaumont didn't see or hear the next story about a vicious assault at a nightclub in Kings Cross. He knew the PR value of being in that surgical team was priceless, yet he hadn't even known about it.

What a shithead you are, Golding. Groundbreaking surgery, but you didn't even mention it to me. You call when you want me in court as an expert witness or to help hack up a few cadavers over Easter. You got one thing wrong, though. If I wasn't the lead plastic surgeon, how could it be the finest team ever assembled, asshole?

The renovations to the surgery were nearly complete when Beaumont had the bright idea of enclosing the entrances with canopies. Patients would enter from the street by opening a gate and would immediately be under a canopy for the short walk to the front or side doors. He knew how important the privacy of his clients was. He'd watched many interviews where male Hollywood film stars adamantly denied having plastic surgery when it was obvious. There was a myth that gravity and time remedied all poor plastic surgery, but Beaumont knew that was all it was. A myth. He had revised many botch-ups in New York, and correcting them was far more involved than starting with a fresh canvas.

A bronze bust of Cleopatra would greet clients entering the main waiting room. Beaumont thought Cleo made a nice change from the statue of Venus de Milo in many other plastic surgeons' waiting rooms. There were half a dozen brown suede chairs and two magazine tables with the obligatory copies of *Vogue, Sports Illustrated* and *Money Magazine* neatly stacked on them. The furniture blended in perfectly with the beige carpet.

The second waiting room for postoperative patients was far smaller with only one magazine table and two chairs, one for the patient and the other for the care-provider. Appointments would be carefully staggered to ensure that patients never bumped into each other.

A central reception serviced both waiting rooms, and smart design meant that it was impossible to see from one waiting room to the other. The only person who would be able to do that would be the receptionist who would look directly into the main waiting room and check on the second via a strategically placed mirror.

The tastefully Egyptian themed brochures that covered every procedure from facelifts to liposuction faced outwards from a thoughtfully designed bookshelf adjacent to the reception counter in the main waiting room. Clients would be seated directly in front of the bookshelf with the intent of enticing them to look at procedures that they may not have considered.

On his last day at The Royal Sydney, Beaumont had only one procedure, a blepharoplasty. The patient was an overweight pensioner whose eyes were nearly closed, and his vision was through narrow slits. A nurse sedated him before Beaumont injected local anesthesia. Beaumont made an incision in the upper eyelid of the man's right eye and removed a large amount of fat. He then excised the excess skin, closed the incision and dressed the eye. He duplicated the process on the other eye and told the man to rest for an hour, after which a nurse would remove the dressing. He finished by saying, "You're going to notice a significant difference, Mr. Parish. I'm sure you'll be pleased. Don't forget, you're not to drive for at least twenty-fours."

"Jeez, Doc, that's the third time you've told me. The missus dropped me off, and she's gonna pick me up when I call her. Don't worry, I'm not gonna drive."

Yes, but if you did and had an accident, smartass lawyers would drag me through the courts. Some bloodsucker would see a quick buck and sue the hospital. Litigiously, Australia was becoming more like the U.S. every day.

The Brown family was Beaumont's last consultation. Timmy's ear had healed, and it was impossible to tell the surgically reconstructed ear from the other ear.

"I'm glad we went ahead and had the surgery," Mrs. Brown gushed, "I knew you would do a fantastic job. I never doubted you."

This was the same Mrs. Brown who had been so negative, and it was young Timmy who had convinced her to consent. Every recipient who was pleased with a good result congratulated themselves on their decision to go ahead with the surgery. Some of those who were displeased raced to their nearest *caring* lawyer and sued their surgeon, seeking revenge and a hefty compensation payment. "Thank you, Mrs. Brown, I'm glad you're pleased."

"Doc, you were bloody terrific," Mr. Brown said. "None of the kids at school pick on Timmy anymore. He's a new boy. Happy, outgoing and confident."

"Don't swear in front of the doctor, Ted," Mrs. Brown said. "You're teaching Timmy bad habits."

Timmy hugged his father's leg and shyly looked at Beaumont. "Thank you," he said with tears in his eyes. "I used to hate looking at myself. Now every time I look in the bathroom mirror, I think of you."

Beaumont was uncomfortable with kids. "Thank you, Timmy," he stiffly replied. "Is there anything else, Mrs. Brown?"

"The nurses told us that you're going into private practice."

"That's right."

"Do you have a card?"

"Yes," Beaumont said, opening his wallet and pushing his card across the desk.

"I have a friend who's thinking about having a facelift. How much would it cost?"

I bet you've got a friend, Beaumont thought discreetly checking Mrs. Brown's face. "Twenty-thousand."

"That much?"

"I'm afraid so. I'm sorry I'm running late for another appointment."

As Beaumont watched them file out, he wondered whether he'd see Mrs. Brown again.

Beaumont was heading for the door when the phone on his desk rang. He momentarily toyed with letting it ring before picking it up. "Dr. Simon Beaumont."

"Simon, it's Brett Golding. I'm sorry I haven't been in touch. You probably know I've been flat out?"

"Have you? I didn't know."

"You must've heard about the conjoined twin's surgery."

61

Cop this you bastard! "No, not a word. I've been busy setting up my surgery. I haven't had time to breathe."

"No one said anything to you? I'm leading a team that's performing groundbreaking surgery on twin girls joined at the head. I thought about asking you to join the team, but realized you didn't have any experience."

Who does, you shithead? That's why it's called groundbreaking. "I'm glad you didn't. I would've had to decline. You know what it's like."

"Yes, yes," Golding spluttered. "I called to wish you well. I hope you make a great success of your practice. I saw your advertisement in *Women's Sport*."

"It's not an ad. It's an editorial."

"It's obviously a paid editorial. Anyhow, I hope it pays for itself."

Prick! "Thanks, that means a lot to me."

"Tony Adamo told me that you signed with that ex-employee of his. That's a big mistake. Why'd you do it?"

None of your fucking business, asshole. "He's just starting out, and I'm just starting out. Tony's pushing sixty. I don't want to go with yesterday's man."

"I'm nearly sixty, and I'm the best plastic surgeon in the country."

No, you're not. "I wasn't talking about you," Beaumont said.

"You've made a big mistake. Levine will be out of business in six months, and you'll be calling Tony with your tail between your legs. Anyhow, I just called to wish you well. I hope Levine doesn't leave you in the lurch."

I bet you don't. Just like I hope I haven't ruined your day. "Thanks, Brett. Oh, I nearly forgot. Debbie Stenson's great, and I mean great."

"You scored with her?"

Now for the coup de gras. "Sorry, Brett. Gentlemen don't screw and tell," Beaumont said. "The Siamese twin's surgery sounds fascinating. Keep me informed."

Chapter 11

At times, the humidity of Sydney's summers had been hard for Beaumont to cope with, but the milder autumns were glorious. The weather forecaster had said to expect another beautiful day with a temperature of 22 which Beaumont converted to 72. Why Australians used Celsius was beyond him.

There was a two-car carport at the rear of Beaumont's surgery, accessible via a narrow lane. It was 8 A.M. when he parked the Ford and made his way to the rear door through a small, overgrown garden. He made himself a cup of coffee, and then inspected the premises for what must have been the fiftieth time. The landlord had saved him a fortune by doing the renovations, but he'd still had to borrow three hundred thousand dollars for equipment and working capital. Once he'd taken out half a million dollars of insurance, it had been surprisingly easy, and he mused that he was worth more dead than alive. He knew that the first couple of weeks would be quiet and didn't envisage performing any surgery until at least the third week.

He'd given Mary Perton a key, and she arrived bright and early. "Good morning, Dr. Beaumont. Days like this make you glad you're alive, don't they?"

"Call me Simon. You're going to be my right hand, and I don't want to stand on ceremony. However, when Julie comes in, you can let her know to address me as Dr. Beaumont at all times. I don't think we're going to be very busy until we start getting referrals from GPs, but within six months this place will be buzzing. You said that you've worked with four plastic surgeons, didn't you?"

"That's right."

"Was Evan Sutcliffe the best plastic surgeon you worked for?"

"They were all excellent."

"Mary, I don't believe in false modesty. Put a scalpel in these," he said, holding up his hands, "and you'll see miracles occur before your very eyes. I feel like Da Vinci must have felt before his artistry became famous. Once there are a few canvasses of mine walking around, the rich and famous will flock to me."

Mary was nonplussed. All plastic surgeons were egotistical, but she'd never heard another as boastful. "I'm sure you're very good."

"Very good? That's how you describe a fine meal, a tasty loaf of bread or the grading of a child's homework. What I do is avant-garde. Did you ever close incisions and sew sutures for the other surgeons?"

"Many times," Mary responded. "You'll be pleas–"

"No, I won't be pleased. You'll never sew sutures for me. My patients will pay for the best, and that is what they'll get. Once you've seen my sutures, you'll understand why."

Mary could feel Beaumont observing her. His arrogance didn't surprise her. It was the nature of the profession, and they were incredibly observant. A rash or tiny zit would never escape them. What surprised Mary was her boss's opinion of his own abilities. He was almost messianic. She was about to respond when Julie Finch pushed the front door open.

"Good morning, Dr. Beaumont. Hello, Mary."

Julie was wearing a lemon colored, sleeveless cotton dress and Beaumont thought she was perfect for her role. Her skin had a freshness that only came with youth, and while attractive, she was far from beautiful. Women in their late thirties and forties would envy her skin, and ask how they could re-attain their youthfulness. He had chosen well.

"Good morning, Julie," they both chorused.

"What would you like me to–?"

As Julie was asking, the phone rang, and Mary said, "Our first call."

"Answer it, Julie," Beaumont said.

A few seconds later, Julie put her hand over the mouthpiece and said, "Mrs. Masterson, for you, Dr. Beaumont."

Beaumont groaned. She had no money. That's why she used the public system. He knew what she wanted. Her areola and nipple tattooed. A minor procedure with a minimal fee that a trained fourth-year resident could perform. "Put her through," he said.

"Mrs. Masterson, this is a surprise. How can I help you?"

"You may not remember, but after my husband died in that terrible car accident, I had to cancel my final appointment when you were going to color match my nipples."

"I do remember, and I'm sorry for your loss. You'll be pleased to know it's a simple procedure, and any number of surgeons at The Royal Sydney can do it."

"I don't want them. I want you."

Damn! How am I going to get rid of her? "I'd love to help you, but the fee I'd have to charge is substantially greater than what you'd pay at The Royal Sydney. It's part of the mastectomy procedure, and is still covered under the public system if you have it performed there."

"Yes, I know, but I've been feeling down, what with losing Tom and all that. I want to have a facelift as well, and thought you could do it at the same time."

Beaumont straightened up in his chair and started jotting on his pad. "Mrs. Masterson, I don't want to appear rude, but you're looking at a procedure for which the fee is twenty thousand dollars."

"I guessed it'd be around that. I'm anxious to get things moving. Can I come and see you today?"

Beaumont was confused. He knew Tom Masterson had been an accounts clerk, the family poor as church mice. What was this woman talking about? "I have a full appointment book today. Can I check and get back to you?"

"Yes," she said. "I'm coming into Sydney this morning to pick up a check from ANL Insurance. It would've been convenient if I could've continued and seen you. I suppose I should be grateful that Tom took out so much life assurance."

Oh no! Big mistake. "Hold on," Beaumont said, and shouted, "Julie, have I got any breaks between consultations today?"

Julie came running into his office, totally confused, as he shook his head and shooed her out with his hands.

"Good news, Mrs. Masterson, I can fit you in at 11:45. Does that work for you?"

"Thank you, Dr. Beaumont, you're very kind. I knew you'd be busy. I better tell my boss's wife to stop procrastinating and call you."

"Your boss's wife?"

"Yes, she saw my breast before and after you operated. She's got three kids, and, well, she's a bit saggy. She's looking at implants and wants to talk to you."

Oh my God! It's getting better. I'll have to be more careful in the future. Folk's financial circumstances can change. "I'd be pleased to see her. I have some free time tomorrow. Why don't you ask her to call and make an appointment?"

"Thank you. I'd better go. I don't want to be late for the insurance company."

"No, we wouldn't want that, would we? I'll see you soon," Beaumont said, putting down the phone and shouting, "Ladies, come in here."

As Mary and Julie hurried into his office, Beaumont said, "When patients call I never want you to say that I'm free or that I don't have any appointments. Ask them when they'd like to come in and then say that you'll have to check my appointment book. When you return their calls say something like, you're fortunate, the doctor can fit you in on Friday."

"I'd just finished telling Julie that," Mary said.

"Good, that's good. One other thing, Julie. Mrs. Masterson's coming in at 11:45. Half an hour later, I want you to buzz and say, I'm sorry, Doctor, your next appointment has just canceled."

"Yes, Dr. Beaumont."

I'll get the first two appointments with Mrs. Masterson out of the way today. I'll get her in to sign the Informed Consent this Friday and to drop in a check. I'll be operating the following Friday. With extras and the tattooing, it'll be twenty-six thousand. Money, money, money. "That's all," Beaumont said. "Dismissed."

The women looked at each other. They had a strange boss.

Chapter 12

Mrs. Masterson arrived right on time and Beaumont saw her immediately. He didn't want her sitting in an empty waiting room for fifteen minutes when he was supposedly busy. He gave her his patient registration forms and said that she could return them when she came back for her second consultation. He examined her breast and admired his artistry. After he had tattooed the areola and nipple, her breasts would be a perfect aesthetic match. No wonder she was pleased.

She was medium build, in her mid-forties and had dyed ash blond hair. Like many others of her generation, she had foolishly spent her younger years in the sun, and needed laser surgery. Her brow was furrowed, and she'd need a forehead lift too. Other than that, she had good genes and skin texture, with high cheekbones and large, captivating blue eyes. Beaumont knew that he could turn the clock back twelve years for any patient, but for those who had good genes, and had looked after themselves, twenty years wasn't out of the question. He examined Mrs. Masterson's face carefully without saying anything. When he had finished, he handed her his glossy *first appointment* facelift brochure.

"Why do you want a facelift, Mrs. Masterson?"

"I'm looking tired and rundown. I think a facelift will pick me up. I'm sick of drooping jowls and wrinkles in my brow."

"A facelift won't resolve the wrinkles in your brow. It only covers the lower face," Beaumont said, lifting one hand below his nose and the other below his chin.

"But I thought it–"

"We'll come back to that after. Is it your decision to have facial enhancement surgery? You're not under stress, are you? Or doing it for someone else?"

"Dr. Beaumont, I've been reading cosmetic surgery magazines.

You're asking me these questions to ensure that I'm of sound mind. I am, and I don't want you examining my mind. I'm here to talk about the surgery. Are those photos in the brochure genuine?"

I just want to make sure you're not a nutcase who could get me into trouble, Beaumont thought. "They certainly are. They are women who had facelifts while I was practicing in New York. Most of them had forehead lifts and laser surgery too."

"Were you their surgeon?"

"Yes."

"Will I have to have those other procedures?"

"Without the forehead lift you'll have a young lower face but your brow will remain the same? Do you want that?"

"No, no. I don't. What about laser?"

"Your skin is badly sun damaged. If you don't have laser, you'll regret it, and I guarantee you'll be back to see me within six weeks. It'll save you time and money if you have all the procedures at one time."

"I understand. I want to look like those ladies in the *after* pics." Mrs. Masterson raised an eyebrow. "I imagine the surgery changed their lives."

"Yes, the impact on some of them was remarkable. They were attractive before the surgery, but nature was starting to take its toll. After the procedures, they were vibrant, confident and full of life. Many said they now had the face that matched the age that they thought they were. You're lucky. You have good genes. I'd like to take some photos." Beaumont reached for his camera.

"Oh, no. I don't want my photos in a brochure. I'm taking a holiday after the operation. When I come back, I'll look rested and rejuvenated."

"Don't worry, I can't use your photos in a brochure without your consent. I need them for your file."

"Will the procedures be painful?"

I'd like to say there'll be minimal pain, but I can't because I'm moving straight to the second consultation. "There will be some pain," he said. "I'll cover it when you come back for your second consultation. I always insist on three consultations. I want my patients to go into the OR with their eyes wide open. I'll go over–"

He was interrupted by the intercom buzzing and hit speaker-mode. "Dr. Beaumont, your next appointment is having car problems and just canceled," Julie said. "Do you want me to try and bring your conference call with Professor Mason and Dr. Colley forward?"

"No, I don't want to mess them around," he said, disconnecting.

"Mrs. Masterson," he said, "if you're free, we could move straight to the second consultation. It's up to you. It'll save you the inconvenience of another trip."

She smiled excitedly. "I'm free and have many more questions. I don't mind if we get all three consultations out of the way today."

"I'm sorry, I can't do that. By the time you reach your car today, you'll have fifty questions that you'll wish you'd asked. You'll be able to ask them when you come in for your next consultation," Beaumont said, handing Mrs. Masterson a second glossy brochure. "Let's go over this."

There was a photo of a man and an attractive woman holding hands and walking through a picturesque, green, treed park. Their faces were easily distinguishable but not like the close-ups in the first brochure. "You'll stay in the hospital overnight after the surgery, preferably for two nights. However, it's not essential if you have someone who can look after you at home."

"I'll be staying two nights."

"Good. You'll be lightly sedated, tired and drowsy. The rest will do you good. There will be some swelling and possibly skin discoloration."

"Doctor, I've seen pics in magazines of actors after they've had facelifts. Most deny it. However, you can always tell because they have almond eyes!"

"Don't worry, that's not going to happen, nor will you have the wind tunnel look. They're the result of old techniques."

"But the magazines are current. How can that be?"

"Sadly, many surgeons don't move with the times and use outdated technology," He sighed. "You should also be aware that you might suffer postoperative depression."

"From the result?" Mrs. Masterson laughed.

"No, you will be delighted with the result. However, some patients think that it's not a major operation. It is, and often one of the after-effects is depression."

"I can assure you, I will not be depressed. I want to know more about the procedures. Will the sutures be visible?"

"I made some short animated videos when I was practicing in New York. Let's watch them. They'll answer many of your questions. The one on facelifts is six minutes." Beaumont inserted the video, flicking the player on and turning the sound off. "I'll explain the procedures in lay person's terms."

Mrs. Masterson sat forward attentively.

"The surgeon's injecting the patient's face with an anesthetic solution of saline, lidocaine, and epinephrine. It constricts the blood vessels, prevents bleeding and minimizes postoperative swelling and bruising. Now he's making a small incision under the chin and pulling the muscle on each side together. It controls the bands under the chin and neck. See it constricting and getting tighter. Now he's sewing sutures to hold it all together. It's called a platysmaplasty. Do you have any questions?" Beaumont asked, pausing the recording.

"No, go on."

"There is a considerable amount of loose skin below the chin which the surgeon's pulling back, nice and tight. Tightening the bands enables him to remove more skin and results in a longer lasting outcome."

The screen flicked to the surgeon making an incision in front of the ear and into the sideburn. He then made a second incision behind the ear that tailed down into the hairline. Then the area was dissected, and the skin pulled away and back over the ear. This lifted the loose skin from under the chin and showed the excess.

"That's a lot of skin," Mrs. Masterson said. "Will I have that much?"

"Every patient's different and for effect, you're watching an exaggerated animation. You will have excess skin under the chin but not that much," Beaumont said and flicked the player back on.

The picture on the screen showed the skin completely pulled away. "You're looking at the SMAS, the subcutaneous musculoaponeurotic system, the fat, some muscle, and connective tissue. See how the jowl and neck tighten when the surgeon pulls the SMAS. Even the cheek is tightened a little. Now he'll remove a section of the SMAS and pull the sections on either side together. When he does, it will tighten the jowl, neck and midface, after which he'll sew sutures. It's called a smasectomy."

"There's a lot of surplus skin. How is it removed?"

"You're jumping a step. Keep watching."

"The surgeon's now liposculpting the excess fat in the neck and jowl line. Once removed, it won't be coming back. Liposculpture is a critical component of the facelift procedure."

"God, there's even more skin."

"The surgeon will remove it with a radio-wave incision machine and then he'll sew dissolvable sutures in the hairline, and in front and behind the ear. The sutures in the tragus will follow the contour of the ear. That, Mrs. Masterson, is your facelift. Now we'll look at the forehead lift and finish with the laser."

"You said that video was six minutes. How long does the operation take?"

"Four to five hours."

"How long will I be on the operating table for in total?"

"I hope to be finished in less than seven hours."

"I see what you mean about it being major surgery. Anyhow, I'm not deterred in the slightest. I am worried about changing my dressings once I'm home, though. That worries me more than the operation."

"That shouldn't concern you. On the morning, you go home, my beauty therapist will wash your hair. There will be no dressings when you leave, and she'll apply light makeup. You'll take Arnica tablets for two days before the procedure, and after, until the bruising has dissipated. I'll give you a prescription for Temazepam to help you sleep. You must not do any heavy lifting or housework until I say so."

"How long will it take before I can go out?"

"I want you to start taking short, non-strenuous walks at night as soon as you get home. You can wear a hat and scarf if you're worried about running into anyone. The exercise will help with the healing."

"That wasn't what I meant. When will I be able to go out again? When will I be able to go to the airport without being stared at?"

"If it wasn't for the laser, and you wore a scarf, five days. However, let's play safe and make it ten. You'll have to apply Vaseline to your face every day. I'll see you the day before you leave, and I don't want you getting any sun. When you come in for your next consultation, I'll give you a detailed list of before and after surgery instructions. On that list, you'll see a moisturizer with a sunscreen that I want you to apply, but not until I say so. Do you have any other questions?"

"Yes. When can you do it and how much will it cost?"

"Let's have another consultation this Friday, and then, if you still want to go ahead, I could operate at The Paragon the following Friday. The total fee will be twenty-six-thousand. If you bring a check, I'll make the necessary arrangements with the hospital."

"Oh, I'm going ahead. Nothing will change my mind."

"Good, let's watch the other videos."

Twenty minutes later, Beaumont stood up, and said, "Mrs. Masterson, before you go I'd like you to meet my assistant, Mary Perton. She'll be getting your medical records from The Royal Sydney, arranging the anesthesiologist, and will be available to answer any questions you might have about the hospital."

After Mrs. Masterson left, Beaumont asked Mary to come into his office. "I take it that the conference call was your idea," he said.

"I thought it added a nice touch," she replied. "By the way, I spoke to that friend of Mrs. Masterson's, Rachel Werner, and she's coming in tomorrow afternoon. Two of my girlfriends called too. They're coming in for some Botox and fillers in the morning. I'll look after them."

Beaumont silently cheered. The injections would cover Julie's wages and part of Mary's. He briefly toyed with the idea of convincing Rachel Werner to have her breast enhancement on the same day he was operating on Mrs. Masterson, but then dismissed it. He knew Mrs. Masterson's medical history but knew nothing about Rachel Werner.

What a great first day, Beaumont thought, as he punched Sonya's number into his cell. *I need to celebrate with some uninhibited action.*

"This is the second invitation I've had. Brett Golding asked me if I'd like to have dinner with him."

Beaumont burst out laughing. "The sly bastard. I know why he asked you out. What did you say?"

"I said I was dating someone and couldn't. He's old enough to be my father. He makes my skin crawl. What do you mean?"

"He knows I've been taking you out. He'd like to get you into bed so he could throw it my face."

"That's disgusting. What am I? The prize in some competition between the pair of you?"

"Hey, it's got nothing to do with me. I'm just letting you know how Brett's warped mind works."

"What a shithead. What time will you pick me up?"

Chapter 13

Rachel Werner was a living, breathing designer label. Black Prada jacket, white Versace jeans, Jimmy Choos and a red Hermes handbag.

Before Beaumont could say anything she extended her hand and said, "Hello. I've heard all about you. Can I call you Simon? You can call me Rachel."

Rings adorned her small fingers, and her face was perfectly made up. *She's well-kept, and has the confidence that only comes with money,* Beaumont thought. "That's fine," he replied. "How can I help you?"

"We can beat around the bush for ages, Simon, but I like to get straight to the point. I'm forty-seven, I've had three kids, and I've got saggy boobs. I want new ones. Big ones. Big round ones." She giggled.

"That's not a good idea. You're petite and let me assure you, you'll grow to hate large implants. I suggest the same size or perhaps one size larger, and with your stature, teardrops will be more becoming. I promise you'll be pleased."

She flicked her honey blonde hair over her shoulder, crossed her arms and smiled. Her teeth were perfect, and her crowns glistened. "Yes, but that isn't what I want. Can you, will you, do as I have asked?"

"If you insist, but trust me, after the novelty has worn off you'll find them uncomfortable, and dare I say, unattractive. I've seen breast implants where clients have insisted on an excessive size. Many of those clients returned to have them replaced. Exaggerated and over-sized breast implants are simply not attractive."

"So as a man, don't you like big boobs?" Rachel's eyes twinkled.

"No, I don't. Everything I do is in proportion, be it face, eyes or breasts. I can create masterpieces with these," he said, holding up his hands. "Yes, I can do large, and my results will be superior to any of my peers. However, if you trust me, you'll be unable to drag your-self away from the mirror. I prefer teardrops, but if you insist, I'll do round. Either will be beautiful so long as you don't go too big. I can't do excessively big and beautiful. No one can."

"God, are all Americans as boastful as you?"

"No, but they weren't blessed with these," he said staring at his hands. "There's a screen behind you. Please remove your top, and I'll see what I can do."

Some women were uncomfortable with this. Rachel Werner was not. "Like a pair of fried eggs, aye Simon?"

"It's the aging process. That's all. I can turn the clock back twenty years."

"Can you insert the implants under my armpits?"

"I can, but I'd prefer not to. Why do you want that procedure?"

"I've read that it hides the scarring, and I used to love sunbaking in the nude. I can't wait to start again, and I don't want anyone seeing horrible scars."

"You can put your top back on. Don't you know that there's nothing that ages like the sun? Use spray tan or gel. Anything's better than the sun. No wonder Australians have the world's highest incidence of skin cancer. If it's scarring you're worried about, I make a periareolar incision, which is virtually invisible."

"Do you use saline or silicone implants?"

"If they're teardrops, they'll have to be silicone."

"Well, that solves one problem. I want saline, which according to you means round. If I agree not to go super-big, can we go up two sizes?"

"I'll answer that when I know more about you. Have you had any serious health problems? Do you smoke? What do you do to exercise?"

"I filled in the answers to all those questions on the registration forms."

"Yes, but I also like clients' to tell me about their health. Do you go to the gym? What do you do to keep fit?"

"If we don't agree on the size, all that's stuff is pointless. I'll be going to see someone else," Rachel pouted.

I'd be happy to take your money and give you a pair of huge bazookas if I didn't think it'd hurt my practice, Beaumont thought. *I know your husband's going to be happy no matter what I do. I'm not worried about him. It's your girlfriends. They're not going to be impressed with a pair of straining melons, but when they see what I can do with just a slight increase, they'll be beating down my door.*

An hour later, Rachel Werner left the surgery. She was carrying Beaumont's glossy brochure espousing all the benefits of breast augmentation including the before and after pics. They had tentatively agreed that she would go up one and a half sizes, even though she wasn't totally convinced. He still hadn't made up his mind whether he would show her his breast augmentation video animation at the next consultation. It might rekindle her ideas of a larger size. He would give her the second brochure, which softly covered swelling, bruising, bleeding and discomfort.

The third consultation would reveal the brutal truth. The Informed Consent.

Chapter 14

When Beaumont called, Debbie Stenson answered her cell phone on the second ring. "How's the king of plastic surgeons this dreary morning?" she asked. "Do you have women falling over themselves asking you to make them beautiful?"

Beaumont cringed. "I've been flat out. I haven't had a minute to myself. And no, I haven't been rushed by clients. However, momentum's building and I'm getting inquiries every day. What about you?"

"The same. You wouldn't be able to cope with what I go through every day. Some people live sad, tragic lives, but you only get to see the shallow ones, rolling in money, panicking because their last lip pump is starting to lose volume."

How many times am I going to hear this? "Jeez, did I pick a bad time to call?"

"You're feeling guilty because you think you should've called me earlier. I'm not concerned. I know how important your practice is to you. Just never call me out of guilt. Call me because you want to talk or be with me. If it's neither, don't bother calling."

She thinks I feel guilty? Unbelievable! I wonder what she'd say if she knew I was calling because I'm feeling horny and looking to get laid. "Christ, I was calling to ask you to have dinner with me in Manly on Saturday night."

She paused before saying, "Why don't you come to my place? Seven-thirty. We'll send out for pizza and watch a movie. Don't drive. Take the ferry."

I'm going to score. "Sure, see you then."

Beaumont closed his office door when he'd called Debbie. There was a sharp knocking and Mary barged in. "Simon," she said, "bad news. Your next appointment is with Mrs. Trentham. She's in the waiting room. That must be her maiden name. I know her as Mrs. Philpott.

She's a vexatious litigant who's sued nearly every plastic surgeon in Sydney."

Beaumont frowned. "You're worrying unnecessarily, Mary. If I get bad vibes, I'll get rid of her."

"You don't understand. She's wealthy and influential. Old money. She can hurt you. You have to be careful. You can't afford to be disrespectful."

While they were talking Julie buzzed and whispered, "Mrs. Trentham's getting annoyed. She said her appointment was for 9:30 and that you're already five minutes late."

"Has she filled out the registration forms?"

"Yes."

"Give them to me and show her in two minutes later."

Beaumont quickly scanned the forms. She was fifty-five and lived in Point Piper. Under the question about previous surgeries she'd said, *various, minor, nothing of significance.*

Julie looked relieved when she showed Mrs. Trentham into Beaumont's office, and he stood to greet her. She was wearing a mink coat and Bulgari framed spectacles. "It's a pleasure to meet you, Mrs. Trentham," he said, examining her face. She was at least seventy and had had surgery, lots of surgery, most of it very good, but there were traces of the wind tunnel look. To the untrained eye, she'd pass for fifty-five. "How can I help you?"

"I'm starting to age, and I'm exploring the possibility of a facelift."

Beaumont looked down at her registration form and said, "I see you've had surgery before. Can we go over the procedures? It'll help me make a proper assessment of your needs."

"They were minor. I don't want to talk about the past."

"It's important. I have to be fully informed before I can advise you."

For the next forty-five minutes, Beaumont extracted information with the same degree of difficulty as extracting molars. Two facelifts, blepharoplasty of the upper and lower eyelids, an endoscopic fore-head lift, a coronal forehead lift, a nose job, liposuction below the chin, Botox and other fillers. He could see that she'd also had cheek implants, but Mrs. Trentham wasn't answering any more questions. She stared defiantly at him; arms crossed and chin thrust out.

The *vanity client* was every plastic surgeon's worst nightmare. Unhappy with previous surgery, they lived in hope that the next surgery would fulfill their unrealistic expectations. Many unhappy vanity clients were litigious, and were to be avoided.

Mrs. Trentham was worse than the typical vanity client. Her lawyers would be the best money could buy. There was no way that Beaumont was going to operate on her, but he had to let her down gently.

"Mrs. Trentham," he said, "I don't think I can help you. The surgery you've had is excellent. I was surprised when you said you were fifty-five on my registration forms. You certainly don't look it." *And that's the truth!*

"Piffle! The fool who did my recent facelift stretched my skin. I looked like a Goddamn Asian for months. I sued hi–"

"What happened in court?"

"The stupid, old judge didn't understand. I don't care to talk about it. I want you to fix what the others have botched. I've heard you're one of the best."

"Oh, you read the article in *Women's Sport.*"

"What? No! I don't read trashy magazines. My good friend, Brett, told me."

"Brett?"

"Brett Golding?"

What an asshole. "Mrs. Trentham, Brett's the best plastic surgeon in Sydney. Why are you here, seeing me?"

"It seems that we're related, and he said he can't operate on a relative for ethical reasons. He said you're the next best."

The next best. What a prick! What am I going to do? "I'm sorry, Mrs. Trentham. I too have ethical problems. I've just commenced practice, and my insurers are naturally cautious. There's a condition in my medical indemnity insurance policy that precludes me from operating on a client who's had major plastic surgery within the past five years, without psychiatric clearance."

"That's stupid! Why?"

"I agree. I have no idea. You know what these insurance companies are like. Here," he said pushing Debbie Stenson's card across his desk,

"I haven't used her before, but I understand she's first-rate. If her opinion satisfies my insurers, I'll be pleased to operate."

Mrs. Trentham looked perplexed, but finally stood up to leave. "Damn insurance companies," she said. "Thank you, Dr. Beaumont. I hope I see you again."

"The feeling's mutual," Beaumont lied.

Chapter 15

Mrs. Masterson was early for her Friday appointment. "Good morning, Dr. Beaumont. Rachel tells me that she and you are on first name terms. Please call me Vicki."

"And you may call me Simon."

"I'm not like Rachel. If it's all the same to you, I prefer Dr. Beaumont, but I'd still like you to call me Vicki. I'm looking forward to next Friday. I'm so excited. I'll be glad when all the paperwork's out the way."

Beaumont pushed a document across his desk to her titled, Informed Consent, which she immediately went to sign. "No, please don't sign until I have been over the contents with you, and then, if you do sign, it must be before a witness. I can't overstress the importance of this document. If there is anything you don't understand, please do not hesitate to raise your concerns."

"I know you want me to be aware of the dangers, but nothing is going to stop me from having the surgery. I can't wait to see the new me."

I'm not doing it for you. I'm doing it so the slimy bloodsuckers have no grounds to sue me if things go awry. "Vicki, do you understand that infection may occur, requiring antibiotics and other treatment?"

"We went over this at the last consultation. Yes, I get it."

Beaumont painstakingly went over each clause, even though he knew he was irritating Vicki. "This is important," he said. "Do you understand that you may suffer a heart attack or stroke due to the strain on the heart? Death as a result of this procedure is possible."

"Yes," Vicki sighed. "Dr. Beaumont, when you operated at The Royal Sydney, how many of your patients had a heart attack, a stroke or suffered brain damage?"

It's not about you. It's about protecting me. "None, fortunately, but that's not the point. Do you understand that the scars in your hairline and behind your ears may be visible?"

For the first time, Vicki seemed disconcerted, and she frowned. "You said that my scars will be almost invisible, and that in time they'll fade."

You dismiss heart attack and stroke but you're worried that the scars might be visible. "Sometimes not everything goes to plan. Do you understand that the scars may thicken and become red and itchy?"

"Yes." Vicki yawned.

Ten minutes later, Beaumont reached the last clause. "Do you understand that bruising and swelling may occur that could cause a blood clot, which might have to be surgically removed?"

"Yes, yes, yes," Vicki said, shaking her head. "Can I sign now?"

"Yes," Beaumont replied, as he buzzed Mary. "Can you come in and witness Mrs. Masterson's signature?"

"Are you going to go over your Informed Consent with Rachel before you do her boobs?"

"Something similar, yes."

"I'd love to be a fly on the wall. She has no patience. Don't be surprised if she throws a hissy fit. Do I sign and date?"

"Yes, and I want you to initial every clause. Mary, initial next to Mrs. Masterson's initials, complete the witness box, and give Mrs. Masterson a copy."

"I don't need a copy. I've got nothing to reconsider," Vicki said, pushing an envelope toward Beaumont. "There's a check for your fee in there."

"Thank you. When you signed, you acknowledged that I had provided you with a copy," Beaumont said.

"Is that all?"

"Yes, unless you have any questions for me."

"Thank goodness I don't."

"Get a good sleep on Thursday night, and remember, no food or drink after midnight."

"Mary gave me the instructions on Monday. I've memorized them. I know precisely what I'm allowed to do and what I have to bring."

After Mrs. Masterson left, Mary came into Beaumont's office. "Can I ask a question?"

"Go for it."

"I've worked with four plastic surgeons. That's the harshest form of Informed Consent I've ever seen. You're going to lose clients. Why is it so severe?"

"I don't like lawyers. They're scumbags. You may not know it, but there are more malpractice suits relating to Informed Consents than all other causes. The surgeon's invariably found to be negligent because he never spelled out all the risks to the client. That's never going to happen to me, and if it costs me a few clients, so be it."

Mary smiled.

"Did I say something funny?"

"Lawyers are scumbags? Who drew up your Informed Consent?"

"Ah, that's funny. I meant to say that all lawyers except the ones who act for me are scumbags," Beaumont said. "Do I have any appointments other than Mrs. Werner this afternoon?"

"Two. One from the editorial in *Women's Sport*. She wants to talk to you about calf implants. The other's an ex-boxer referred to you by Dr. Kruse. He has a badly twisted, broken nose with an ugly hump."

"Why isn't he going through the public system?"

"He has private insurance, and it seems that Dr. Kruse spoke very highly of you."

He's Timmy Brown's GP. No wonder he's sending referrals to me. "Yes, I know him."

Chapter 16

There was a chill in the early evening air, and Beaumont zipped his jacket up to the neck as the ferry pulled into Manly. It was Saturday, and The Corso was buzzing with families, and the young getting primed at the pubs. He stopped at a bottle shop and with the help of the shop assistant bought a bottle of Hunter Valley red.

Five minutes later he knocked on Debbie's door and was greeted with, "You slimy bastard. I didn't think you'd have the cheek to show your face."

"Whoa," Beaumont said, holding up his hands, "what's wrong?"

"As if you don't know. Does Mrs. Trentham ring any bells with you?"

"Oh, shit. I didn't think she'd contact you."

"Liar! You gave her my card and fed her some bullshit about not being able to perform surgery without your insurer's consent. Then you said they wouldn't consent without a psychiatrist's report and told her to come and see me. Bastard!"

Beaumont tried to keep a serious face. "I never thought she'd get to see you. You told me you had appointments and meetings every minute of the day. Why did you see her?"

"You can't be that thick. Her family have been generous donors to The Royal Sydney for decades. She called the higher-ups. They told me to drop everything. I could've killed you. I'm seeing bashed wives, out of control drug addicts and potential suicides, and you waste my time because you're too gutless to tell her you won't operate."

"What did you say to her? Jeez, can I come in?"

Debbie stepped away from the entrance. "I should put you back on the ferry," she said. "I was honest with her. I asked her if she wanted to take the risk of surgery at this stage of her life. I suggested that she'd be far better off enjoying her grandchildren, rather than lying bruised and battered in a hospital bed."

"She wouldn't have liked that."

"No, not at first. She got uppity and told me about her family and how rich they were. Then she calmed down and said how refreshing it was to talk to someone who was upfront with her. It seems that most people tell her what they think she wants to hear. She thinks you're full of shit. Those were her exact words. She contacted her insurance broker, and he said that he'd never heard of anything like the insurance condition you conveniently created. She asked me if I had, and I responded in the negative. She thinks you treated her like a fool."

"Shit! Is she coming back to see me?"

"Thanks to me, no. She asked if I knew you. I said you were a passing acquaintance."

"And then what?"

"She told me that Brett Golding was a distant relative and ethically it precluded him from operating on her. I nearly puked. She thought it was bullshit too and asked me what I thought. I wasn't as honest with my response. I was wary of getting caught in Golding's cross hairs again, so I said that I didn't know. She told me she admired my diplomacy. Do you and that fool, Golding, think she got rich by being stupid?" Debbie angrily tossed the salad.

"Did she ask you why Golding and I didn't want to operate on her?"

"Yes, and I asked her if she'd ever sued any negligent plastic surgeons."

She didn't answer. She just slapped her thigh and laughed.

"I said that the pair of you were probably worried about litigation."

"Yes, I was worried. I could achieve perfect results, and she'd still sue. Is she going back to see Golding?"

"No. She's reconsidering whether she needs surgery. She did ask what I'd heard about you. I said that the nurses in the OR think you're competent but there are others who are better."

"Shit! You didn't say that."

"I did. You didn't want her coming back to see you. Well, I've solved your problem. Why are you worried?"

"I don't want her badmouthing me to her family and wealthy friends."

"You should have thought of that before you got me involved."

"Jesus, Debbie, you're always saying that those contemplating plastic surgery should see a psychiatrist, and when I refer a client to you, you shit all over me."

"Don't you dare get self-righteous with me, Simon Beaumont! If you were concerned, you should have told her of your concerns and said that you'd like her to see a psychiatrist. Instead, you went on with that charade about your insurers. You and Gold-digger make a fine pair."

"I never thought she'd go to see you," Beaumont said, trying not to grin

"Yes, that's your problem. You don't think," Debbie said, opening the wine. "I need this."

"Can we declare another truce? I won't do anything like that again."

"I don't know. I've been simmering for days and wanted to blast you. I'm not going to be good company tonight."

"If you don't stop tossing that salad, you'll liquefy it. Why don't I order the pizzas? You'll feel better after you've eaten. What are you having?"

"A small vegetarian on a gluten free, thin and crispy base."

"That'd be right," Beaumont muttered.

"What did you say?"

"That'll be nice."

"Oh? Yes, it's my favorite."

Beaumont took out his cell phone and called Natalia's Pizza Shop. Twenty minutes later, two pizzas were delivered.

"Smells great," Beaumont said, opening the lid of the box containing the larger pizza.

"A family sized pepperoni on thick crust. Could you have chosen anything unhealthier?" Debbie said.

"I love it," Beaumont grinned. "How was your week?"

"God, what have I just been talking about?"

The next five minutes they ate in uncomfortable silence until Debbie said, "Sorry, tell me how it is being back in practice?"

"Surprisingly busy. I'm operating this Friday. A facelift, and I'm doing a breast augmentation the following week. I've got a long way to go, but it's a good start. I'm sure the practice is going to be very successful."

"What's your definition of success?"

"Three facelifts in a day," he said. "You know how much I'd make in fees? Sixty thousand. Sixty thousand in one day."

Debbie shook her head. "The inequity of it. That's what I earn in a year, and I'm saving lives. The nurses do talk about you. They marveled when you gave that Aboriginal girl an eye socket. Surely you got more satisfaction out of that than taking ten years off the face of a superficial social climber?"

I got to bed one of those appreciative nurses because of that operation. That was satisfying. "So you think I'm shallow. Well, I didn't put in all those hours studying and kissing up to surgeons, to end up a pauper. I want to be wealthy. Secure. Happy. If I have to operate on superficial, socialite millionaires to achieve my goals, then that's what I'll do."

"I don't think you're as bad as what you make out. You just portray yourself that way because you know it annoys me. Let's not talk shop anymore. I've rented a great movie. Sleepless in Seattle."

Can the night get worse? "Good choice, let's take our glasses over to the sofa and settle in."

A few minutes later, he leaned over and kissed her. She responded half-heartedly, and said, "We're missing the movie."

That's okay. I've got all night. "We wouldn't want to do that, would we?"

For the next hour and a half, Beaumont sipped wine and feigned interest in the movie. Debbie was engrossed. *Unbelievable!*

As the movie credits ran down the screen, she glanced at her watch and said, "Oh my God, look at the time. I was going to make coffee, but you don't have time. You'll have to hurry to make the last ferry."

Beaumont was about to laugh, but when he looked at Debbie, she wasn't smiling. He thought about saying something but decided against it. "Yes, I better get going."

She kissed him lightly on the lips. "It was nice to see you, Simon. Thanks for the pizza and wine. It's my treat the next time."

There won't be a next time. "Sounds good," he said, as she closed the door.

It was cold, and a light drizzle was falling. He zipped his jacket to the neck and put his hands deep into his pockets. The drunks were out in force on The Corso, and young girls who had spent hours preparing for the night now looked scruffy and bedraggled. It was after midnight when he boarded the ferry. He sat inside the cabin staring out the window. It was a moonless night and he could barely make out the white of the waves but could feel the ferry being buffeted. He was fuming. *How dare she treat me like that? I could've been with Sonya, Connie or many others, all far more attractive than that bitch. I won't be wasting any more time on her. Good riddance.*

Chapter 17

The second week of Beaumont's practice was busy with appointments coming from the editorial in *Women's Sport,* a friend of Rachel Werner's looking to freshen up her eyes, and referrals from GPs. He had been unable to forget what Debbie had done to him, and each night when his head hit the pillow, she was on his mind. Now on a cold morning, six days after she'd kicked him out, he was still thinking of her as he scrubbed up for his first cosmetic procedure in over two years.

He gloved with Mary's help. Vicki Masterson lay supine on the operating table, a sedated smile on her face. The anesthesiologist asked her to count to ten and by the time she reached five she was in dreamland. Mary nodded to one of the hospital nurses and Bizet's Carmen permeated the operating theater. Beaumont watched as the breathing tube was inserted and then looked at the clock and said, "Commencing at 6:35."

He injected a solution of saline, lidocaine, and epinephrine into Vicki's jowls, mouth, and hairline where he would be making incisions. Mary had arranged his tray of instruments atop a Mayo stand. She passed him a scalpel, and he made a small incision under the chin. A few minutes later he said, "She has redundant platysma muscle that I'll have to remove."

Mary held the skin back with a retractor while Beaumont removed the excess and started to elevate the platysma muscle. Thirty minutes had elapsed. The Toreador Song echoed around the theater, but the anesthesiologist and the two hospital nurses' chatted loudly about their plans for the weekend. Beaumont looked up and glared. "For Chrissake, shut the fuck up. I can't enjoy Bizet with that din going on."

The chatter stopped, and the anesthesiologist nervously said, "Sorry," before refocusing on the gauges in front of him.

Six and a half hours later the facelift and forehead lift had been completed, and Beaumont was finishing tattooing Mrs. Masterson's nipple. "Can you tell the difference, Mary?" he asked.

"No," she said, "They look identical. It's perfect."

"I know."

At 1:15 he said, "We're all done. Take her to recovery." He felt invigorated and not in the slightest fatigued.

Ten minutes later, Beaumont sat in the cafeteria enjoying a latte with Mary. "I imagine Hollywood hospitals look like this," she said. "Who'd ever imagine a cafeteria with polished timber tables and cushioned chairs? It wreaks of money."

"You're right, and they sure know how to charge for the OR. I'll have my own hospital in the not too distant future," Beaumont said. "Mary, it helped to have you anticipating my every need. One small point, though. You have a tendency to slap the instruments into my hands. I'd like to you be gentler in future."

"I was trained that way. I've never had a complaint before."

"I'm not complaining. I'm telling you how I'd like to have the instruments passed to me. Did you see anything that you hadn't seen before today?"

"Yes, a few minor differences, but basically it was the same as countless other face and forehead lift procedures that I've assisted in."

Beaumont clicked his tongue. "Wait until you see Mrs. Masterson in a week's time. I guarantee you'll be surprised. In three months when we take photos, you won't believe your eyes."

"Why wait three months? No one who I've worked for has waited that long."

"Subtle changes will still be occurring then and will continue for at least a year. However, nothing noticeable will occur after three months. I'm a little surprised that you didn't notice any differences in the OR."

"Oh, but I did. I've never seen a surgeon get so angry over a little banter before, and worse, you spoke to the anesthesiologist like he was your slave. I doubt he'll ever work with you again."

"When I was training, I worked for some surgeons who cracked jokes and told stories. I don't. I concentrate. One false move and I nick a nerve, or complete a procedure where the patient's face ends up lopsided, and I'm out of business. My patients will be my billboards, my works of art. I have to deliver perfection. Nothing less is acceptable. If I lose an anesthesiologist along the way, do you think I care? There are plenty more where he came from."

Mary took a sip from her cup and peered over the rim. "I don't know what to make of you? You're obviously a perfectionist, and I like that. However, is it because you care for your patients; or are you worried that poor surgery will hurt your practice?"

"Look at it this way. My current patients are the beneficiaries of my need for future patients."

"More like your need for money."

"Mary, I'll never apologize for being ambitious. Why don't you head back to the surgery? I'm going to wait for Mrs. Masterson to recover. I'll be another hour."

The following morning Beaumont pulled into The Paragon's underground parking garage. There were two Porsches and a Mercedes, but it was nearly empty. His was the only Ford. *Not for much longer, though,* he thought, as he looked enviously at a glistening red Porsche. How different this was to The Royal Sydney, where despite it being Saturday morning, there wouldn't be any vacant spaces.

Mrs. Masterson had had a peaceful night, and while her face was swollen, the bruising was minimal. She had already looked at her face in the mirror in the bathroom that adjoined her private room. "I'm thrilled, Dr. Beaumont, I think you did a marvelous job," she gushed.

"You're seeing yourself at the worst possible time, Vicki. Each day you'll see a marked improvement. Is anyone coming to visit?"

"My daughter and Rachel Werner. No one else knows."

"That's good. Right now, you need rest. I'll be in tomorrow morning before you leave. After that, my beauty therapist will wash your hair. It will pick you up."

"Doctor, I don't need picking up. I'm delighted. Oh, I nearly forgot. What you did with my breast defies description. Do you remember the horribly scarred mess? I knew what I wanted was difficult compared to an implant, but I am so pleased. You are a surgical magician."

"I'm glad you're happy. I'll see you in the morning."

Beaumont got out of the elevator on the ground floor. The reception was quiet, but it reminded him more of a five-star hotel than a hospital. Patients entered through automatic, sliding, glass doors that opened onto a large white marble tiled foyer that led to an expansive polished, black, granite counter. To the left of the counter was a waiting area. The plush leather chairs and walnut coffee tables surrounded by bookshelves smelled of money. Coffee machines like those in the lounges of international airlines were positioned next to racks filled with the latest magazines and newspapers. *When I build my hospital, it will put this to shame,* Beaumont thought as he got back into the elevator.

Chapter 18

The week after Mrs. Masterson's facelift, Beaumont scheduled Rachel Werner's breast augmentation. He was busy with referrals from GPs for reconstructive cosmetic surgery. He wasn't worried. He knew that he'd have to build up the pipeline. Broken noses were the order of the day with three clients looking to improve their appearance and breathing. Another client in her mid-forties had what she described as a drooping, lazy right eye that not only looked unsightly but also impaired her vision. An attractive nineteen-year-old girl had seen the editorial in *Women's Sport* and wanted, but didn't need, a facelift. The fee was tempting but Beaumont, wary of possible adverse publicity was short with her, saying that she should see a psychiatrist, but he didn't mention Debbie Stenson. Rachel Werner came in for her third consultation and got angry when Beaumont spent more than thirty minutes going over the Informed Consent in minute detail. She was a feisty, crass woman used to getting her own way, but Beaumont finally convinced her that going up one and a half sizes would produce the optimum result. As she was leaving, she turned and said, "If I'm not happy there'll be hell to pay. I'm not going up two sizes because I've listened to you. I hope for your sake that you're right."

On Thursday, a twenty-two-year-old Asian girl came to see him looking for round eyes. It was an increasingly popular procedure that Beaumont had no reservations about performing. His last appointment was a fifty-four-year-old male executive whose sagging jowls, droopy eyes, and wrinkled forehead were making it increasingly difficult for him to compete with his younger peers. He had visited two other plastic surgeons and knew what the surgery entailed.

Beaumont complimented him on his choice of surgeons and said that their work was excellent, adding, "The results they achieve using older techniques are remarkable." He knew the response this would elicit. Who in their right didn't want the latest technology whether it be a television or facial rejuvenation? He would become adept at using this tactic when competing for work with other plastic surgeons, with one notable exception, Brett Golding. It was far too early to get on Golding's wrong side by stealing his clients.

By the end of the week, Mary had booked The Paragon for three clients the following Wednesday. Rachel Werner's breast augmentation, the boxer's nose reconstruction and a simple blepharoplasty where Beaumont would incise the skin from the patient's right eyelid and remove the fat and excess skin. He gloated as he read an article in *The Daily Telegraph* citing the average Australian weekly wage as seven hundred and twenty dollars a week – his fees for Wednesday would be seventeen thousand. He quickly read the social pages. There was a photo of Western Australian mining billionaire, Joe Milgate, and his much younger, svelte wife, Barbara, who were looking to buy an eastern states retreat in Wolseley Road. Beaumont read the accompanying article about the billionaire, who had been prospecting for gold when he stumbled across a massive nickel deposit. *Wealth acquired by luck is so unfair,* Beaumont thought.

On Monday morning, Mrs. Masterson became the first client to use the second waiting room for postoperative patients. She was wearing a scarf and large lensed sunglasses, but there was no longer any need for them. "I'm over the moon," she gushed.

Beaumont came around from behind his desk and examined her face. The swelling had subsided, and fresh pink skin glistened. "You're healing nicely," he said, pulling out his camera. "Let's take a few pics."

"You said you wouldn't take the *after* pics for ninety days?"

"These aren't the *after* pics; they're just to track your progress. Don't worry, no one else is ever going to see them."

"I haven't been able to drag myself away from a mirror. Am I vain?"

"Probably, but you have every right to be. Don't question your actions. Enjoy your new face."

"Rachel Werner wants you to do the same for her as soon as her boobs heal. I think she's jealous."

That's hardly unexpected. Thanks to me, you look a million dollars. A walking, talking billboard. "The main thing is that you're pleased."

"Did you and Rachel settle on a size? She said you were trying to talk her into going small. Why would you do that?"

"Vicki, I can't talk about my other patients."

"I'm sorry. I didn't think. I'm on such a high. You thought I'd be depressed. No way."

"Good. Please go behind the screen and take your top off. I need to check your breast for color."

"It's perfect. It's impossible to tell the difference."

A few minutes later, Beaumont said, "You're right. I hope you're not going out in the sun on your holiday."

"I'm not. I'm going to a health spa in the Dandenongs. Healthy food, freshly squeezed fruit juice, rest, long walks in the hills and yummy massages."

"Excellent. Mary has a little bag of lotions and potions for you to take on your holiday. I'll ask her to come in." He hit the intercom.

Mary stopped, open-mouthed, as she came in and said, "Oh my God, you look marvelous. You don't look a day over thirty."

"Thank you. It's Dr. Beaumont who's marvelous."

Yes, I am. "I'll see you after you get back," Beaumont said, glancing at his watch.

After Mrs. Masterson left, Beaumont asked, "What do you think, Mary?"

"The transformation is amazing."

"The best facial rejuvenation you've ever seen?"

Mary paused before saying, "Yes, in twenty years I haven't seen better."

Beaumont gloated and looked down at his hands.

On Friday afternoon, Beaumont returned to The Royal Sydney for his first pro bono procedure, the pinning back of a young, orphan boy's ears. Known as otoplasty, it was a relatively simple procedure.

As usual, the parking garage was packed, and the only two vacant spaces were Brett Golding's. Beaumont carefully reversed into one of Golding's spaces, leaving as much room in the other as he could. The probability was that Golding was at his Sydney surgery, and if he wasn't, there was ample room for his Bentley.

The procedure went smoothly, and in a little over two hours Beaumont was back in the parking garage, but his car wasn't. Brett Golding's Bentley occupied both spaces. Beaumont rushed back into the hospital only to be told by the receptionist that his car had been towed away at the instruction of Dr. Golding. "I don't think he knew it was your car, Dr. Beaumont. He said that some bum had pinched his car space and told me to call for a tow truck. Here are the company's details," she said, handing Beaumont a card. "The tow truck driver said you'll have to pay three hundred dollars before they release it."

"Fuck! Fuck him. Where is he?"

"The-the tow truck driver?"

"For Chrissake. No. Dr. Golding."

"I-I don't know. I-I'll page him."

"Don't bother," Beaumont said, pulling out his cell phone.

"Brett," he shouted, "what do you think you're doing having my car towed?"

"Was that old rust bucket yours? I didn't know. It shouldn't have been in my parking spaces."

"It's not a rust bucket, and I left you plenty of room. Why couldn't you have parked in the other space? I have to get a taxi to Canterbury and pay three hundred dollars before the tow truck company releases it. Who's paying?"

"I know who's not," Golding grunted. "You read the sign and ran the risk. Next time you'll know better."

"Fuck you."

"I'll forget you said that this time. Be careful, Simon. It'll take me all of an hour to put you out of business. Do you want that?"

I'm going to be the laughing stock of the hospital and the profession when this gets out, but I can't afford to upset this asshole. "Sorry, Brett."

"Apology accepted," Golding replied and terminated the call.

Chapter 19

Monday was another busy day for Beaumont at The Paragon with two rhinoplasties and a mid-face facelift. He had chosen to operate on Mondays and Wednesdays in an attempt to avoid weekend follow-ups.

He had tried to talk a fifty-three-year-old woman out of a mid-face facelift, where a platysmaplasty isn't performed, and incisions aren't made behind the ears. The media promoted it as being harder to detect, but that was because it was impossible to get the same tightening as a full facelift. As such the results were nowhere near as good, and obviously not as noticeable. If he hadn't needed the fee, which wasn't much less than he charged for a full facelift, he would've declined the surgery. It always amused him when clients came in wanting to look ten to fifteen years younger but didn't want anyone to notice. Vicki Masterson was going to return from her holiday and tell her friends that she had metamorphosed because she'd spent two weeks at a Victorian spa. She had looked tired and drawn, but would return looking youthful and vibrant. No one was going to believe her.

Beaumont had checked on Rachel Werner in the two days following her breast augmentation when she was still on pain killers. She'd been bright and bubbly, and told him that she wanted the same facial procedures he'd performed on Vicki Masterson, plus the rejuvenation of her upper and lower eyelids.

Six days after the procedure it was a different Rachel Werner who Mary showed into his office. She was wearing a loose-fitting, black top, matching tracksuit pants and sandals. Before he could greet her, she said, "I'm sore, tight, and I have a swollen stomach. You have to do something. Oh, and I hate this post-op bra. Yuk! And I hate having to sleep on my back."

Every issue she raised was covered in the postoperative instructions, which she either hadn't read or had forgotten. "Let me have a look at you," he said, nodding toward the screen.

"What do you think?" she asked. "The scarring looks horrible."

"You have virtually no bruising, and the swelling has already started to subside. You will notice a rapid change from now on and in three weeks, eighty percent of the swelling will have gone. It will be six months before it completely subsides," Beaumont said, resisting the urge to say *I've already been over this with you, and it's in the instructions.*

"What about the scars?"

"They're healing well. There's a little pleating that will resolve itself in time. The incisions were made on the edge of the areola so they won't be noticeable. Have you been using the antibiotic ointment?"

"Yes, just as you said."

"Good, I want you to stop," Beaumont said, "and start using the vitamin E oil. Remember, massage gently. It'll speed up the healing process. The scars will get softer, flatter and start to fade. In three months, you won't notice them." Beaumont took a step back. "The size is perfect and they look superb. I'll get my camera."

"Yes, they do. I love them. I just wish they weren't so tight."

"The tightness will go as the swelling subsides. It might be more comfortable to sleep on a sofa or recliner for the next few days. You can put your top back on."

"Sleeping's not all that uncomfortable."

One compliment about how superb her boobs look, and she's no longer feeling the pain. What a great job this is. So long as I get the aesthetics right, all else is forgiven and forgotten. "I'll see you in three weeks, Rachel. They're only going to get better."

"Good, we can talk about my facelift then."

Chapter 20

Beaumont sat on his balcony sipping a cup of coffee and staring out at the harbor. It was Saturday, and he was at a loose end. He toyed with calling Steve Levine and arranging to go to The Level 20 Club tonight but thought better of it. Instead, he scanned the contacts in his cell phone. There were plenty of nurses he could call. He got to S and saw Sonya's name and realized that he didn't know her surname. The number immediately below Sonya's was Debbie Stenson's and he silently cursed. It had been three weeks since he'd seen her, and yet not a day had gone by when he hadn't thought of her. He was still angry, and she needed to be taught a lesson.

She answered her cell phone on the second ring. "Simon, how nice to hear from you. How is the practice going?"

"Getting busier by the day," he responded. "How are things with you?"

"Same old, same old. I see them every day, but I can't believe the lives some people live. They almost bring me to tears, but I have to remain stoic. That is the only way I can help. While you're giving some socialite from the north shore a new set of boobs, I'm comforting a mother whose drug addict son has just copped two years hard time in Long Bay."

Shit, it's like listening to a dull recording on loop. "Let's not go there."

"I'm not being catty or spiteful, Simon. You know what I said is true. I studied medicine to help others. You, Brett Golding and the many others like you, pursued medicine to help yourselves. I'm not resentful; rather I feel sorry for you. You're going to wake up one day and realize that you're worshipping a false god in the almighty dollar. Anyhow, that's my last word. I promise. Why did you call?"

Jesus, what a drone she is. "Do you remember I talked about going to that new Italian restaurant? The reviews are outstanding, and the food is to die for. If I can get a table, would you like to go there tonight?"

"Sounds good. I'll take the ferry over. Will you meet me at Circular Quay?"

"I will. Say 7:30."

"When will you let me know if we have a booking?"

"Assume we do."

"I'm glad you called. I'll see you tonight."

Beaumont hit the end button and then punched in Steve Levine's number.

"Yeah, Simon, what I can do for you?"

"Get me a quiet table for two at Botticelli's at eight o'clock tonight, Steve."

"If you don't hear from me within fifteen minutes, consider it done."

Beaumont opened *The Daily Telegraph* and turned to the social pages. A photo of Joe and Barbara Milgate standing in front of a grand mansion in Wolseley Road stared at him. The caption was *$8 Million Bargain,* and the article said that the Milgates had acquired the property so they'd have somewhere to stay on their frequent trips to Sydney. The article quoted Mrs. Milgate saying, "It's terribly difficult to find good servants these days. I don't know what we're going to do." *I'd love her money,* Beaumont thought, turning to the front page.

The harbor was flat, and the weather mild when Debbie's ferry berthed. She was wearing a black dress, a matching jacket, and three-inch heels. "You look great," Beaumont said, kissing her lightly on the lips.

"Thank you. I hope this place isn't very far because I'm not used to heels."

"Less than five minutes," he said, putting his arm around her.

The entrance to Botticelli's was understated, the lights were dim, and Renaissance murals adorned the walls. The plush chocolate-brown carpet still had the new smell about it, and red leather chairs complemented double-damask tables set with fine crockery and hallmark silverware. The waiter showed them to a table below a mural of The Tower of Babel. Beaumont ordered sparkling mineral water, and the waiter left them with menus, saying that he'd be back in a few minutes.

"Check the prices out," Debbie said. "I should've been a chef."

"Don't look at the prices. Just order what appeals to you."

"I can't. Twenty-two dollars for a tomato and basil side salad. It's obscene."

"If you keep this up, you're going to spoil the night."

"I'm sorry. I've never been impressed by places like this. What are you having?"

"Tasmanian oysters followed by charcoal grilled swordfish and red pepper agrodolce. Have you made up your mind?"

"Tuna and squid salad for starters and then King George whiting. It's such an indulgence," Debbie said.

"Just enjoy," Beaumont said, beckoning their waiter. He ordered their meals and a 1994 Hofstatter Pinot Grigio.

"How's the practice coming along, Simon?"

"I can't complain. Next week's appointment book is nearly full, and I'm operating two days. Not bad, when you consider I only hung my shingle out four weeks ago."

"Do you do specialize or do you have a broad brush?"

"A broad brush? I've never heard surgery described like that before. I like it. There isn't any cosmetic procedure that I won't perform."

"What about labia reductions?"

"Of course. There's growing demand for labiaplasty and vaginoplasty. If you have a problem, I'd be pleased to help you, at friend's rates of course," Beaumont winked.

"I don't have a problem," Debbie said, turning red. "Vaginoplasty? Who comes up with those names? You just add plasty to any body part and voila, you have a new procedure. I guess you plastic surgeons have Ogilvy and Mather on retainer?"

"I hope you aren't that sarcastic with your clients. If it makes women feel better about themselves why shouldn't they avail themselves of the procedures?"

"Because there's no reason for women to feel bad. What happens to their bodies is natural. It's only glossy magazines and greedy plastic surgeons who create doubt and false expectations. I presume you do penile enlargements too?"

"No, I don't," Beaumont glared.

"Oh, how come? Hasn't anyone come up with a suitable name? How about dickaplasty?"

"You're not funny. It's called penoplasty. It's something I don't offer."

The waiter served their entrees and poured the wine. After he'd left, Debbie said, "You claim that you perform all plastic surgical procedures. You don't. You're happy to carve up women's genitalia, but not men's. Do you know what I think?"

"Would it make any difference if I said I don't, and nor do I want to know?"

"No. I think you're homophobic. You can't stand the thought of handling another man's penis."

Beaumont sighed, as he popped an oyster into his mouth. "If that's the case, there are an awful lot of homophobic plastic surgeons in Sydney. I don't know anyone who performs penoplasties. Can we drop the subject?"

"Penoplasties?" Debbie giggled. "Do you know how hilarious and stupid that sounds? You'd better find a replacement for Ogilvy and Mather."

"You're not amusing. Are you finished?"

"Not quite. Do you remember telling me that women's confidence significantly improves after breast augmentation? Is it the same for men?"

"How would I know?"

"So you've never suffered dick envy in the showers at the gym?" She angled her face accusingly.

"No. I guess others might have been envious of me, though."

"God, you're serious. You must be the most arrogant man in the world. You make me want to puke."

"I was joking."

"No, you weren't."

They finished their entrees in silence and the conversation over their main courses was strained. The waiter cleared the table and left them with dessert menus. Beaumont didn't open his.

Debbie ran her finger down the menu and said, "I don't think I can fit anything more in, but I'd love to try the tiramisu. Will you share it with me?"

Beaumont felt himself relaxing again. *She's like a little girl in a candy store.* "Sure, but you'll have to have the big half." He leaned back and crossed his legs. "I'm having a cappuccino. What about you?"

"Just tiramisu, thanks."

As they lingered at the front of Botticelli's, Beaumont said, "I can walk you back to the ferry or we can grab a taxi and you come back to my place for a nightcap."

"What would you like me to do?"

"It'd be nice if you at least got to see my place before I vacate."

"You're leaving."

"I'm not leaving Wolseley Road, but I need a two-bedroom place, so I'll have a home office. I want something nicer too."

"And more expensive."

"Of course."

"Does it have it to be Wolseley Road?"

"Yes. I like the harbor views."

"There are many other less expensive suburbs with views of the harbor. Why do you have to stay in such a prestigious, or should I say snobby road?"

"I like it. I'm never going to leave. Within three years, I'll own a house."

Debbie laughed. "God, is there that much money in plastic surgery? The worst house in Wolseley Road will set you back three to four million. Mosman's an upmarket suburb, and you can buy a superb home there for two million."

"No thanks. Look, are you coming back to my place? You can get a taxi when you're ready to go home."

"You mean if I don't stay." She laced her fingers with his. "I'll ask you again. Do you want me to?"

"Of course I do. You are the most exasperating woman."
""You're such a charmer. I sure hope I enjoy the nightcap."
And I sure hope I enjoy you.

Chapter 21

By mid-1997, Beaumont had purchased the freehold from where he practiced and four adjoining old houses. He had extended the renovations to his surgery to accommodate three injectors, and two therapists specializing in dermabrasion and laser resurfacing. Mary Perton had taken on the role of practice manager and two consultants reported to her. The first helped interview prospective clients, and the second arranged finance for those who didn't have the funds to pay for their procedures. Beaumont had become something of a celebrity, and many 'sticky beaks' made appointments just to meet him. The standard fee for a medical consultation was forty-five dollars with eighty percent rebateable from the government health insurer. His growing reputation had become a burden, and he increased his consultation fee to five hundred dollars to deter sticky beaks. If the women of Sydney were going to waste his time, they were going to pay for it. He was doing between eight and twelve surgeries a week and making a fortune. He still hadn't achieved his goal of three face and forehead lifts in a day but in one great week had managed to earn fees of nearly two hundred thousand. The Ford was gone, replaced with a gleaming, new, silver Mercedes convertible. He had discharged his mother's mortgage and was sending her a thousand a month. Despite this, she still wasn't happy and nagged him incessantly about his mean behavior.

Brett Golding was still the A-listers surgeon of choice. Beaumont had made no attempt to steal his clients but Golding was starting to lose them anyway. He had performed a face and brow lift on the Governor General's wife, which to the trained eye, had produced a pronounced lopsided result. Beaumont had studied the photos in the *Woman's Day* and knew that gravity would not improve the outcome. It was second-rate surgery, but it was still too early to make an enemy of Golding. Interestingly, every time Beaumont increased his fees,

Golding followed with a slightly larger increase. Market leaders in any field were always the priciest, and Golding was sending a message that he was still the leader of the pack, but his clients were starting to wonder if his results justified his exorbitant fees.

While Beaumont was raking in the cash, he was also spending big. Architects had drawn up plans for a two-level, sixteen room, boutique hospital, with two operating theaters and an underground parking garage. Two adjoining houses were being demolished so that his dream could be realized. The other two would eventually be torn down and replaced with a luxurious motel style aftercare facility for clients flying in from Asia. He knew he wouldn't have enough business to fully utilize the aftercare facility, and this was the reason the hospital had been designed with two operating theaters. He would make one available to other plastic surgeons who were looking for an extended aftercare facility for their clients.

When Beaumont told Debbie where he was going for Christmas, she said, "I haven't been to New York. I'd love to spend Christmas in the snow."

It won't be with me, Beaumont thought. *I'll be having some fun with Vance and don't want you cramping my style.* "It's not a holiday," he lied. "I'll only be there two weeks, and I'll be meeting with surgeons."

"Over Christmas?"

"Yes."

"I wanted to spend Christmas with you," she said, trying to conceal her hurt.

Now you know how I felt when you kicked me out of your apartment. "Sorry, we'll catch up when I get back."

The last major procedure that Beaumont performed for the year was a facelift for a thirty-nine-year-old woman, Karen Blackman, from the rich, rural Southern Highlands of New South Wales. Beaumont had been struck by her beauty. She had great bone structure and perfect skin texture. She'd also done extensive research and was one of the most informed clients he'd ever consulted. She had no laxity below the chin and told Beaumont she did not need a platysmaplasty. Nor was she looking for a mid-face facelift that she thought would be ineffective after a few years. She wanted a full facelift without the platysmaplasty; to remove the minute looseness in her jowls and around her cheeks. Beaumont didn't think she needed surgery, but he wasn't about to tell her and cost himself a fee.

There was minimal swelling when Karen attended her first postoperative consultation, but no bruising. She looked vibrant and any trace of facial laxity had disappeared. Better still, she was happy, and that was all that counted.

It was bitterly cold when Beaumont's flight landed at LaGuardia the day before Christmas. Vance was waiting for him, and as they left the terminal, Beaumont pulled his overcoat up in a futile attempt to keep the arctic wind out. "Jeez, it's cold. What's the temperature?"

"What's wrong, Jack? You're not getting soft down under, are you? It's 44. You'll soon get used to it again."

No, I won't. I'm glad I'm only here for two weeks. "Jesus, in the middle of winter in Sydney it's in the low sixties. I don't miss this one bit. Oh, and no one's called me Jack for years. I prefer Simon."

"Are you staying with your mom?" Vance teased. "Will she call you Simon?"

"Are you kidding? Of course not. I'm in the Hyatt, Times Square. I'll do my duty and spend Christmas Day with her, but I'm not going to listen to her whine about me changing my name for two weeks. I want to have some fun with you."

"I'm in a serious relationship. I met her in Soho a year ago and she moved in the month after."

"So? You can still have a bit on the side," Beaumont grinned. "You're not stupid enough to tell her everything, are you?"

"We've got no secrets."

"Hell! What happened to the old Vance Morgan?"

"He grew up. I've built up a practice here. Nothing like what you have in Sydney, but we both know I'll never be the surgeon you are. I'd love to have you around for dinner to meet Liz, but my fooling around days are over."

Christ, what did I come back for? The weather's shithouse. Vance is not up for any fun, and I'm stuck home listening to my Mom. Fucking great Christmas! I'll see if I can get a flight to Sydney on New Year's Day. "Sounds good, Vance. I'm looking forward to it," Beaumont lied.

BOOK 2

1997 - 2002 SYDNEY — MAKING IT BIG

Chapter 22

Beaumont returned to Sydney running a fever. Debbie had called him four times in New York but he'd let her calls go through to voicemail. When the taxi dropped him at his new apartment, he made himself a hot lemon drink, popped two disprin, and was about to jump into bed when his cell phone rang. It was Debbie. *Fuck!*

"Why didn't you return my calls?" she demanded.

"I didn't get them until I got off the plane. I had problems with the carrier in New York."

"I need to see you. Where are you?"

"I'm sick. I got in this morning. I'm going to bed."

"You're at your apartment?"

"Yes."

"I'll be there in ten minutes. I won't hold you long."

"Can't it wait?"

"No."

"I've moved. The address is—"

"I know where it is. I'll see you soon."

Beaumont poured himself a large brandy and downed it in one gulp. He refilled the glass and sat on the sofa.

Fifteen minutes later, Debbie knocked sharply on Beaumont's door. He answered, glass and hand, and said, "Couldn't it have waited?"

"No." She pushed past him into the apartment. "You look terrible How many drinks have you had? You're slurring."

"I'm alright. What's so urgent?"

"It's not urgent. I'm just curious, and I want you to be truthful. The night before you left I went to the hospital Christmas party. Brett Golding cornered me and asked if I'd had you on my couch. He gave me the grubbiest look when he said it. He made my skin crawl, and when I tried to push past him, he asked when I could fit him in for an appointment. He emphasized 'fit' in the crudest of ways. What did you tell him?"

"So that's what this is about. I didn't say anything."

"Simon, I'm a big girl. I'm not worried, but while you were in New York, I was repeatedly propositioned. Gold-digger must've spread some nasty rumors about me. Was I just another conquest? Did you boast about it?"

Beaumont downed another brandy and emptied the remains of the bottle into his glass. "No, I never breathed a word."

"You never hinted, or gave him a nod and a wink like men do when they boast about their conquests?"

"No," Beaumont said, giving her a dopey smile, but I did say something about asking you to move in with me," Beaumont lied.

"That's sweet. Why didn't you ask me?"

What did I just say? How stupid am I? It must be the brandy. "I know how much you value your independence. I knew you'd say no."

"I could compromise," Debbie said. "I like the idea and think we'd get on just fine. Is the invitation still open?'

"Of course."

"Fantastic! I'll terminate my lease and start moving my stuff in. I knew you weren't as shallow as you made out. Now come on, let's get you to bed before you get seriously sick."

What did I just do? God, please cut my tongue out. "Thanns Deb, youse a real pal."

"I think you've had too much to drink." Debbie put her arm around his waist and helped him into bed.

Chapter 23

The Olympics were more than two years away, but a large number of the surgeries Beaumont had been performing were for clients wanting to look good for the Games. He had a fourteen-week waiting list, and it was getting longer by the day. The city was in a frenzy as preparations continued unabated to make the Games successful. Sydney had always played second fiddle to Melbourne when it came to hosting international sporting events. Now it was time to show the world what it could do.

The waiting room was always full of clients waiting to see Mary, the consultants, injectors, and therapists. Plus there were those prepared to pay five hundred dollars to see Beaumont. Julie looked stressed when she came into his office. "There's a woman who insists on seeing you. She doesn't have an appointment. I told her you wouldn't be able to see her for three weeks. She became aggressive and said that once you knew who she was, you'd see her. Her name's Barbara Milgate."

Beaumont smiled. He certainly knew who Barbara Milgate was. Her family had owned a huge pastoral empire in Western Australia, and she was queen of the Perth social scene. When the family had fallen on hard times, she had married mining billionaire, Joe Milgate, a union the media described as class for cash. Milgate had been a hard drinking, hard playing womanizer but under the tutelage of Barbara, had become semi-respectable. A condition of the marriage was that she provide him with a son and heir, something she'd failed to do and had no intention of doing.

"Show her in, Julie."

She was a tall, slim brunette in her early forties who sat down without extending her hand. "Sit down, Milly," she said to the frumpy teenager with her.

Who in their right mind would call their kid, Mildred Millgate? Was it payback because she wasn't a boy? She's got her father's long horsey face and hawk-like nose. I could remedy that. The only thing she's got going for her is her lustrous, wavy black hair. "Good morning, Mrs. Milgate. How can I be of service?"

"My husband is relocating the head office of his business to Sydney, and we're looking for suitable accommodation."

You've already got an eight million dollar pad in Wolseley Road. What's not suitable? "Welcome to Sydney. And who might this be?" Beaumont looked at Milly.

"I hadn't finished," she said. "Last week I was at a luncheon for The Epilepsy Foundation, and I met this obnoxious woman. She was loud, vulgar and totally out of place, however, she looked stunning. Her name's Rachel Werner, and she raved about you. She said that if I thought her face looked good, I had to see her breasts, and she offered to show me them in the restrooms. Naturally I declined."

Beaumont fought back a smile. *A billboard doing its job.* "I'm please–"

Barbara Milgate held her hand up. "I'm not finished. I'll tell you when I am."

What a bitch. I wonder if her husband regrets his desire to buy respectability.

"I've been having work done in Harley Street. We have a place in London, and I enjoy shopping there. However, since meeting that woman I've had you thoroughly checked out. You've achieved some amazing results. What can you do for me? I feel that I'm a little too hard looking. Now you can talk."

I thought you were here to see me about your daughter. Barbara Milgate had good genes and skin. Her face was aristocratic but severe. Her small, defined biceps talked when she moved her arms, and she had a gym-hardened body. The work she'd had done was excellent and the facelift she'd had within the past two years was first-rate. Her problem was attitudinal as much as it was aesthetic. If she wasn't so domineering, she would naturally have a softer expression, but Beaumont knew she didn't want to hear that. "Mrs. Milgate, I think we can achieve the subtle changes you desire with some laser treatment and Botox around the eyes."

"Is that all?"

"I was about to say and the forehead."

"When can you do it? I have some free time this Wednesday afternoon."

Beaumont suppressed a smile. "It's not a one treatment solution. It will require three consultations. I have surgery on Mondays and Wednesdays, so they're out."

"Hmmph! I'll get my personal assistant to contact you with a list of dates when I'm available."

"Ask her to contact my practice manager, Mary Perton," Beaumont said, pushing Mary's card across the desk. "She handles my appointments."

"Very well, Doctor. Come on, Milly, I'm running late."

As they left, Beaumont thought, *my first genuine A-lister and she sits at the top of the tree. I don't want her in the waiting room on future visits, though. Her dog ugly daughter might scare my clients away.*

After the parking garage incident, the call from Brett Golding was totally unexpected. "Simon," he said, "you're enjoying the benefits of the actions of your peers, but not putting in. You've been practicing here for five years but every time we've asked to you appear in court as an expert witness, you've come up with an excuse. You've done nothing to stop GPs, dermatologists, gynecologists, and other quacks infringing on our territory. It's about time you stepped up to the plate. I gave Samantha Armstrong your number. She's a partner at Mordant & Hewitt. Don't refuse her when she calls. If you do, your peers and I will take a very dim view of it."

What a time to get stuck with this. I'm flat out, but I can't say no. Golding can hurt me, and if he gets the others to join him, they could do some serious damage. "You couldn't have asked at a worse time. I've got surgery booked for three months and a full appointment book."

"And when I'm asked, I haven't?" Beaumont held the phone away from his ear to keep from going deaf. Golding continued. "Everyone's busy. These are great times. The Olympics have a put a rocket under the city. I'm just asking you to do your bit. The lawyers will work around the days you operate, and you'll just have to reschedule your consultations. You're not being asked to do anything your peers haven't done."

"Yes, alright. What choice do I have?"

"None. You could find the experience enlightening," Golding said.

"Before you go, Brett, Sonya tells me that you've been asking her out. You know she's one of my playthings on the side. I'd hate to think you're trying to pay me back because I beat you to Debbie. It won't work. Sonya thinks you're a sleaze, and there's no way you're getting between her legs. Why don't you try one of my castoffs? There are plenty."

"You've got a smart mouth."

"Debbie sends her love," Beaumont said and hung up.

On the drive home, Beaumont struggled to come up with an excuse that would allow him to welch on his commitment to appear as an expert witness. The heavy traffic didn't help. Sydney seemed to have a twenty-four-hour peak period. Perhaps it was the work on the Olympic venues. The three-mile trip from his surgery to Point Piper took thirty-five minutes, no matter what the time of day. He parked in the underground garage and caught the elevator to the third level of the low-rise apartment block. His renovated apartment was super modern and had an extended balcony that overlooked the harbor, opera house, and bridge. He thought of it as ten-million-dollar view, as that was the price of houses further up the road.

"How was your day?" Debbie asked.

"Okay."

"You're pensive. Is there something wrong?"

"I have to appear in court as an expert witness. It's something I'm not looking forward to. I don't want to talk about it."

"How did that happen? Were you subpoenaed?"

"I said I didn't want to talk about it," Beaumont grunted.

"You don't have to snap. I was only asking."

If hadn't got sick and drank the brandy you wouldn't be here! Questions, questions, questions. Another year of this and I'll be up the wall. "I'm tired. I don't want to think about it," Beaumont said, picking up the remote and turning on the television. "Let's watch the news."

Chapter 24

Mordant & Hewitt's offices were on the 40th level of a high-rise, glass tower in Chifley Square. Samantha Armstrong had agreed to meet with Beaumont at 5:30 P.M. on Tuesday so as to only minimally disrupt his day. The reception was typical of large legal firms, with a marble counter and an adjoining waiting area containing coffee tables, leather chairs and bookcases. There were four high-backed stools behind the counter, but at this time of day, only one was occupied. The receptionist said that Ms. Armstrong was on the phone and would be a few minutes.

Beaumont sat down at one of the coffee tables and started to read the *Financial Review*. On the third page, there was an article about Milgate Mining Limited and its plans to be Australia's largest nickel miner. He was engrossed in the article when he felt someone standing beside him. "Are you into the markets?"

Beaumont looked up to see a good looking, fortyish woman dressed in a smart gray suit and white blouse. She had shoulder length blonde hair, sparkling blue eyes and a warm smile. "Samantha Armstrong, I presume," he said, standing and extending his hand. "How long do you think we'll be?"

"As long as it takes," she replied, "all-nighters are the norm around here, but I doubt that it will take more than two hours to go over the surgery performed by Dr. Gerald Curnow. Come down to my office."

He followed her down the corridor visualizing how much more attractive she'd be if she lost ten pounds. She had a large corner office, definitely for a senior partner. He glanced at the sheer drapes and could see the Botanical Gardens, and the harbor in the background. Folded over one of the chairs was a black robe and a traditional horsehair wig sat atop it.

She nodded at a coffee table with four large recliners around it and said, "Before we start, would you like mineral water, coffee, tea or perhaps a light ale?"

"Thank you, nothing. No offense, but I don't want to spend a second longer here than I have to."

"Oh, do you have to rush off somewhere?"

"No."

"I see," Samantha frowned. "Let's get down to it then. The defendant, Dr. Gerald Curnow, is a gynecologist. The plaintiff, our client, Helen Fenton is a nineteen-year-old university student."

"Why was Ms. Fenton seeing Dr. Curnow?"

"She had a urinary tract infection, and was referred to Dr. Curnow by her GP."

"Go on."

"Antibiotics resolved the problem, but at the follow-up appointment, she mentioned that she was uncomfortable with the size of her breasts and suffering back pain. He suggested breast reduction surgery and said he was qualified to perform it. I believe the medical terminology is bilateral reduction mammoplasty or surgery to reduce the size of both her breasts."

"That's right. Let me see the photos. It'll speed things up."

"I was about to, but wanted you to have the case background first," she said, tapping her fingers impatiently on the coffee table while handing him a file.

Beaumont opened the file and said, "Shit! That's terrible. In layman's terms, the nipples are out of alignment, the left breast is significantly smaller than the right, and there's unnecessary scarring. What a stuff-up."

"You'll need to be less colorful in court."

"Yes, I know. When can I examine her?"

"Aren't the photos enough? I'll have them entered into evidence."

"I'm surprised you'd even ask, counselor," Beaumont said. "I'm testifying about the surgery of another surgeon. Before I do that, I want to see what I'm testifying about. Not some photos that might have been doctored."

"Doctored photos?" Samantha angrily crossed and uncrossed her ankles. "Who do you think you're dealing with?"

"I don't care. I want to examine Helen Fenton. If I don't, I don't testify."

"I'll arrange it for Thursday. We're in court on Friday."

"Are you going to depose me?"

"No, I'll examine you and defense counsel will cross. You shouldn't be in the box for any longer than three hours."

"How do I get paid?"

"You invoice us for your time and expenses."

"At my normal rates?"

"What are your normal rates, Doctor?"

"Six thousand an hour which will include this meeting, my examination of Helen Fenton and my time in court."

Samantha scoffed. "You don't get six thousand an hour for consulting."

"No, I don't, but I do when I'm in the operating theater. When I'm in court on Friday, who's to say that I mightn't be losing a twenty-five thousand dollar facelift?"

"Doctor, we've never paid a surgeon more than a thousand dollars an hour."

"Call me Simon, Sam. I can call you Sam, can't I?" Beaumont said. "You've never had a surgeon with my skill sit in this chair before. I won't testify for less than two thousand an hour. Now come on, you must be on a contingency of thirty percent, and with my testimony, your client's looking at five million. You're going to pocket one and a half mil. You can afford my fee."

The barrister looked at him quizzically. "Did you ever study the law?"

"Never. It didn't pay enough."

"You have a surprisingly good understanding of the law. Far better than any of your peers."

"I watch a lot of television," Beaumont lied. "Would you like me to call after I've examined Helen?"

"Yes. You may discover something that alters my strategy."

Beaumont completed his last procedure at The Paragon just after 5:30 P.M. on Wednesday and was in the cafeteria enjoying a cup of coffee while checking his voice messages. Helen Fenton was coming in at midday tomorrow, and Barbara Milgate had called to say that she'd be in for her first treatment at 10 A.M. She was going to be a problem turning up at any time and expecting to be attended to immediately. *That's the price I'll have to pay if I want a billionaire's wife as a client,* he thought.

Chapter 25

Beaumont showed Mrs. Milgate and Milly to a small operating room at the rear of his surgery containing a large chair on castors, similar to a dentist's chair. "Can I get you anything, Milly? A magazine or a glass of water?"

The young girl turned red and shook her head.

"If you had a chocolate bar she'd wolf it down, wouldn't you, my little darling? Well not so little," Mrs. Milgate laughed with the enthusiastic condescension of a bullying school girl. When she regained her composure she glared at Beaumont as if the distraction was his fault. "Doctor, I haven't much time. I barely managed to squeeze you in."

What a bitch! If you weren't so rich, I'd throw you out. "I won't take long."

"Before you touch me with that laser I want to see what it does."

"That's easy," Beaumont said, holding it above his hand. Small puffs of smoke came from his palm. "It only removes the outer layer of dead skin. It's not painful and after the third treatment, you'll see a distinct difference around your eyes."

"Good, you may commence."

"Did you find a house?"

"Fortunately, yes. We couldn't find exactly what we wanted, but with some renovations, it will do."

"Good, now a little Botox. I won't hold you much longer," Beaumont said, glancing over at Milly, who looked bored.

"Are you alright, Milly?" he asked.

Again the young girl turned red.

"Don't worry about her. Get on with it, and be careful. One of my girlfriends had Botox injections in her forehead. It drooped and closed her right eye. She couldn't go out for a fortnight. I don't want that."

"That's never going to happen with me. Would you like numbing cream?"

"That's a stupid question. Of course, I do."

Ten minutes later, Beaumont held up a mirror and said, "It'll be about four days before you see any difference. I want you to apply Retin-A every–"

"I know. Some of the finest surgeons in the world have Botoxed my forehead and eyes before. Come on, Milly."

What a pain in the ass. "After today, you can say *the* finest plastic surgeon in the world has Botoxed your forehead," Beaumont said.

Mrs. Milgate turned abruptly to look at him, shook her head and left without another word.

Just after midday on Friday, Beaumont made his way to the 13th floor of the Law Courts Building in Queens Square. Samantha Armstrong was wearing a black suit and white blouse. She led him to a meeting room where she briefed him on the questions she, and the defense counsel, would ask. He didn't say anything, but knew what was coming and was sure that he'd read as much case law as her.

"How are you feeling?" she asked.

"Great. Why wouldn't I be?"

"This is the first time you've appeared as an expert witness. Many witnesses suffer nerves before appearing in the Supreme Court."

"It'll be a soda."

"Really? We'll see if you feel that way in three hours."

The clerk called Beaumont and swore him in just before 2 P.M. The jury were seated forty-five degrees to his left. He was surprised to see the attire of the barristers. Samantha was wearing a black robe and wig, as was her junior counsel and the three defense counsel. The judge wore a red robe and a longer wig. It was theater and vastly different to Beaumont's only other court appearance in New York.

It was a different Samantha Armstrong to the one he'd met three nights ago. She had a real presence when she stood at the Bar table. Unlike her U.S. contemporaries, she didn't pace around, but added emphasis to her questions by changing the inflection in her voice.

For fifteen minutes, she took him through his background, his academic qualifications, his work at The Royal Sydney, the pro bono surgeries that he'd performed and his experience in his practice. She questioned him extensively about mammoplasties and his experience. His answers were clear and concise. By the time she had finished she'd established that he was a highly qualified plastic surgeon, vastly experienced in reconstructive surgery and that he contributed to the community by performing pro bono surgery.

Looking over the top of her black, thick-rimmed spectacles, Samantha asked, "Doctor, in respect of Ms. Fenton's nipple misplacement, was there, in your opinion, a departure from proper care in performing the surgery?"

"The preoperative markings should be done while the patient is an upright position and should accurately depict the placement of the nipples. It should be done symmetrically. It was a departure when they were placed asymmetrically."

"How could such a misplacement occur?"

"The measurements were made inaccurately, or if made accurately, the lines drawn were not followed during the procedure."

"If the lines weren't marked accurately, would that be a departure from proper practice?"

"Yes."

"If the lines were marked accurately and not followed, would that be a departure from proper practice?"

"Yes."

"Are you able to state whether the departures that you have described, resulted in the misplacement of Ms. Fenton's nipples?"

"Yes, one or both departures caused the misplacement. The nipples are asymmetric because they were placed asymmetrically. The departure or departures are elementary and indicate that the surgeon had no previous experience in this area, or perhaps had a late night before operating."

A smattering of laughter went around the courtroom.

Defense counsel leaped to his feet. "Move to strike the last part of the witness's response, your Honor."

Beaumont put his hand to his forehead and subtly winked at Samantha.

"The jury will disregard everything after elementary, and the witness will confine his responses to the questions asked."

"I'm sorry, your Honor," Beaumont said.

For the next thirty minutes, Samantha examined Beaumont about the reasons there was a difference in the size of the plaintiff's breasts.

"In your opinion, was the use of a bra to determine the size of Ms. Fenton's breasts a departure from proper practice?"

"Yes, it is elastic and flexible. A large breast of a woman in a supine position can assume almost any position. There is a lot of flexibility as to where the breast can be placed. Markings for breast reductions are typically done when the patient is sitting or standing. When the patient is lying flat, there is a high probability that the markings will be inaccurate."

"Possibility or probability."

"Probability."

"In this case, how reliable do you think the markings were?"

"Reliable?" Beaumont scoffed. "About as reliable as Sydney's weather."

"No," defense counsel shouted as he again leaped to his feet. "Move to strike, your Honor. The witness is being given too much latitude."

"The jury will disregard the last response, and, Doctor, please respond without embellishments or theatrics."

"Yes, your Honor."

"Do you think that the method Dr. Curnow used was reliable?" Samantha repeated.

"No, on the contrary, highly unreliable."

"Doctor, when did you examine the patient's scars?"

"Yesterday."

"How does the surgeon determine where he will make the incisions?"

"Preoperative markings."

"In your opinion was there a departure from this procedure?"

Beaumont paused for quite some time.

"The witness will answer the question," the judge intoned.

"I can't say. I don't know what markings the surgeon made. I can say with certainty that the result was horrific. The worst surgery I've ever seen."

"Your Honor, he's doing it again," defense counsel shouted. "Move to strike."

"No," the judge said. "The witness is an expert who is expressing an opinion. "Continue, Ms. Armstrong."

"Why did you say it was the worst surgery that you have ever seen?"

"I have studied the patient's preoperative photographs. There is nothing to indicate why it was necessary to make the scars asymmetric."

"You've used the word asymmetric many times during your testimony. Can you tell the court why?"

"Yes. Symmetry is about balance, flow, and lines. Subconsciously it is the first thing you notice when you enter a house. Consciously you pay no attention to it unless one of two scenarios is evident. The symmetry is so perfect that it takes your breath away and–"

"And the other?" Samantha cleverly interrupted so as to give more emphasis to Beaumont's answer.

"It's so bad that your eyes are drawn to it because of its sheer ugliness."

"Is that what happened when you saw Ms. Fenton's breasts?"

Helen Fenton was sitting in the second row, and Beaumont looked directly into her eyes and said, "Yes."

Loud sobs echoed around the courtroom. Beaumont looked at Samantha, rubbed his mouth as if he was considering something so the judge couldn't see his smirk.

"Your witness," Samantha said.

Defense counsel rose and ask the judge for a ten-minute recess.

"I'll give you a little longer, counsel. Court's adjourned for thirty minutes."

"All rise," the clerk of courts shouted as the judge left the bench.

Beaumont walked over to the Bar table and said, "That was fun, Sam, but I'm glad it's over. I was getting bored."

"It's not over. You're going to be cross-examined."

"You know that's not true. The other side's working out a settlement right now. I made sure of that. They're going to make a substantial offer within the next few minutes. Why would you say they're going to cross-examine me?"

"Okay," Samantha said. "I agree. On the off-chance they don't settle, I wanted to keep you alert and on edge."

"Oh, you kept me alert. You were superb. You dominated the court-room and commanded the respect of the other side and the judge. It was a compelling performance. You know what I was thinking about when you were examining me."

"You're going to tell me no matter what I say."

"I kept looking at you standing next to the Bar table in your black robe, and thinking about how exciting it'd be to take you on top of the table, wig and all."

Samantha colored a little but her brown eyes sparkled. "Now that's a first. In twenty years of appearing in court, no one's ever said anything like that to me."

"You're a sexy woman. I was getting worried in the witness box that it was becoming apparent, and the judge might say something. What could I have said if he'd asked about my hard-on? And worse, what if he'd followed up with why?"

"Stop it. You're not funny."

"Really? That's not what your eyes are saying."

Samantha was about to respond when the clerk appeared and said, "Ms. Armstrong, they want you in meeting room number four."

"I've done all the hard work for you," Beaumont said. "You should get at least an extra mil courtesy of my efforts."

When the court reconvened the parties to the action advised the judge that settlement had been reached. The judge thanked and discharged the jury.

As Beaumont and Samantha chatted at the front of the court, he asked, "How much did you get?"

"That's none of your business."

"It is you know. It was my testimony that got you over the line. We both know the jury didn't ignore my supposed slip-ups, despite what the judge told them. I guess you got six million. That's an extra three hundred thousand in fees thanks to me. If you had any conscience, you'd pay me six thousand an hour. I earned it."

"A lawyer with a conscience," she said. "Now that would be a rare find. Are you sure you haven't read the law? You're almost too good. I was worried you'd come across as a professional witness. You should

125

remember that next time. Juries don't like witnesses who come across as smartasses."

"If I have any say in it, there won't be a next time. You don't pay enough. Besides, I've done my duty. Thirty-six other plastic surgeons have to take their turn before it gets around to me again. Let's not talk shop. I see you're not married. Are you in a relationship?"

"That's none of your business."

"That answer's getting repetitive. Would you like a drink?"

"Okay. Just one. Not around here, though. I've got a reputation to maintain, and it won't do any good if I was seen with a George Clooney lookalike. There's a quiet little bar about three miles away. We'll grab a taxi."

"Now there's something I've never been called before. George should be so lucky. Oh, and my car's just around the corner."

"Oh my God. Now I've heard it all. I have some male partners who think they're God's gift, but you make them look modest."

"I was just having some fun," Beaumont said, holding the door of the Merc open.

"Nice car, and no, you weren't."

Bar 77 in Double Bay was small and intimate, and the tables were illuminated by small lamps. "I'm only staying for one drink," Samantha repeated, as Beaumont took her coat, and placed it on an adjoining chair.

After ordering two house Chardonnays, Beaumont said, "I meant what I said in court. You had the judge eating out of your hand and the lawyers for the other side in awe. It was a powerful performance. It turned me on something shocking."

"Do powerful women do that to you?"

"Not all of them. You did. Is the black suit you're wearing one of your power suits? Perhaps the one you wear when you're about to lower the guillotine?"

"You have a vivid imagination, Doctor."

"Simon. It's Simon. When I was in the witness box, I figured out what else you were wearing. A lacy black bra's a certainty, and then I wondered, is it black panties or a G-string? I went with the G string.

It's a powerful way of privately expressing your sexuality. How did I do?"

"Unbelievable! Is that what you were thinking about when I was examining you?" Samantha asked, resting her chin on her hands.

"No. I thought about what you were wearing when you were addressing the judge before examining me. Once you started, I was thinking about doing you on the Bar table. You ended up with only high heels, your barrister's gown, spectacles and wig. Jeez, I'm getting hot and bothered thinking about it." He signaled the barman to bring two more Chardonnays. "How do you feel about finding a motel?"

"It's not going to happen, but you know what it tells me. You have a fetish for gray-haired women or horsehair."

"Okay, if it's not a motel can we go back to your offices? I know it's not the Bar table, but we could improvise. Have you ever done it on your desk?"

"No and no, and that's another first. You're the first witness who's ever propositioned me. And to think, it took you all of a day."

"Two days. You forgot Tuesday night. I wouldn't want you to think that I thought you were easy."

Samantha stood up and picked up her coat. "I won't say I'm not tempted, but men like you ruin the careers of women like me, and then walk away unscathed."

"It wouldn't be like that."

"You're so insincere. It's been an interesting day. One to put in my memory bank. How come a good looking man like you, isn't married?"

"I'm not marrying type."

"Is there anyone serious?'

"No. Will I see you again?"

"I have to go. I'll grab a taxi. You can call me, but I want you to know where you stand. There's two out, you're on first, and the probability of a home run is minimal."

"Possibility or probability?"

"Oh, you're good."

"Don't lose your wig."

It was dark by the time Beaumont got home.

"How was the court case?" Debbie asked.

"I'm glad it's over," he said. "Can you turn on the television? I want so see if it makes the news?"

When the first advertisement came on, Debbie asked, "Did you think about what we talked about?"

"What?"

"About having babies."

All I'm thinking about is Samantha Armstrong. "Oh, hell no."

"We've been together for more than two years. I want to know if you want kids."

Have I put up with you for that long? "I want to make hay while the sun's shining. There's plenty of time to think about kids after."

"No, there's not. My biological clock is ticking. I'm not going to have babies in my mid-forties. I want to be a mother to my kids, not a grandmother. I'm thinking about going off the pill."

"One minute you ask me if I want kids, and the next you're going off the pill. Maybe I wasn't clear. I don't know if I want kids. I do know that I don't want them in the next three years. I'm on the verge of something big. I don't want any obstacles impeding me."

Debbie squinted and fought back tears. She'd always thought that deep down he was a good man, but his obsession with money sickened her. Exasperation overcame her and for the first time she wondered if he had any redeeming qualities. "Obstacles? To what? You have wealth. You have freedom. You mingle with your super-rich clients all day. I smell their perfume on your clothes."

Beaumont felt himself color. "We've been over this before. Unlike you, I have to get close to my clients. I have to examine their faces, and God forbid, touch their boobs. What am I supposed to do? Ask millionaires not to wear perfume."

Debbie stood up and folded her arms across her chest. She was gruff, but didn't look him in the eye. "If I ever find out that you're doing after-hours vaginaplasmys, that'll be the finish. Do you understand?"

I'm sick of you. I don't care. I have to get out of this relationship, and I'm not paying you a cent when we split. "Not vaginaplasmys," he said, "vaginoplasties."

"Whatever."

"I've never cheated on you," Beaumont lied, "but if you go off the pill, that's the end of sex."

"And the end of us?"

"You said it."

Chapter 26

Beaumont woke at 8:30 on Saturday morning. It was a working day for Debbie, and she'd already left. He lay in bed fantasizing about Samantha Armstrong for a few minutes before jumping under a badly needed cold shower. Ten minutes later, he strolled to the local shops and bought *The Daily Telegraph*. As had become his habit, he flicked to the social pages first. There was a photo of the Milgates' standing in front of a stately mansion with the short caption *Twenty million*. The article quoted Mrs. Milgate, "It's old, but we like the house and expect the interior decorators and renovators to work miracles." The journalist noted that the Milgates had sold a smaller residence in Wolseley Road for twelve million and that Mrs. Milgate was using it to pay for modifications to their new house. *Shit! Who buys a house for twenty mil and then spends another twelve mil fixing it up? And how could they have got twelve mil for the other place? They only paid eight, and they've owned it less than two years. That's more than twenty percent per annum, for just sitting on their hands.* Beaumont thought, picking up his cell phone.

He punched in Steve Levine's number and before he could answer, said, "What's the entry level price for a house in Wolseley Road with views of the harbor?"

"Good morning to you too, Simon," Levine laughed.

"Steve, I don't have time to root around."

"Okay, keep your shirt on. Five million will buy you a shitbox."

"That's an expensive shitbox."

"It's the highest priced street in the country. Everyone wants to live there. Very few can afford to."

Beaumont related what the Milgates had done and were doing. "Steve, I need you to get me five mil. Can you do it?"

"You've got loans on the five Darlinghurst properties, the construction loan for the hospital, and you're going to have to borrow to build your aftercare accommodation. Then you've got your taxes and the two new lasers to pay for."

"You told me those Darlinghurst properties were great investments. Plus I'll be rolling in cash after the hospital's built, and I've never been late for a loan repayment."

"They're great investments. You could sell the two you haven't built on and clear more than a million in profit. It could be the deposit for Wolseley Road."

"I'm not selling. I'm building the best aftercare facility that Sydney's ever seen. Asians will fly down, I'll operate, and then they'll stay in my hospital for two or three nights. After they're discharged, they'll go into my aftercare accommodation for a week. I'll make a fortune on every one of them. I'm not selling anything."

"All the interest you're currently paying is tax deductible. The interest you pay on money borrowed to buy a residence won't be. It makes it very expensive. Why don't you wait a few more years?"

"Steve, you're either not listening or not hearing me. Prices in Wolseley Road are going up by twenty percent per annum. If I don't get in now, I'll never be able to afford to. I want to tell the real estate agents that I'm in the market. Can you get me the money? I know if I ask Tony Adamo, he'll have no problems setting me."

"You can start looking, and, Simon, that Tony Adamo line's wearing thin. There was a time when you were the only surgeon on my books. Not anymore."

"I'm no longer your most important client?"

Steve laughed. "You know you are."

"Good. I nearly forgot. Get me another fifty thousand and nominate me for Level 20 Club membership. The hospital will be finished soon, and I'm having a grand opening. There are a few club VIPs who I want to make sure are there."

"Have you got a name?"

"I'm torn between Darlinghurst Private and The Phoenician."

"Darlinghurst Private sounds stuffy and government owned. And if I was looking for a brothel or a casino, I'd call The Phoenician."

"Well, what would you call it smartass?"

"That's easy. The first thing I notice when I drive down your street.

The trees on either side. Why don't you call it The Boulevard? It's understated and classy."

"I don't know. It sounds like the sidewalk to me. I don't know. I still like The Phoenician."

"I've got the Yellow Pages in front of me, and I've just flicked to Escort Agencies," Steve said. "I have to tell you that both the Phoenician and Cleopatra's are listed."

"Okay, you've made your point. The Boulevard it is. I'll get invitations printed."

"Simon, you're building a nice portfolio of assets, and becoming quite wealthy."

"Bullshit! The Milgates are wealthy. Compared to them I'm a pauper."

It was mid-morning, and Beaumont heard a commotion outside his door. A few minutes later Julie hurried into his office with Mary right behind her. "Nicole Kinnane's manager called from Hollywood. He wants to arrange surgery when she visits next month. I thought it was a prank, so I put the call through to Mary."

"I spoke to him, and it's no prank," Mary said.

"Jesus, don't keep him holding, put him through," Beaumont shouted.

"He couldn't wait," Mary said. "She's coming down for a six-week holiday. Her manager made an appointment for 2 November. He said that she wants to have the procedure the following week. Oh, Julie, there's someone at reception."

"Yes, yes, but what procedure?"

"Do you remember Karen Blackman?"

"No. Fill me in."

"Late-thirties. Great skin and bone structure. Cheekbones to die for. She had a full facelift without a platysmaplasty. She's Nicole Kinnane's sister."

"Yes, I remember. She's classically beautiful. I should have picked the likeness. It's strange that Karen didn't say anything, though."

"What was she going to say?" Mary said. "I'm the sister of a triple Academy Award winner. Nicole wants the identical procedure and no doubt the identical result. It's a great compliment. Oh, her manager is paranoid about privacy. She won't be able to come here. You'll have to go to her hotel for the consultations."

"Yes, of course. We'll do the procedure in the new hospital. It won't officially open until the following week. Only those in the operating theater will know, and I'll swear them to secrecy. It's perfect. Make sure that Julie doesn't blab to anyone."

When Debbie found out that Beaumont was looking for a house they had a terrible fight. "What's wrong with staying here?" she said. "You're wasting your meaningless life making money and impressing people who couldn't care less about you."

"It's for the future. I can afford it. Why shouldn't I buy a house?"

"Oh yes, you can afford it. That's why you're borrowing five million. The average mortgage is eighty thousand. You're borrowing sixty average mortgages. It's stupid."

"So you say."

"You've missed your last three procedures at The Royal Sydney. I didn't tell you, but I saw the little boy who you were meant to operate on last week. He has a cleft lip. A simple procedure, but you were too busy. You broke his heart. Even Gold-digger turns up for his pro bono commitments. That little boy is back on the waiting list. It'll be at least eighteen months before he sees the inside of an operating theater. Are you proud of yourself?"

Chapter 27

Nicole Kinnane was staying in the presidential suite at the Ambassador, and her entourage was as large as a baseball team. Beaumont had to pass by her bodyguards as he entered the suite, and found her cocooned amid media agents, hairdressers, beauticians, and even her personal trainer. Her manager cleared the room, and Beaumont examined her face. She was seven years older than her sister, with even more pronounced cheekbones. Beaumont thought of the suntanned women he had tried to talk out of sunbaking. He doubted that Nicole had ever offered herself to the sun, and was sure that when outdoors, she used sunscreen. Her sister's skin had had a tinge of color, but Nicole's was porcelain.

"My sister speaks very highly of you, Doctor. You understand that I want the same procedure that she underwent? Nothing more, nothing less."

"Simon," he said. "Yes, your manager's emails were quite explicit. You have unique genes like your sister, which helps produce optimal results. I'm sure you're going to be pleased."

"Yes, I know I am. You realize that our meeting and the surgery must remain private. Some surgeons in Beverley Hills are intentionally accident prone at parties and like to drop the names of the stars who are clients. I don't want anyone to know I've had surgery, and if asked, I'll deny it. That's another reason I'm glad I've found you. Hollywood's a long way from Sydney."

"When you get off the plane in LA in six weeks, you're going to look even more fantastic than you do now, which will be a feat in itself. The only sign of surgery will be tiny, fine scars behind your ears. No one will be able to tell."

"Yes, I know. Karen emailed me pics. I know she's had three subsequent consultations and that you lasered the scars. Her husband says that he can no longer see them. I intend to have laser when I get back home."

"I thought this was your home."

"I wish. Hollywood is my home. Oh, I nearly forgot. The next time Seth Hawke is back in Australia, he wants to see you. His people will contact yours."

Beaumont looked puzzled. "I'm sorry. I was under the impression that you were looking for privacy. Have you told Seth you're having surgery?"

"Of course. We've worked on half a dozen movies together. I co-starred as his wife in *The Centurion*. I was so pleased when he picked up his Oscar. We have no secrets."

Nicole's manager rejoined them. "We have to go," he said. "Nicole's a guest on *Sydney Today,* and the Channel 8 folks are panicking that she might be late. Did you park in the sub-basement garage, and do you have sunglasses?"

"Yes and yes," Beaumont replied.

"Good, there's a media throng in the foyer, and we wouldn't want anyone to recognize you."

"I'm sorry," Nicole said placing her hand over his. It was cold, and he thought of Samantha Armstrong. Nicole Kinnane was classically beautiful, but Samantha had it all over her when it came to sheer sex appeal.

As the elevator zoomed down, Beaumont reflected. Hollywood was coming to him. When the other stars saw Nicole Kinnane and Seth Hawke they too would journey down under. *I don't need to go back to the U.S. to prove I'm the best. The U.S. will come to me. Fantastic. The world is about to find out what I've always known.*

Beaumont knew Debbie had been working late into the night to avoid him. They were falling apart, not that he cared. The only times they had sex were when their hot bodies touched by chance in the early hours of the morning. It was fast and brutal. He would close his eyes and imagine he was thrusting himself deep into Samantha Armstrong. He cursed the day he'd invited Debbie to shack up with him and blamed the brandy. She was a socialist who believed the rich should be taxed out of existence to subsidize the lazy and talentless. *Well, fuck that!*

The lease on Beaumont's apartment expired in two weeks and then he moved into his shitbox. It was more than a shitbox, though. It was large and quite livable. Its major shortcoming was that it was old. He wasn't worried. In time, he would knock it down and rebuild. He finally had a toehold in one of the most expensive streets on the planet.

"Do you want me to come with you?" Debbie had asked.

No way, but I'm too gutless to tell you. "It's up to you."

"If you want me to come, you have to ask me."

Shit. I'll be glad when I don't have to listen to her psycho-babble anymore. "Do what you want to," he said, no longer listening.

He turned the television on and started channel surfing when he saw Gold-digger sitting around a table with three women and another guy. The female presenter was saying, "We're lucky to have eminent plastic surgeon, Brett Golding, as our guest today. You've been very successful, Dr. Golding."

"Yes, I've been lucky. There are those who have worked far harder than me, and sadly, have achieved far less."

You asshole! You've just told everyone how smart you are while trying to appear modest.

"I think it's far more than luck," the guy said. "You've been recognized as Australia's finest plastic and reconstructive surgeon."

"Oh, I don't know about that."

"You're very modest. Your achievements could fill a scrapbook."

Modest? Bullshit!

Another panelist leaned forward to speak. "You've devoted many hours performing pro bono surgery, Mr. Golding."

"Yes, I'm a great believer in giving back to the community. Helping those who haven't been as lucky as me."

"That's noble," the presenter said.

I'm going to puke.

"You keep saying that you've been lucky," another panelist said. "I don't think luck's played any part in what you've achieved. Is there anyone else who could have led the team that successfully separated the conjoined twins?"

Golding rested his chin in his hand like The Thinker. ""You've caught me on the hop. I'm sure there is. I just can't think of anyone this minute."

"I don't think there's anyone else in your league," the panelist added.

I'd buy and sell him on my worst day. He's not the best!

One of the panelists, a woman in her mid-thirties sitting opposite Golding, looked at her notes and then at him. "I hope you're not offended," she said, her eyelids fluttering. "I just checked your age. You're sixty-one, but you don't look a day over forty-five. Have you had work done, and if so, can I have the name of your surgeon?"

The panel, including Golding, burst out laughing.

"I'm often asked that question. I'm not in the least offended, young lady. I'm quite flattered. In answer to your question, no, I've never had surgery. Fortunately, I was blessed with good genes. As I said, I've led a charmed life."

You lying bastard. You've had work done, lots of it.

"We have to go to an ad break," the presenter said. "We'll be back in a few minutes." As the camera panned away, Golding was glowing, and the women were fawning over him.

Chapter 28

Beaumont had a restless night, unable to stop thinking about Golding and the unjustifiably high esteem in which he was held. He'd only been in the office a few minutes when he asked Mary to join him.

"I want to increase my fees," he said, "ten percent across the board."

"You put them up six months ago, and the others didn't follow. Not even Brett Golding. People aren't happy."

"People aren't happy? What's that supposed to mean."

"I'd rather not say. I don't want to make you angry."

"I promise I won't get upset."

"Some clients and referring doctors are saying that you're greedy."

"Is that right? Forget the clients. Tell me, who do these doctors think is the best plastic surgeon in town?"

"Everyone knows you're the best, Simon. Even your peers."

"Good. Answer me this question. If you were buying a car and looking at a Ford and a Mercedes, which one would you expect to be the most expensive?"

"You can't compare the price of cars with the fees charged for surgery."

"I'm not. I'm trying to show you that folk always pay more for the best."

"The others won't follow you. They didn't last time; they won't this time. You'll lose clients."

"Sheep always follow leaders," Beaumont laughed scornfully. "These sheep are dumb. They still think Golding's the leader. I've never tried to steal his clients. I've praised his surgery, and told you to do the same. I've gone out of my way not to upset or get on the wrong side of him. That's about to change. He's yesterday's man. From now on we'll tell his clients that he's using old techniques, and subtly leave pictures of the Governor General's wife lying around. When we're asked what happened to her, we'll say we'd rather not comment, before, with great reluctance, we tip a bucket of shit all over him. When the smoke dies down, I'll be the new leader and I guarantee the others will increase their fees. Everyone likes more money."

"You're going to make a terrible enemy. He's very influential."

"By the time I'm finished with him, he'll be a lot less influential. Oh, I nearly forgot. Increase my consultation fee with to a thousand dollars commencing immediately. I want to drive consultations to you while I spend more time operating. I read about a surgeon in Beverley Hills last night. Get this. He did seven hundred procedures last year. If I can do the same, I'll gross more than ten million a year. Ten million!"

"That's great for you," Mary frowned, and slowly shook her head. "I don't know whether I should be elated or depressed.

"I'm not interested in what you feel. However, I want you in the theater with me when I operate on Nicole Kinnane."

"I haven't been in an OR for more than a year. I'll be rusty. Why?"

"Privacy. I only want people in the OR who I'm sure I can trust."

"Do I have any choice?"

"No."

The stressed voice of Julie came over the intercom. "Mrs. Milgate's here to see you, Dr. Beaumont."

"Show her in."

"She never makes appointments. That's what the super-rich do, Mary."

Barbara Milgate flounced into Beaumont's office with Milly in tow. "I just managed to fit you in," she said.

What a pain in the ass. She expects me to thank her. "Hello, Milly. Why aren't you at school today?"

"There are two physical training periods this morning, and Mom doesn't like me doing PT," Milly replied. It was the first time she had spoken to Beaumont.

"Why's that?"

"Look at her! And you ask a question like that. It makes me wonder how you ever became a doctor. Can we get started? I'm running desperately short of time."

"I'll be as quick as I can. Come down to my operating theater."

Milly had picked up a breast prosthesis and was flicking it from hand to hand. She looked up and timidly asked, "Is this a fake breast?"

"Put it down," her mother snapped.

Fifteen minutes later Beaumont injected the last of the Botox and wiped Mrs. Milgate's forehead. "The next treatment you'll see the full effect. Your expression is already softer."

"Yes, I know. Milly, go and wait in the waiting room. I have a few personal questions for the doctor."

No way she's sitting in my waiting room. "Wait in my office, Milly. I'm sure we won't be long."

"What is it, Mrs. Milgate?"

"I was in Armani yesterday doing some Christmas shopping, and bumped into that vulgar Werner woman. She wanted to show me her breasts in one of the change rooms, and the only way I could quieten her was by agreeing. I never realized those change rooms were so small. She poked them in my face and in the loudest voice told me to have a feel. I prayed that there was no one in the adjoining rooms who I knew. How embarrassing would that have been? I hope I never set eyes on her again. I digress. They were sensational. Can you do the same for me? I'd like to go a little larger than her."

Of course, you would. "I'll have to examine you."

"I can be a few minutes late for my next appointment," she said, looking at her watch. "You can do it now."

Beaumont raised his hand to conceal his smile. *Now the boot's on the other foot. I have something you want. More than want – something you're desperate for – obviously tits by Beaumont are more desirable than a dress by Armani.* "Sorry, I don't have time. I have clients backed up in the waiting room," he said, as he put his hand on her elbow and steered her toward the door. "Call Mary, and make a time to come in. I have a full appointment book, but I'll ask her to fit you in."

After Mrs. Milgate and Milly left, Beaumont called Mary into his office. "When the Milgates are here I don't want Milly in the waiting room. If I'm with a client take them down to the operating room."

"Why?"

"Do you need to ask? Milly's as ugly as sin and we're selling beauty. She'll frighten clients away."

"Oh my God. I can't believe you're that shallow. You want to listen to yourself."

"Just do it, Mary, and don't question me. That's all. You can go."

Just before 6 A.M., Nicole Kinnane made a low-key arrival for her surgery, accompanied by her manager, and sister, Karen Blackman. The bodyguards would come later, and position themselves inside The Boulevard. The drapes would remain drawn. To prying eyes, the new hospital, which wasn't due to open for another week was unoccupied.

Nicole Kinnane had been sedated and just before the anesthesiologist placed the mask over her face, she looked up at Beaumont and said, "I feel privileged to christen your splendid new hospital, Simon. I love the name."

"Enjoy your sleep, Nicole. I'll see you when you wake up."

"Let's test the sound system, Mary," he said, and a few seconds later Wagner's Flying Dutchman filled the operating theater. "Commencing at 6:35."

Mary gently put a scalpel in his hand, and he made an incision at the front of the right ear.

Five hours later, he sewed the last of the sutures. He was always meticulous and careful, but given who it was; he spent an additional hour ensuring a perfect result. Nicole Kinnane would be his most famous billboard.

Beaumont was pleasantly surprised when he received numerous inquiries from plastic surgeons expressing interest in his operating theaters and boutique hospital. If he was ever going to earn more than ten million dollars a year in fees he'd need to operate three days a week. With this in mind, he permanently booked the first operating theater on Mondays, Wednesdays, and Fridays. Four of his peers took the remaining two days and the second theater. Their patients would pay a pretty penny for the resource.

Two of them had indicated that they would like to keep their patients in The Boulevard for three nights after major surgery. They had also queried whether the private rooms might be available for admitting patients the night before early morning procedures. Beaumont was charging slightly less than The Paragon, but the rates were still astronomical, and his accountants had forecast accommodation revenue of one and a half million in the first year. His worry was that sixteen rooms wouldn't be enough. Steve Levine had suggested holding off on building the aftercare facility for a year. That advice was impractical, and waiting would cost him a fortune. He knew he could fill it with Asian women looking for round eyes, breast implants, and facelifts.

Chapter 29

More than a hundred guests crammed into the foyer of The Boulevard for the grand opening. The Premier of New South Wales and the Lord Mayor of Sydney, together with their wives, were on the dais. As were Brett Golding as President of the Institute, and his wife.

Debbie had declined to attend, saying that she wouldn't feel comfortable with *those people*.

Beaumont looked at the crowd and was surprised to see Joe, Barbara and Milly Milgate sitting in the second row. Joe Milgate was even uglier than his photos, and it was easy to see where Milly's looks came from.

The Premier was effusive about the young American and said that New South Wales would always welcome surgeons of his caliber. He then looked at Beaumont and said that he could pull some strings with visas if Beaumont knew any other American doctors wanting to come to Sydney. The crowd laughed, and The Premier finished by wishing Beaumont luck and success in his new venture.

The Mayor gave a short speech and spoke glowingly of the enormous contribution that the highly skilled surgeon from New York had made to Australia, and more particularly, Sydney.

Brett Golding then rose from his chair. "It seems like only yesterday that Simon Beaumont was working under me at The Royal Sydney. It's hard to believe that nearly eight years have flown by so rapidly. I remember a nervous, young man who sought my counsel about surgery, and flatteringly, personal problems in his new home. I knew that he was a quality person and was pleased to be able to help him find his feet. For someone so comparatively inexperienced, he is a highly skilled young surgeon, and long after I've retired, I'm sure he'll prove to be one of the finest plastic surgeons in the state. Simon, congratulations and good luck on your new venture. Remember, you have many friends and should you have any problems, surgical, personal or business, I'm only a phone call away." The crowd applauded warmly, and there were cries of "hear, hear."

Beaumont was fuming. He clasped his hands together and gritted his teeth. Golding's self-serving bullshit had stolen what should have been his day. *Why does the little prick always have to pump himself up?* Beaumont took the microphone, looked at his notes but didn't see them. He was ropeable and forgot to specifically thank the Premier, the Mayor, and their wives. As he started to speak he looked at the conceited face of Golding and was hit by a burst of inspiration.

"Ladies and gentlemen, honored guests, thank you for taking time out of your busy day to celebrate the opening of my hospital. While Brett and I have never operated in the same theater, his reputation precedes him. As he said, we first met at The Royal Sydney where he was performing simple pro bono procedures. Plastic surgery has made remarkable advances in the past thirty years, and more significantly in the last decade. At Brett's age it can't be easy trying to keep up with the ever-changing technology. It is a credit to him that he has made such an effort to educate himself about new techniques." Beaumont stared at Golding. "I doubt that I'll need to access your wise counsel on personal and business matters, Brett, but thank you for offering. I know that there are many new techniques that you are not familiar with, and I want to let you know my door is always open. To my staff, clients and friends, I want to thank you for making me so welcome in this wonderful city. I hope to personally thank each of you." There was a smattering of applause and Beaumont looked down at Golding and winked. *Cop that, you bastard!* The little man was trembling with rage and his face was scarlet.

As Beaumont left the dais, he was approached by Barbara Milgate, who said, "I'd like you to meet my husband, Joseph."

He was tall, bony, all angles, and at least, twenty years older than Barbara. He had an elongated face, huge forehead, and a hawkish nose, but all Beaumont focused on was his large, calloused hands and nicotine stained fingers.

"Call me Joe," he said, thrusting out a hand.

In response Beaumont held up his hand and said, "Sorry, Joe. I can't shake; I sprained my fingers changing a tire."

"Oh no," Barbara said. "Can you still operate?"

As if I'd ever change a tire. "I don't have any procedures scheduled until Friday. I'm sure I'll be okay by then. How are you enjoying Sydney, Joe?"

"It's okay. Most of my drinking buddies are in the west. Besides that, it's alright."

"They're bums," Barbara said. "Good riddance, I say. It's a pity you had to bring Harry with you. Perth is just a big town where everyone knows everyone. Sydney has so much more to offer."

"You forget that our money came from the west. I'm hardly like to make a significant nickel find in New South Wales. Those bums you're talking about are self-made men who'd buy and sell your family. And you need to remember, Harry Cusack's been with me for longer than you have." He turned to Beaumont. "She comes from old money. Ya know, the born to rule type. Trouble is her family's collectively got the ass hanging out of its pants. Old money's fine when there's still some left. When there's not, new money like mine's quite acceptable. That's right, isn't it, darling?"

"You delight in humiliating me," Barbara responded.

In one short statement, Joe Milgate had shown who wore the pants in the Milgate family.

"He who owns the gold makes the rules," Joe said. "Have ya heard that saying before, Simon?"

I'm not getting involved in this. "No, Joe." Beaumont looked up as Milly approached. "Hello, Milly, are you enjoying yourself?"

"It's no fun. Can we go, Dad?"

"Yeah, kiddo, I'm with you, and I'm busting for a cigarette. Tell Harry to bring the car around," Joe said, handing his cell phone to Milly.

A few minutes later a squat, heavyset man with tattoos on his hands and across his neck approached Joe and said, "The car's out the front, boss."

"Simon, I'd like you to meet Harry Cusack. Harry's been with me since Milgate Mining was just a shitty little explorer going nowhere. Harry, you can't shake the doc's hand. He hurt it changing a tire."

Cusack narrowed his eyes and nodded. Beaumont felt a chill run down his spine. Something about Harry Cusack was truly menacing.

"Good luck with the hospital, Simon, and I sure hope ya hand heals up," Joe said, as he turned to leave.

"I'll be in touch," Barbara said.

"Thanks for coming," Beaumont said, his eyes scanning the thinning crowd. There was no sign of Brett Golding, but he saw Steve Levine sharing a joke with Mary and Julie. "Steve," he said, butting in, "I need to see you for a few minutes."

"The only thing you ever want to see me about these days is money. When was the last time we had a drink or went to the Level 20? You're working too hard. You're going to burn yourself out."

"Yes, yes. Every bed in the hospital is going to be taken within two months. We need to get the aftercare facility built. We're not going to be able to cope without it. If I can't offer the proper facilities, my clients are going to go elsewhere."

"Simon, I don't know how to say this, but every dollar in the world doesn't have your name on it. You're making a fortune, have a great practice, and you're highly respected. What more do you want?"

"I just told you," Beaumont frowned. "We've got the plans and permits. If you work on a figure of four million, you won't be far off the mark. All we need is the finance. As soon as it's approved we'll call for tenders. I think we can start building in February and be up and running within six months. How long do you think it'll take to get the finance approved?"

"Work on the basis that it is," Levine replied. "I wish you'd slow down, though. You're going to end up being the richest corpse in the cemetery."

"Now you're talking, buddy. That's why I pay you the big bucks. Well done."

"I'm glad you're pleased because I've got a favor to ask."

"What?"

"I have a close friend who's worried sick about his daughter. He says that she's carrying a little weight around the tummy and is self-conscious about the size of her boobs. I think she's looking at having a tummy tuck, a boob job and fat removal from her thighs. There might be more. She had a fight with him and now won't tell him anything. She's only twenty-five and doesn't have much money. She's seen three surgeons and their quotes have been between sixteen and eighteen thousand."

"Whatever their fees are, mine will be more exp–"

"Let me finish. She found a place on the internet in Bangkok that'll do the lot for eight thousand. That's airfares, accommodation, anesthesiologist and surgery. She's got four thousand and a friend who'll lend her the rest. That's what started the fight with her dad. He told her she was a fool, and they've hardly spoken since."

"Jesus, you're not asking me to operate for eight thousand, are you?"

"No, of course not. I'd like you to have a consultation with her, pro bono, and talk her out of this madness."

"I can try. What's her name?"

"Felicity Mott."

"Text it to me. I'll make sure Mary squeezes her in when she calls."

Two weeks later, Beaumont was again summoned to the Ambassador. Nicole Kinnane was in the same suite but other than her manager, and bodyguards, most of her entourage had disappeared. "Once I finished my television interviews and media commitments, I didn't need them," she explained. "I've been staying at Karen's place in the Southern Highlands. We were raised there. It's nice getting back to nature. The air is crisp, and it's lovely to wake up to the sounds of birds singing. I nearly didn't come today. I have no pain and look marvelous. Karen and I call you God's plastic surgeon. You fix the parts that he missed," she said, her eyes dancing. "Do you think it will be alright if I go horse riding?"

I'm in awe of myself. No other surgeon in the world could have achieved such perfection. God's plastic surgeon – they're not wrong. "Let's go over near the window," Beaumont said, "so I can get a better look at you. There's no bruising and only minimal swelling. I agree, you look marvelous, yet little has changed. No one will know that you've had work done; you just look fresher and more vibrant."

"A perfect description, Simon. Now please make my day and tell me that I can go riding. Please. I'm going back to the Highlands in the morning."

What's she talking about? Does she want to be back on my operating table? It proves you don't have to be bright to be a Hollywood star. "I'd love to say yes, but you have sutures under the skin, and we can't run the risk."

"I'm here for another three weeks. Surely it'll be okay to ride in the last week before I go back home?"

Thick as a brick. "No, it won't. If you get thrown, the damage might be severe, and that aside, I don't want you bouncing around on the back of a horse."

"You're the doctor," she pouted. "If that's all, I won't hold you."

Hmmm. God's plastic surgeon just got the ass. "Enjoy the rest of your stay, and say hello to Karen for me."

On the way back to his surgery, he called Samantha Armstrong on her private line.

"I had a feeling it was you," she said.

"How about a drink or dinner?"

"I told you the other times you called that I can't. Nothing's changed. I'm aiming to be the first female managing partner in this firm's illustrious one hundred year history. Messing around with a bad boy like you won't help me."

"Okay, I can compromise. We don't have to do it on your desk or boardroom table. We can do it miles from your office. No one need know. Just bring the spectacles, gown, wig, and high heels."

"You're a bad, bad boy. "You couldn't care less about me or my ambitions. You just want to put it in."

"Yes, and you want me too, just as badly."

"Oh, you're so sure of yourself. How many other women have you regaled with dirty phone calls?"

"None. I've been saving myself for you."

"You're such a liar."

"Come on, Sam, you know you want it as bad as me. It's called chemistry."

"Sorry, Simon. I have to take another call."

Each call she'd teased and flirted just enough to keep him hot. *I will have my way with you, Samantha Armstrong. It's just a matter of time,* he thought.

Chapter 30

At Beaumont's instruction, Mary had always praised the surgery of Brett Golding when one of his clients was seeking a second opinion. She never used the line that he was an excellent surgeon using old techniques, which they had so successfully used to win other surgeons' clients. Golding became so confident that he referred his clients, seeking a second opinion, to Beaumont.

Now, Mary had a copy of the *Woman's Day* on her desk opened at the article on the Governor General's wife, and was looking at the poor woman's lopsided face. When Beaumont found out that Jennifer Byrne had made an appointment to see Mary, he told her it was time to take the gloves off. The Byrne family, seriously wealthy A-listers had been Golding's clients for years. When Jennifer sat down opposite Mary, she said, "I've just turned the big four-o and look tired. I have furrows in my forehead and bags under my eyes. Brett suggested a facelift, platysmaplasty, a brow lift and blepharoplasty of the upper and lower eyelids. I'm worried about general anesthesia and was hoping for rejuvenation without surgery."

Mary could diagnose with the expertise of most plastic surgeons and thought that Jennifer's face belied her years. Her chin was taut, and Mary couldn't see any reason for a platysmaplasty. She had lost a little volume from the cheeks, and there was minimal laxity around the jowls. Mary examined Jennifer's eyes and saw no reason to touch the upper eyelids. Usually, at this stage, Mary would agree with Golding's diagnosis, but today she did not.

"The good news is that if you decide to go with Dr. Beaumont, you won't need general anesthesia and the surgery will be minimal. The doctor will perform a lower lid blepharoplasty under local anesthesia, and that will be the full extent of the surgery. He will make a small incision, excise the fat, and perhaps remove a small amount of muscle, excise the skin, and close. The effect will be amazing."

"I don't understand."

"Rather than surgery we'll use Botox, fillers and laser to achieve the same results. You have excellent skin texture, minimal laxity, and the tiredness that you see will vanish after the blepharoplasty. Not only that, it will save you a considerable amount in fees."

"I still don't understand. Why wouldn't Brett have recommended the same procedures?"

"I don't know. Perhaps it's because Dr. Beaumont is so much younger. Techniques change, and the fillers of thirty-five years ago, if they had any, are far more sophisticated today."

Jennifer looked thoughtful. "The treatment you're suggesting, when compared with the alternative, is quite appealing."

Mary closed the *Woman's Day*. She wouldn't need it. "I'm glad I could provide you with another option. Call me if you require any more information."

Felicity Mott was a pretty, gum chewing brunette with a button nose, cheeky smile and a ring pierced upper lip. She was solid rather than fat. Beaumont told her that he only had fifteen minutes and asked her to go behind the screen and strip down to her panties. She had small breasts accentuated by broad shoulders and was carrying excess weight around the abdomen and thighs. Beaumont didn't like performing abdominoplasties because the scar was long and ugly. It could be hidden below the bikini line, but couldn't be hidden from patients, and they often regretted having the procedure. "Why do you want breast implants?" he asked.

"I thought that was obvious she said. They're small. I want big ones."

They all want big ones. "And you want to lose some weight from your abdomen and thighs?"

"Yes."

"Who suggested an abdominoplasty?"

"I looked it up on the internet."

"What did the other surgeons you consulted say?"

"Two of them said they'd liposuction my tummy, and after it had healed, I should enroll in an exercise program for six months. They said they'd only consider an abdominoplasty if the loose skin didn't resolve itself with exercise."

"That's good advice. Why didn't you have the surgery with one of them?"

"Far too expensive. Then I found this hospital in Bangkok. It's more like a five-star hotel. They said they could do everything, and I could even have a holiday, all for eight thousand dollars."

Beaumont paused. "You shouldn't even think about it. The risks are enormous starting from poor quality surgery to infection, perhaps even death."

"They said that's what Australian surgeons would say and that it was just scaremongering. Some of their surgeons are board certified in the U.S."

"Listen to me, young lady, and listen carefully. Some of the surgery in Asia is first-rate and is performed by highly qualified surgeons. The problem is that there's no consistency. If you're lucky, you'll get a first-class surgeon and a first-rate result. However, you might get a butcher. If that's the case, the results will be disastrous. Going up there for surgery is like buying a lottery ticket. What are you going to do when you're back in Australia, and something goes wrong?"

Felicity Mott blew a bubble. "The same thing could happen here. Steve Levine says that you're the best plastic surgeon in Sydney. If he's right, it means I'd get a better result with you than any other surgeon here."

"You can't afford me, but what Steve says is true. Here's the difference between Sydney and Asia. With me, you'd get an outstanding result. With my peers, you'd get an excellent result. Focus on those two words, outstanding and excellent! In Asia, your result could be excellent. It could also be terrible, and if that's the case, you'll go through postoperative hell. Is that what you want?"

"You're trying to scare me."

"Yes, I am. Steve tells me that your father loves you dearly. Have you thought about the angst he'll go through if you go to Bangkok? It's about time you thought of someone else besides yourself." He waved his hands dismissively. "I have another appointment. Think about what I said."

She had lost some of her bluster. "Can you do the surgery? I could pay you when I get a job."

She's only got four thousand and doesn't have a job. There's no way she's getting finance. What a waste of time. "You can't afford me. Here's my advice. Stop eating, begin exercising, get a job, and start saving." Beaumont smiled cruelly. "When you've got some money, come back and see me."

"Thanks, but I won't be coming back to see you. Not ever," Felicity sneered.

Barbara Milgate arrived right on time for her appointment. Beaumont lasered her eyes and injected Botox.

"I'm not sure that I want breast augmentation now."

"Really? You were so enthusiastic. What's changed your mind?"

"I've done a lot of reading," Mrs. Milgate said, "and I don't like pain."

"I won't lie to you. There will be some postoperative pain, but it will be no worse than what you experienced after your facelift."

"That does nothing to assuage my concern. I was in pain for two weeks after my facelift."

"I understand. Could I suggest that instead of staying in my hospital for two nights, you extend your stay to seven nights?"

"I've thought about that. I don't like the idea of you filling me up with drugs."

"Perhaps surgery is premature. Go behind the screen and take your top off."

"I wish that was true. My breasts were fine until I had Milly, but after the pregnancy, they never returned to what they were. Joe wanted to try again for a boy. That was never going to happen."

"Did you breastfeed Milly?"

"Are you stupid? Of course not. She'd already done enough damage," Mrs. Milgate said, stepping behind the screen.

Barbara Milgate was fit and toned. She had taut stomach muscles, and defined shoulders and arms. Her breasts weren't saggy, but had lost a lot of volume. "You're in great shape. You can put your top back on."

"Tell me something I don't know. I work out for at least an hour every day. I put myself through agony for Joe, and he hardly notices. He'd take notice if I looked like Rachel Werner. Damn that woman and damn you. I never wanted implants until she gave me an eyeful of what you did. Do you think I need breast augmentation?"

"Only you can answer that, Mrs. Milgate. If you decide to have surgery, it should be for yourself and not to please others."

"That's crap. If I don't look good for Joe, he'll replace me. We're only having sex twice a month, and I know what an insatiable appetite he has. I can look the other way when he dallies, but I don't want to lose him. If it wasn't for the pain, I'd get you to operate tomorrow. As it is, I need to think about it."

You're postponing the inevitable. You know what Rachel Werner looks like, and you want to look the same. You'll soon put the thought of pain to one side. "You're a fit, young woman. There's no rush. Feel free to call me if I can be of any help."

"Thank you. I'm pleased with my forehead and eyes. You've softened my expression."

You'd look even more relaxed if you weren't so aggressive, but I can't say that. Not if I want to keep you as a client for the next fifteen years. "I'm glad."

Chapter 31

There was little warmth in Beaumont's and Debbie Stenson's relationship, but they hadn't fought for more than a fortnight and were being civil. Beaumont was on the sofa watching television when she sat next to him. "Can I ask you a favor?"

"You can ask," he said, turning the volume down.

"I have a conference to attend from Wednesday to Friday next week that concludes with a dinner at the Pinnacle-Regency. Can you accompany me?"

He stared at the television. "You couldn't bring yourself to attend the opening of my hospital but want me to go to dinner with you. How's that work?"

"That's unfair. I had nothing in common with the people at your function. All big-timers who've never wanted for anything in their comfortable lives."

"What do you think I've got in common with a herd of psycho-babblers? If they're anything like you, they'll be disgusted when they learn how I earn my living. Can I say I'm a social worker? That should win me some brownie points."

"I'm sorry I asked. I should've guessed your response. There's only one person in the world you care about, and you look at him while you're shaving every morning," Debbie said, standing up.

"Here I was thinking the sarcasm genie had got lost when she was only snoozing. Look, if it's that bloody important to you, I'll go. Anything's better than the silent treatment for the next ten days."

"Thank you. It means a lot to me. I know you hate me saying it, but you do have a good side. It just takes a long time to surface."

"I don't know if that's a compliment or an insult," He sneered, turning up the volume. "If it's all the same with you I want to watch this program. It's about botched up cosmetic surgery in Miami. It's rampant. I can't stand Brett Golding, but he's put a lot of medicos who aren't plastic surgeons out of business. Largely because of him, we don't have the problems that LA and Miami are experiencing. The profession's in his debt."

"Yes, and thanks to him, you've all got plenty to pay it with."

"I was talking a debt of gratitude. How about putting the sarcasm genie back in her bottle? I want to watch this."

Julie sounded stressed when she said, "Dr. Beaumont, it's Mr. Golding for you. He's not happy."

"Brett, this is an unexpected pleasure. I was only singing your praises to Debbie last night."

"Don't give me that shit. What was that crap you were talking about at the opening of your hospital when you said you'd help me with new techniques?"

"Whoa. You lied about me working under you. I know you did it to help me with credibility. That's right, isn't it? I was just doing the same for you."

"What? What are you on about?"

"Well, at your age I knew there'd be those in the audience who'd think you weren't up with the latest techniques. I wanted to let them know that if they used your services, they didn't have to worry. You could access them through me." Beaumont grinned and held the phone away from his ear.

"You, you slimy piece of shit," Golding shouted, "there's nothing you could show me, and you damn well know it. I'm the best plastic surgeon in Australia."

"Really? Do think the Governor General and his wife would agree?" Beaumont taunted. "I'm getting a patient of yours every week for revision. I didn't say anything because I didn't want to offend you. Face it, you're yesterday's man."

"The Governor General's wife never complained. Those photos in the *Woman Day* were doctored. I'm surprised you fell for them."

"I saw her on television sitting next to her husband at a national-ization ceremony. You should be ashamed of yourself. You're lucky, she's a sweet lady who'd never kick up a fuss. It was shocking surgery and the *Woman's Day* didn't have to doctor the photos after you'd doctored her. Brett, you're in the worst few surgeons practicing. What is it? Is old age catching up with you?"

"You damn, arrogant Yank. Who do you think you're talking to? I can break you with just three phone calls. Think about it, before you go any further."

"I'm not worried about you, Golding."

"You should be. Jennifer Byrne said that one of your consultants told her that I was using old techniques. Understandably, Jennifer was very upset when I informed her that your consultant didn't have any qualifications and that her advice was a load of rubbish. I said that I'd talk to you and that you'd call her and apologize for your consultant's ill-advised comments."

"Hell will freeze over before I make that call."

There was a long pause, and Beaumont could hear Golding breathing. "Brett, are we all done?" he asked. "I've got a practice to run."

"I thought you might like to know that I was in New York last week. I visited the Fielding family. Valerie's still in a wheelchair. She's a vegetable. The money didn't help, and they still hate you, Jack Donovan."

Beaumont felt his lungs compress. "You bastard!"

"Do yourself a favor, Jack or Simon or whatever your name is. Call Jennifer Byrne and tell her that your consultant made a mistake. Oh, and if I hear any more of this new techniques rubbish, the media might just get to hear about your past."

"That information's private. If the media finds out about my background, I'll sue you and the Institute."

Golding cackled. "I know my duties and responsibilities. I won't say a word, but sometimes leaks occur, and it's impossible to find out where they originated. Call Jennifer. Clear up this little misunderstanding, and then stay off my turf. There's more than enough money for both of us if you don't do anything stupid."

"I'll call her, but I'm not changing Mary's diagnosis. I'll tell her that I've got a six-month waiting list and that she should talk to you about the procedures Mary discussed. I'm sure you'll be able to slime your way out of your earlier diagnosis."

"I can live with that."

"You're too old, Brett. You've lost it. You're not helping your clients. You don't need the money. Retire."

"I'm still the best plastic surgeon in the land. You're just too young and inexperienced to know. Take me on again, and I promise you'll lose everything."

Beaumont was about to respond when he heard the dial tone.

Slimy bastard. I underestimated him. I have no choice but to call Jennifer Byrne. Damn!

"Mary," Beaumont shouted, "come and see me."

"What's wrong?" she asked.

"Policy change. I don't want to chase Brett Golding's clients. I've got enough on as it is."

"I don't understand. You were gung ho last week. What are we going to do about Jennifer Byrne?"

"Don't worry, I'll call her. I'll apologize and say that I have too much on to take on new clients."

Mary had a quizzical look on her face. "Simon, you do many things that I don't like. I think you're ruthless and obsessed with money. If you weren't so talented, I would've left you long ago."

"That and the fact that you're Sydney's highest paid practice manager. That let's you drive your sportscar and take overseas holidays. Don't get sanctimonious, you're no different than me."

"And you're shallow enough to believe that. Yes, you pay me well, but I'm nothing like you. I like working with you because your surgery is remarkable and often life-changing. However, I think you just met your match in ruthlessness. What did Brett Golding do to make you back off?"

"Nothing," Beaumont grimaced. "You know how busy we are."

"If you say so," Mary said, "but I don't believe you."

Chapter 32

After finishing their conference, psychiatrists congregated with their partners in a large room in the Pinnacle-Regency enjoying drinks and Hors d'oeuvres. Debbie was involved in deep discussion with a group of colleagues about youth suicide. Beaumont stood next to her pretending to be interested while he checked out the room for talent. There were some good looking women, and he thought, with a bit of luck, he might end up at a table with some of them. He was still angry about the kicking that Golding had given him. His aggravation didn't improve after he'd called Samantha Armstrong. She had flirted with him, but he was no closer to getting into her pants. Perhaps she was just a tease.

As he was thinking about Samantha, there was movement in the crowd. Debbie grabbed his arm and said, "We're going into the dining room. Are you enjoying yourself? Are you hungry?"

"It's okay," he said, "and I'm famished."

"We're on table number sixteen," she said, "it's at the back of the room."

It didn't take long to find. Four couples were sitting at the table, and there were two vacant chairs to the right of Beaumont's. None of the hot women that he'd spied were at their table. Debbie did the introductions, and the couples engaged in small talk while waiters poured drinks. Five minutes later, Beaumont felt the chair next to his getting pulled out. He looked up to see two guys in their forties sitting down. The one nearest to him extended his hand and lisped, "Hi, I'm Phil, and this is my partner, Jonathon." Beaumont felt his body involuntarily stiffen.

Most of the couples at the table seemed to know the two men and greeted them warmly.

"Are you are a psychiatrist, Simon?" Jonathon asked.

"No, I'm a plastic surgeon."

"Ooh," Phil said, "I need to get my lips done, and I'm thinking about cheek implants. Do you have a card?"

Beaumont didn't move. "I have a six-month waiting list. I'm sorry, I'm not taking on new clients."

"Oh, you must be good?" Phil simpered. "What do you think of my lips? Do you think they need doing?"

"Phil, I made Simon promise that he wouldn't talk about plastic surgery tonight," Debbie laughed. "You're going to get him into trouble with me."

"Oops, I'm sorry, Deb. We can't have that, can we?"

The waiters served tripe in a Riesling tomato sauce for the entree. Lively conversation was taking place around the table, and Debbie squeezed Beaumont's thigh, but he didn't respond.

When the waiters returned to top up the wine glasses, Beaumont put his hand over his glass and said to Debbie, "I'm not feeling very well. I think the entree disagreed with me. I'm going to grab a breath of fresh air."

A few minutes later Debbie joined him at the front of the hotel. "I'm sorry," she said, "I had nothing to do with the seating. I promise."

"I'm not comfortable around queers," he said. "I'm going to get a taxi home."

Debbie shook her head. "You said you weren't homophobic. Jesus, in two months it'll be 2000. What century are you living in?" When he turned away, she grabbed his elbow and made him face her. "It's not like they have any interest in, or are a threat to you. Why shouldn't Phil and Jonathon love each other? They care for each other more than most heterosexual couples. Look at us. What am I going to say if you don't come back?"

"Poo jabbers," Beaumont sneered. "I don't give a stuff what you say. I'm in the first taxi that pulls up."

"Now you're showing your true colors. You are a homophobe."

"No, I'm not," Beaumont smirked. "I don't hate lesbians."

"You're sick. If you let me, I can help you."

"I'm not into psycho-babble," he said, as climbed into a taxi. "I think it's crap."

When Debbie got home from the psychiatrists' dinner, they had a terrible fight, and Beaumont had hoped that she'd walk out. She hadn't, and things gradually drifted back to normal. Their relationship was passionless, other than the occasional accidental contact in bed. He wished that she would leave but didn't have the guts to throw her out. Her parents were flying in from New Zealand on Friday week on a stopover on the way to a holiday in Hawaii. She told him how much they were looking forward to meeting him. He could think of nothing worse.

With the Olympics just around the corner the demand for plastic surgery by those who wanted to look their best at the opening ceremony intensified. Beaumont hadn't seen Mrs. Milgate for over six months but wasn't surprised to hear that she was in the waiting room with Milly, demanding to see him. *Jesus, I don't want Milly out there.* "Bring them in, Julie," he said.

"I've decided to go ahead. When can you operate?" Mrs. Milgate said.

"Good morning, Mrs. Milgate. Hello, Milly," Beaumont said. Milly was turning into a woman, but she was grossly overweight. Joe Milgate was lean, and his wife was slim. Milly's weight problem wasn't genetic; she probably ate out of misery. After all she had inherited her father's facial features.

Milly looked at her feet, turned red, and mumbled, "Hello, Dr. Beaumont."

"Can we just get on with it? I have a busy morning in front of me."

"The last time we talked, you were concerned about postoperative pain. Why the change of mind?"

"Joe's losing interest in me. I need to do something to spice things up. I've just finished telling Milly how men are driven by sex. Still, she's not likely to have a problem." Mrs. Milgate patted Milly's face.

You're right about that. "Are you sure? Have you thought about seeing a psychiatrist or marriage counselor?"

"Spare me the crap. I know far more about men and their lust than you could ever hope to."

Beaumont fought back a grin. *That's how I talk to Debbie. No wonder she gets aggro.* "Alright, let's discuss the options."

"No need to," Mrs. Milgate said. "I've read every magazine available on cosmetic surgery and spent hours on the internet. I probably know more than you. I want round, saline, and two and a half sizes larger. When can you operate?"

"You didn't answer my question. You were in fear of surgery and pain the last time we talked. What's changed?"

"I told you. Listen to me! I can't afford to lose Joe. I'll stay in your hospital for seven nights. You'll sedate me, and the pain will be minimal. No heavy drugs!"

Can't afford. What an interesting choice of words. "You're slim, and teardrops will look far more natural. You'll also regret going up two and a half sizes."

"Doctor, didn't I just finish telling you that I'd spent hours researching breast implants? I even visited that horrible Rachel Werner woman."

"Then you know she only went up a size and a half."

"Yes, I do," Mrs. Milgate said. "I know exactly what I want. If you won't operate, I'll find a surgeon who will. I know how ambitious you are, Doctor. I have many girlfriends around my age, here and in the west. Do you understand?"

"How could I not?"

"When's the earliest you can operate?"

"Friday week, but you'll need to come in and see me this Friday. I need to go over the Informed Consent with you."

"I'm too busy. I know all about it. Just give it to me and I'll sign it now."

"No. You don't know the contents of my Informed Consent. I can fit you in at midday. Allow half an hour for the consultation."

"If I must! Come on, Milly, we've wasted enough time here."

Chapter 33

When Beaumont looked down at his cell phone and saw who was calling, he smiled. "Hello, Samantha, this is a pleasant surprise."

"Would you like to have dinner on Friday week?" she asked.

"That's an even more pleasant surprise. Where?"

"I have a conference in Melbourne over the weekend. I'm going down on Friday morning. I'll be staying at the Hyatt on Collins. Can you make it?"

"Are you taking the spectacles, robe, and wig?"

"If you want to know, you'll have to jump on a plane," She giggled.

I've got Barbara Milgate's surgery on Friday, and I'll need to see her the following morning. Oh, and I'm meeting Debbie's parents. Oops, was meeting Debbie's parents. "I'll be there. It's quite convenient because I want to catch up with a Melbourne surgeon."

"Convenient?" She laughed. "I've been called lots of things, but never convenient."

"Sorry, a slip of the tongue, I'll make it up to you on Friday night."

Beaumont immediately called Andrew Houghton, the surgeon from Melbourne, who he'd dissected cadavers with five years earlier. They had stayed in contact on a professional basis, and, fortunately, Houghton was available on Friday.

When Beaumont told Debbie he'd been called away to perform emergency surgery with one of his colleagues in Melbourne, she was furious. "It's one night," she said. "One night. I don't ask much of you. My parents were looking forward to meeting you."

"Can I help it if emergencies arise? I didn't plan it. Why can't you ask your parents to stay over, and we'll have dinner on Saturday night?"

"I told you their flight's on Saturday morning. They got a special deal and can't change it. Not everyone's rolling in money like you. Surely you're not the only surgeon who can perform this procedure? Your friend in Melbourne must be able to find someone else? Why don't you ask him? It's one night; that's all I ask."

"I can't let him down."

"The surgery won't take all night. Why can't you get a flight back on Friday night? You'll still get to meet them and then we can drive them to the airport."

Jesus, do you have to make it so hard? "I have no idea how long the surgery will take. It's complex. It could go well into the night. I'm on an early flight on Saturday, so I'll be back at the hospital in time to do my morning rounds."

Mrs. Milgate's surgery went smoothly, and Beaumont took a little license by going up just over two sizes rather than the two and a half she had wanted. He finished just before midday and at 12:45 visited her in recovery. She was drowsy and would remain sedated through-out the night.

Mascot Airport was relatively quiet when Beaumont parked the Mercedes in the short-term parking and boarded a flight to Melbourne. Eighty minutes later he was in a Hertz driving out to Andrew Houghton's practice in the posh suburb of Toorak. Houghton was a happily married family man in his early forties with a serious demeanor. Other than surgery they had nothing in common, but Beaumont respected his skills and thought he was the second best plastic surgeon in the country. "What is it that you want to see me about, Simon?"

"What I'm going to tell you must not go further than this office. Do you understand?"

"Yes. You have me intrigued. Go on."

"Did you see the photos of the Governor General's wife in the *Woman's Day?*"

"Yes, it wasn't Brett's finest surgery. What's it have to do with me?"

"It's occurring frequently. I'm worried about Brett. Perhaps he's getting too old."

"Rubbish," Houghton said, "he's only in his early sixties. I've known competent surgeons who've practiced to their early eighties."

"I saw a woman a few weeks ago. Her right eye was nearly closed, the result of a brow lift. Not only that, her face was asymmetric. She asked me to operate."

"What did you do?"

"I refused. If I'd accepted, it would've undermined Brett. He's a good friend, and besides, I didn't want to get on the wrong side of him. I told her to go back and see Brett, and that if he thought it was warranted, he'd operate again."

"How did she respond?"

"I won't tell you exactly what she said, but if I say it was along the lines of *I'll never set foot in that butcher's surgery again* you'll get the general gist."

"He's a good surgeon. It sounds like there's something wrong with him. I wonder if he's got the yips," Houghton said.

"I think he'd put his hand up and call time out if that was the case."

"Sadly, many surgeons don't. They think it'll cure itself. I hate it when patients are compromised, but why are you telling me? There's nothing I can do."

"There's not a surgeon in Sydney who'll do revision work on Brett's clients. I was wondering what you'd think if I was to refer them to you. You don't have the same obstacles down here that I do."

Houghton's glasses slid down his nose, and he put his hand under his chin. "In principle, I don't have a problem with the idea. However, I don't like patients paying Brett and then having to pay me. That's morally reprehensible. If Brett continues with surgery, the problems will be exacerbated. Have you thought about confronting him?"

"Of course, but I don't want to lose a dear friend and nor do I want to lose my practice. Brett is very influential in Sydney. Someone to keep as a friend. God forbid that he becomes an enemy. I would only refer the worst cases to you and then only after I'd suggested that they return to Brett. I'm looking for an option if they decline."

Houghton tapped his long fingers on his desk. "I'm prepared to help, but only after all other avenues have been pursued. You are not to tell your Sydney peers about our arrangement. It sounds like there may be a large number of cases, and my clients must take priority. I don't want to get bogged down doing revision work."

I've just hammered the first nail in your coffin, Brett Golding, and the beauty is that you'll never know it was me. "I won't hold you any longer, Andrew. Thank you for seeing me. When you're next in Sydney, we must have dinner."

Before Beaumont got back into the Hertz, he called Samantha. She answered on the second ring. "Are you in Melbourne?"

"Of course. Are we going out for dinner?"

"Where are you?"

"Toorak."

"Park under the Hyatt. I'm in the Premier Suite on the thirty-third level. We'll work out what we're doing when you get here."

Thirty minutes later, Beaumont knocked on Samantha's door. She was wearing a black suit, and he took her hand and kissed her. "You look stunning," he said, his eyes sweeping the suite. There was a large open living area with a dining table set for eight guests, an oversized desk and a huge, suede sofa set back from a sixty-inch television. Floor to ceiling windows afforded panoramic views of Melbourne's skyline. "All this for one person. You lawyers certainly know how to live. While I shower and shave, work out what we're going to do. I'm sure they've got a great dining room here."

"I thought we'd eat in. I'll tell you why after you've cleaned up."

The bathroom was black marble, featuring a sunken spa, and a rain shower, with water body jets. Beaumont enjoyed the hot water pounding against his body. It had been a great day starting with Mrs. Milgate, and then Andrew Houghton. His thoughts turned to Samantha, and he was immediately aroused. After he'd shaved, he threw on a soft, white Hyatt dressing gown, matching slippers and nothing else.

Samantha was looking out the window when he came out of the bathroom and put his arms around her. "I sometimes doubted this was ever going to happen. Your call was a fantastic surprise, even though I had to travel six hundred miles."

"I have a partner in Sydney," she said. "He runs another law firm.

We've been together for five years. Like me, he lives for the law. We have an open relationship. This is the first time I've exercised the open option. We attend many functions and are seen as an item. We have a rule that the open option must never be flaunted or exercised in public."

"So that's why you wouldn't go out with me in Sydney," Beaumont said, turning her around and kissing her.

"That, and I wasn't sure about you. I enjoyed the banter and your fantasy but didn't know whether I wanted to live it." She slid her hand under his dressing gown, giggling. "You can't afford jocks?"

"Not on what you paid me," he said, pulling her closer, his breathing becoming shallow.

"Don't lose that," she said, taking her hand from around his penis, and putting a condom pack in his hand. "Put this on while I change into something a little more comfortable."

A few minutes later, she returned wearing her wig, black, thick-rimmed spectacles, and robe and high heels.

"Oh my God, my fantasy," Beaumont gasped, taking lifting her onto the desk. He kissed her passionately while opening her gown to reveal a black G-string and nothing else.

She carried a little too much weight, and her boobs were bigger than he liked, but she exuded sexuality. Her face was filled with desire and her eyes glazed over as she ran her fingers up and down his penis barely touching the skin. He was more turned on by her face than he was by looking at any bikini clad model. He reached down and slowly took her G-string off, his fingers gently massaging her clitoris. She was wet, and he started to feel like he was losing control. He pulled away from her hand, dropped his dressing gown to the floor, dragged her closer to the edge of the desk and thrust himself into her. Two minutes later she orgasmed with a scream, and he simultaneously exploded. Sweat was pouring off him, and Samantha reached up and said, "I have to get this off," and threw her wig on the carpet.

"That was fantastic. You're the best fuck I've ever had."

"That's so romantic." She giggled. "Is that what you say to all your lovers?"

"I think you enjoyed hearing it. Was it fantastic for you too?"

"You were okay."

"Okay?" he said. "Before this night is out you'll say I'm wonderful."

"Simon, Simon, you should listen to yourself. Sex isn't a competition where you get awards and rankings. Relax, enjoy the moment."

In the next few hours, they took pleasure in each other's bodies and around midnight Beaumont asked, "When will I see you again?"

"You won't. Tonight was the enactment of a fantasy for me too. I'm like you, but probably not as bad. I'm shallow, ambitious, determined to get to the top, and I'll remove anyone who gets in my way. The difference is that there are people in my life who I care for, whereas you are a narcissist who cares for no one but yourself. Yes, you're charming, amusing, good-looking, and that little boy smile will get you a lot of action, just not with me."

"That's not fair."

"Isn't it? Think of all the women you've lied to and dumped in your lifetime. Then ask yourself if what I said is fair."

"It's not!"

"Let's not have this conversation. We have a few more hours left to enjoy each other. Let's not waste them."

"God, you're worse than a man," he said, pulling her toward him.

Chapter 34

It was a little after 9:30 A.M. on Saturday when Beaumont entered The Boulevard. Barbara Milgate was in good spirits. "Good morning, Doctor," she said. "I made one of your nurses help me take this terrible bra off in the bathroom. I just had to see them. They're magnificent. I don't know how to thank you."

"You just did, Mrs. Milgate. Have you experienced any pain?"

"A little. It's nothing when measured against the outcome. I wish I'd had the procedure when we first talked about it. I can't wait to get rid of this horrible bra and show Joe. He's going to love them."

"The bra is crucial. You only have to wear it for six weeks. If you don't, you'll find yourself back in the operating theater." Beaumont frowned.

"I'm not stupid, Doctor. I read your instructions. I know what I'm allowed to do. In forty-two days, I'm going on a lingerie shopping spree. I can't wait."

Beaumont looked up, and Milly was standing at the door. "Hello, Milly, how did you get here?"

"Joe bought her a car," Mrs. Milgate said. "She's independent now."

"I didn't think you were eighteen."

"I'm nearly nineteen," Milly said, turning bright red.

She's so lacking in confidence? She drew a bad hand when looks were being handed out, but her parents are super-wealthy. Most wealthy kids are obnoxious and think they were born to rule the world. "Are you a good driver?"

"Dad, says I am," she responded, still looking at her feet.

"She ought to be," Mrs. Milgate laughed. "Her driving instructor told us that he'd never given anyone so many lessons."

You're a cruel woman. I wonder what Milly's done to you? "Mrs. Milgate, I'll see you in the morning at the same time. Have a restful day."

Beaumont wasn't looking forward to facing Debbie, but there was no point in delaying the inevitable. He drove slowly along Wolseley Road, admiring the huge mansions before doing a U-turn and driving into his garage. Debbie was on the veranda. Her eyes were red, and she looked run down. "How were your parents?"

"I needed you here," she said, "but you had to run off to Melbourne."

"I told you I didn't have a choice. It was a tricky procedure that only a few surgeons could've performed."

"I'm pregnant," she blurted out.

"You're what?" he shouted.

"I told you I wanted a baby."

"And I told you I didn't. What were you going to do? Make the big announcement in front of your parents and expect me to play the doting, expectant dad. It's just as well I wasn't here because I would've said exactly what I'm going to say now. Abort it. If I had of known you'd stopped taking the pill, we would've separated. I'm not getting stuck with a kid on a whim of yours."

"I didn't say a word to my parents, and I wouldn't have without you agreeing. I just wanted to talk to you before they got here. I was hoping you'd feel the same joy as me. Your son or daughter is in here," she said, placing her hands on her tummy. "Don't you feel anything?"

"Nothing. Get rid of it."

"No. I want this baby. I won't ask you for anything."

"You lied and used me. We had a deal. I told you that it would be at least three years before I'd be ready to think about kids. You took no notice of me."

"You didn't listen. I told you I was going to stop taking the pill."

"Bullshit! You would've been out the door in a flash. Anyhow, what do you intend to you?"

"I'm having our baby."

"I want you to have an abortion. If you don't, we're finished."

"We've been finished for ages."

"I want you out of here," Beaumont said, pushing the front door open.

There were three suitcases in the hallway. "I knew what you'd say," Debbie said, wiping a tear away, "but I hoped you wouldn't. Don't worry, I won't ask you for anything. I'll call a taxi."

That's until you see a lawyer, and then you'll be after half what I've got. Well, you won't get a cent off me, Beaumont thought. Ten minutes later he watched the taxi pull away. He felt nothing, other than relief.

For the rest of the year, Beaumont buried himself in his practice. In most weeks, he was operating three days, and on target to perform more than seven hundred procedures for the year. He was generating enormous amounts of cash and traded the Mercedes in on the latest Lamborghini. Not satisfied, he put a twenty percent deposit down on a three-million-dollar cabin cruiser, due for completion early in the New Year.

The Olympics came and went in November. Afterward Sydney basked in having hosted one of the most successful Games. Just before Christmas, Sydney's Lord Mayor opened the aftercare facility in what was a low-key ceremony. Had it been grander, Beaumont would have had to conform to protocol and invite the president of the Institute to the opening. He'd had more than enough of Brett Golding in 2000.

Chapter 35

On a balmy late summer's day, Beaumont launched the Boulevard of Dreams. It was a state of the art cabin cruiser, and pretty waitresses plied guests with caviar and Dom Perignon. No expense was spared and many of the movers and shakers who frequented the Level 20 Club were celebrating with their wives and partners. As the boat pushed further out into the harbor, Beaumont reflected on his achievements.

"You've been very successful, Simon," Steve Levine said.

"I'm not so sure. I live in the worst house in Wolseley Road."

"Which you couldn't buy for less than ten million today. Don't look at it as the worst house. Look at it as living in the best shitbox." Levine sipped his wine and watched the windsurfers spectacularly leaping waves.

"Not funny, Steve. I want to tear it down and build a mansion."

"Why can't you be satisfied? Why do you always have to have more?"

Beaumont ignored the questions. "I'm getting plans drawn up. The architect said there won't be much change out of ten million. Can you get it for me?"

"Yes, but you're paying millions a year in interest. Why can't you slow down? You'll be in debt for more than twenty million after you've paid for the new house."

"Yes, and I'll have more than forty million in assets."

"You've done exceptionally well."

"I'm the best in the world. When you relate that to my assets, I've hardly achieved anything. Denzel Washington gets twenty million for one movie. That's my net worth, and what's he do to get it? Spends six months on a film set."

"You can't compare yourself with a Hollywood superstar."

"Why? I've got more talent in my little finger than he has."

"I'll tell you again, Simon. Not every dollar in the world is destined to finish up in your pocket. That's an attractive woman you're with," Steve said, nodding toward Sonya. "Nice rack. Talking of racks, how many sizes did Barbara Milgate go up?"

"None of your business. You know I can't talk about clients."

"You don't need to. She's flaunting them everywhere, and giving you the credit. Low-cut dresses and blouses, and tight sweaters. Old Joe's running around her like a horny teenager. You sure saved her ass."

"What? I'm not with you."

"Rumor is that he made her sign a watertight prenup before they walked down the aisle. So long as they're together, she can spend like there's no tomorrow. However, if he dumps her, she's cut off without a penny."

"Jesus."

"Yep, so right now you're the flavor of the month, but that could change at the drop of a hat."

"You're talking in riddles," Beaumont said, as they cruised past the opera house. "Get to the point."

"Well, if Joe gets too excited over Barbara's tits and carks it, your name's gonna be shit. Rumor has it that he's left everything to Milly and Barbara's not mentioned in his will. When Milly's turns twenty-one, she's supposedly on a hundred million dollars a year out of a trust fund Joe created when she was born. I guess when Joe created the fund he never envisaged it growing to that extent. The trust owns the shares he controls in Milgate Mining Limited. You're walking a fine line with Barbara, but right now, you're her favorite person."

"So that's why Barbara treats Milly so poorly. If something happens to Joe, Barbara will need to watch her step."

Sonya joined them, and Beaumont slipped his arm around her waist. "Are you enjoying yourself?" He asked.

She was about to respond when the boat tilted and Steve cannoned into them. "Jesus! What was that?"

Sonya regained her balance and said, "That's the Packer yacht. It supposedly cost them more than a hundred and twenty million."

"Bastards!" Steve said. "They were too close and going too fast. What gives them the right to kick up a wake like that?

"Simple. The super-wealthy make their own rules," Beaumont

said scornfully. "And you call me rich." He turned toward the stairs. "Sonya, tell the captain to turn around and head back in. I've had enough of the harbor."

As they drove toward Beaumont's home, Sonya asked, "Do you want me to stay tonight?"

"It'd be better if you didn't. I think I got too much sun today. I'm tired and feel a headache coming on," he lied.

"A headache?" Sonya teased. "I thought only women used that excuse."

"It's true. Is it an excuse you use, Sonya?"

"Never. I'm always up for it."

Beaumont glanced at her. She was young, uninhibited and tempting, but he needed to do some serious thinking. "Sorry, I'll make it up to you."

"Have you heard from Dr. Stenson? You know she's due any time now?"

"No and no."

"She looks fantastic. Glowing and so healthy. She'll make a great mom."

"I don't want to talk about her."

"Don't you care? Don't you want to see your baby?"

Beaumont ignored her questions. "I need to get some sleep. I'm operating in the morning."

"I can take a hint," Sonya said. "I know when I'm not wanted. You're a cold man."

Beaumont poured himself a glass of wine and lay on the sofa staring at the faded ceiling. What should have been a day of crowning glory had turned into a disaster. Why should some twenty-one-year-old loser be entitled to a hundred million a year just because she was lucky enough to have come out of the right womb? On reflection, it could've been any womb so long as it was Joe Milgate's seed. *I would've had more chance of becoming rich if I'd walked all over Western Australia with a metal detector. Life is so unfair.* Then there was the Packer superyacht that had made the Boulevard of Dreams look like a dinghy. *Vance Morgan's dad told me I'd never get really wealthy providing a service. Now I know what he meant. No matter how successful I become, I'll never rub shoulders with the Milgates or Packers unless they invite me.* He sipped the wine and put a hand to his forehead lightly massaging it. He had never felt so depressed. The uninvited black dog was tearing him apart.

The following morning Beaumont struggled to get out of bed. On the drive to The Boulevard, he slapped his face telling himself to snap out of it. He had four procedures scheduled for the day and knew that he had to focus.

Chapter 36

When Steve Levine called, Beaumont told him that he was having second thoughts about the new house, and to hold off on the loan.

"I wasn't calling about that," Levine responded. "I was seeing a client at The Royal Sydney, and I bumped into Sonya. She told me that Debbie had a little boy. She named him Jack. Jack Beaumont has a nice ring to it. Congratulations."

"Jack Stenson, and it's not something I care to talk about."

"Are you going to visit them? I'm sure Debbie would love to see you."

"Steve, I don't appreciate you meddling in my personal life. It has nothing to do with you. If you know what's good for you, you'll butt out."

There was a long pause. "I'll butt out, but I think of you more as a friend than a client. If you have nothing to do with your son, you'll live to regret it."

"Thanks for the advice, but in future, keep it to yourself. Goodbye."

Beaumont was still a perfectionist with his surgery, but he'd lost something that day on the harbor. It was the zing and the ambition to achieve more. When Julie buzzed to tell him his next appointment was in the waiting room, he ran his hand down the consultation sheet that Mary had prepared. Yvonne Chapman was a forty-five-year-old merchant banker and another of Brett Golding's dissatisfied clients. Beaumont would listen to her, empathize and then send her back to Golding. There was nothing else he could do. "Show her in, Julie."

She was tall, dressed in a smart, charcoal gray suit and her long black hair cascaded over her shoulders. One eye was smaller than the other and her nose was large, bulbous and ugly. Despite this, she commanded a presence, and Beaumont sensed a volcano primed to erupt. After they'd exchanged pleasantries, she said, "I had a Roman nose that wasn't very attractive. I went to see Mr. Golding, and he told me that he could remove the hump and make my nose slimmer. This is the result." She glared at him as she touched the end of her nose. "It's hideous and far worse than it was. Can you help me?"

The redraping of the excess skin is terrible. That's why you have a bulbous, ill-defined nose. "Have you been back to see, Mr. Golding?"

"The only place I'll see that weasel, is in a courtroom. Look what he did to my left eye. He was meant to remove the fat from under my eyes and excise the excess skin. I look like I should be in a circus."

What are you doing, Gold-digger? You removed far too much skin. "Has it impacted your work?"

"I resigned. How could I face clients looking like this?"

"It must be tough going, living without a salary?"

"No. It's fine. I'm more than comfortable, but I miss my job. If I was available, my services would be heavily in demand. I have a group of loyal, wealthy clients. If I looked anything like normal, I'd be back working tomorrow. You are highly spoken of, Dr. Beaumont. Can you help me? I'm desperate."

"Tell me what you'd like me to do."

A line of color raced up Yvonne Chapman's face, and she squeezed her hands vigorously. "That's obvious. I want you to repair my facial deformities and return me to normal."

You have a quick temper, lady. I like it. "Is there anything else?"

"Oh yes. After you've restored my face, I'd like to sue that little bastard's ass off. I earned more than a million dollars a year. I don't need the money, but that butcher ruined my lifestyle. I'd like to repay him."

You're my dream woman. "I can't help you and nor can any other surgeon in Sydney."

"But why–"

Beaumont raised a hand. "Hear me out. You don't want to know about the politics, but take my word, what I said is true. However, all is not lost. There's a first-class surgeon in Melbourne, Andrew Houghton, who'll be pleased to help you. Here, I'll give you his card," Beaumont said, pushing it across the table. "I'll call to let him know that you'll be contacting him. He'll remedy your surgical and aesthetic problems. You'll be pleased with his work."

"I know all about politics," she said with a weary sigh. "Thank you."

"Good." Beaumont held his hands below his nose as if he were praying. "Everything I say from now on is off the record. If asked, I'll deny ever saying it. Do you understand?"

A puzzled look came over Yvonne Chapman's face. "Yes, but–"

Again Beaumont held his hand up. "If you mention that you're going to sue Brett Golding, Andrew Houghton will not perform the corrective surgery. Plastic surgeons don't like testifying against other plastic surgeons. Do not under any circumstances mention litigation. If he asks if you're going to sue, say no, and that you're only interested in getting back to normality."

"I think I know where this is going," she said.

"Andrew will take before and after photos and will document why you have come to see him. Should you wish to institute legal action after he's performed the corrective surgery, it would be a simple matter for your lawyers to subpoena him and his records."

"God, I'm talking to a reincarnation of Machiavelli. What did Golding do to you?"

"Nothing, Ms. Chapman," Beaumont said. "This conversation never took place. It was nice of you to drop in," he said, extending his hand.

As Yvonne Chapman reached the door, she turned and said, "Thanks again, Dr. Beaumont. Remind me never to get on your bad side. If you ever get sick of plastic surgery, give me a call. You're a natural as a merchant banker."

After she left, Beaumont put his hands behind his head and threw his legs up on the desk. It was the best he had felt since that day on the harbor.

Chapter 37

The Boulevard of Dreams was an expensive folly that Beaumont had only taken out on the harbor that one time. It was not that he didn't like the water, but rather that he didn't want to run across the monstrosities of Greg Norman or the Packers. Steve Levine knew what was bugging Beaumont when he called him. "You have one of the best boats moored in the harbor. How you can you be ashamed of it? If you're not going to use it, I'll take it out. Some of the girls from the Level 20 would love to spend a few nights on a boat like that."

"It's yours, Steve. Do what you like with it. Maybe you could set it on fire, and I'd get my three mil back from the insurance company."

"I don't understand you. By any measure, you're a wealthy man, and you've only just turned forty. You've got your whole life in front of you, yet you mope around like it's a battle to get through the day. You have to snap out of it. The old Simon Beaumont, who loved borrowing, frightened me, but he was far more exciting than the moribund 2001 version. In six weeks, the year will be over, and you won't have built anything or acquired any new equipment. Are you sure you don't want me to get the ten mil so that you can build your new house?"

Beaumont grimaced. "For years, you've been telling me to slow down and consolidate. I've paid off a lot of debt this year. You should be congratulating me."

"If I thought your motivation was consolidation, I'd be praising you. It's not. Why don't we go to the club tonight? Let our hair hang down like the old times."

"I'll take a raincheck, Steve."

"The old Simon Beaumont could be a prick, but at least he was alive. You've gotta snap out of it."

"I have to go, Steve."

The week before Christmas, Julie buzzed Beaumont just after 9 A.M.

and nervously said, "Mrs. Milgate is in reception demanding to see you."

A few minutes later Barbara Milgate barged into his office with Milly following close behind. She was wearing a low-cut, bright red top that showed far too much cleavage. "My chauffeur's got gout," she said. "Have you ever heard of a chauffeur with gout? Milly's driving me around, and it's not a pleasant experience."

"Hello, Mrs. Milgate. How are you, Milly?"

"We don't have time for pleasantries. We have a lot of shopping to do. Do you think my eyes and forehead need doing again? After seeing what you did for Suzie Kemp, I thought I might have a facelift. She looks fifteen years younger. Suzie and my other girlfriends are very pleased with you. So am I. No one has breasts like mine."

You should be in here for your daughter, not yourself. She turns twenty-one next year and is dog ugly. Jesus, why didn't I think of Milly before? "I think we should stay with the laser and Botox. It's far too early to have another facelift, and you certainly don't need one. You look vibrant."

I need to talk to Milly by herself but how? "Thank you, Doctor. I'm so happy. Joe's like what he was when I first met him. It's all because of you. Will it be three treatments again?"

"Yes," Beaumont said, jotting on a loose piece of paper.

"What are you doing?"

"I always make file notes about how my clients look," Beaumont said. "Fantastic would cover you, but I like to be a little more elaborate."

"When do you start back?"

"Fifteenth of January."

"I'll see you then," Mrs. Milgate said, bouncing up from her chair, and opening the door. "Come on, Milly, we have lots to do."

Beaumont reacted quickly, and as Milly reached the door, he caught her by the wrist and put the piece of paper in her hand. "Our secret," he whispered.

I wonder if she'll call me. God, I hope she doesn't tell her mother.

When he left the surgery that night, he still hadn't heard from Milly, and he put his plan down to a rush of blood. *What was I thinking?*

There was a 9/11 documentary that Beaumont wanted to watch, and he poured himself a glass of wine before turning on the television. He cursed when he saw the first plane crash into the south tower. As the documentary was finishing, his cell phone rang, and private caller appeared on the screen. He was about to hit the red button, but sensed it might be Milly. "Dr. Simon Beaumont," he answered.

"Dr. Beaumont, it's Milly. You wanted me to call."

"Thank you, Milly. I wanted to talk to you, preferably away from the surgery."

"What about?"

"I'd rather discuss it face to face. Do you have any time over Christmas?"

Beaumont thought he heard a muffled laugh. "I have all the time in the world. You're just down the road. I can come and see you tonight, if you'd like."

He looked at his watch. It was nearly ten o'clock. "How do you know where I live?"

"Every time my mother drives past she says, there's the dump my plastic surgeon lives in."

Beaumont felt himself color. *What a bitch that woman is.* "If it's not too late for you, you're welcome to come now. Park up near the house, where your car can't be seen from the road."

"I'll be there in five minutes."

Beaumont put his camera on the coffee table next to the sofa before turning the veranda lights on. Milly had sounded nervous, but not as nervous as when she was with her mother.

Chapter 38

Milly was wearing a floppy, black T-shirt, jeans, and sandals. Beaumont studied her as she sat down. She had narrow shoulders and hips but a large stomach and arms. "Thank you for coming, Milly. Can I get you something to drink?"

"No, thanks," she said, staring at the carpet. "Why do you want to see me?"

Beaumont sat on the end of the sofa so that he was only a few feet from her. "I'll answer that in good time. First, I have some questions for you. If you feel they're too personal, just say so, and I'll stop."

Milly turned red. "Don't be nervous," Beaumont said, turning on a coffee table light while switching the living room lights off.

In semi-darkness, Milly said, "This is very strange. If I don't like your questions, I'll leave."

"Fair enough. Are you happy?"

"Oh, I thought you were going to ask me about my health," Milly replied, sounding relieved. "No, I'm not happy. I have no friends. No one to talk to. Most nights I cry myself to sleep. People think I'm lucky because I have wealthy parents. If only, they knew."

"What about your mother?"

"She married my father for his money. They made a deal. Can you believe that? He'd marry her, and she'd give him a son. I'm that son. Neither of them are happy."

"How do you get on with her?"

"I don't. I might as well not exist. She delights in telling me how fat I am. I heard her sniggering with her girlfriends and saying, *she's her father's daughter, just look at her nose.* The only time she talks to me is when her chauffeur's not available, and she wants me to drive her somewhere."

"How about your father?"

"I think he loves me in his own way, but he doesn't have time for me. He's either with her, Harry Cusack and his mates, or putting some business deal together. However, he'd give me anything I asked for. It's faster and easier to give money than time," she sniffled. "If it wasn't for you, he might have had more time for me."

"How's that?"

"Their marriage was on the rocks. Daddy was playing around, and it was only a matter of time before they divorced. Then you got involved and enhanced her. Daddy went gaga and was soon back under her thumb. I hated you. Men are so fickle. He fell under her spell again because you gave her new boobs."

"If it hadn't of been me, it would've been someone else."

"Yes, but they mightn't have achieved the same results. When she's in your surgery, she plays the sophisticated lady. Well, about three months after the surgery she was in the sunroom with some of her girlfriends. They'd just finished playing tennis when I walked in. She was naked from the waist up and flaunting herself."

Beaumont put his hand to his mouth and grinned. "Go on."

"Two of our gardeners were behind a tree looking through the window getting a real eyeful. I'm certain she knew they were there. Some lady."

"Are you going to university?"

No. I was mid-way through law at Sydney University when I had a bad experience and dropped out."

"Tell me about it."

"It's personal," she said, folding her arms. "I've never told anyone, and I'm not going to tell you."

Surprisingly she held his eyes and said, "Why am I here?"

Beaumont paused and then reached over and put his hand over hers. "When your mother was having surgery in London, and then later with me, did you ever think about yourself? Some procedure that you thought you might like to have?"

"Are you joking? I know what I look like. I asked Mother, and she told me I was too young to have surgery. She said that plastic surgery slowed down the aging process, but surgeons couldn't change a person's looks. I didn't believe her, so I went on the internet. She was right. I read about women wanting to look like Angelina Jolie, and surgeons saying it was impossible."

"Go on."

"She said I'd been unlucky, that I'd had inherited Daddy's genes, and nothing could be done," Milly said, lifting her free hand up to her nose. "Please tell me why you wanted to see me?"

"But you would've known that surgery could correct the hump in your nose?"

"Yes, but she said Daddy would be upset if I had surgery to make it smaller."

"Did you ask him?"

"How could I ask him something like that?"

"Milly, your mother, didn't tell you the truth," Beaumont said, drawing closer and putting his hand under her chin. "And you also misinterpreted the internet articles. I could work wonders with your face."

"Could...could you make me beautiful?"

"Yes."

Milly paused, deep in thought. "Mother will never let me have surgery."

"You turn twenty-one next year. Isn't it time you did your own thing? Got yourself an apartment and became independent? Haven't you lived in your mother's shadow for far too long? Would your father give you enough to live on?"

"Daddy would give me a million dollars if I asked him, and she'd pleased to see the back of me. Then she'd have him all to herself. Witch!" She looked at him skeptically. "How much will the surgery cost?"

"Nothing. You've had a rough deal, Milly, and I don't want you to think I'm exploiting you because I'm chasing fees. There are some conditions, though."

"Anything."

Mr. Morgan was wrong. I don't need to invest wisely or sell a product. I just need to marry a super-rich trust beneficiary and heiress. "It's to be our secret. You are not to breathe a word to anyone. Most importantly, you must do everything I say."

"I will. I will."

"Good," Beaumont said, picking up his camera. "I'm going to take a few pics. First thing tomorrow I want you to find a place to rent. Somewhere nearby."

"I'll have an apartment by lunchtime."

"How much do you weigh?"

"The last time I weighed myself I was one hundred and seventy pounds."

"If I'm going to make a fox out of you, you're going to have to lose more than fifty pounds. Can you imagine your mom's face when she sees the new you?"

"I'd kill to see it."

"Take a long walk in the morning, and whatever you ate today, eat less tomorrow. Also, drink two liters of water a day. It'll curb your appetite. I don't want to have to do an abdominoplasty, and you should do everything to ensure that I don't have to."

"What's an abdominoplasty?"

"Your mother's girlfriends would giggle and call it a tummy tuck. It's serious surgery with unavoidable scarring."

"That's why you want me to lose weight."

"Yes. You're young and hopefully won't end up with ugly, loose skin around your tummy. We don't want the weight to fall off. Slow and gradual will produce the best results."

"Can I email you if I have any questions?"

"Of course."

"I'm so excited," she said.

Me too. I have big plans for you. "I'm glad."

Chapter 39

Beaumont bounced into his surgery and said, "Good morning, Mary. Beautiful day. What do you have planned for Christmas?"

"My, we're in good spirits today. Did you win the lottery?"

No, something far bigger. "No such luck. I've been feeling a little run down. I'm looking forward to the break."

"You work far too hard, Simon. I'm glad we have no more surgery planned until the New Year."

Beaumont booted up his laptop and downloaded the pictures of Milly's face to the laptop and started drawing lines over it. *This will be more than a facelift. It will be a total face recreation. I'll lower her hairline and reduce the size of her forehead. Her nose will be a big job. I'll get rid of the hump and make it smaller. I'll insert cheek implants that will lift and make her cheekbones more pronounced. Her chin is problematic. Can I get away with just shaving it? No. I'll have to sculpt it by removing bone and muscle. Her teeth are far too large, and she needs to see a dental surgeon. Her lips are fine, but I could give her Angelina Jolie's lips with the use of a little body fat. I'll ask her if she'd like Angelina's lips. I know what her answer will be.*

When Milly called Beaumont, he could feel her excitement. She had rented a two-bedroom apartment in Point Piper and asked if she could see him in the evening. "I'll be home after seven o'clock. Come around anytime, I'll only be watching television. Did you think about what we talked about?"

"I've been unable to think of anything else. I'm bubbling."

"It's the first time I've ever heard you sound happy."

"I'm on such a high. When are you going to operate?"

"I'll arrange it now and let you know tonight."

The hospital administrator at The Paragon was surprised when Beaumont called. He didn't usually speak to surgeons as their support staff made theater bookings. "I need a theater for ten hours on January the third with a full support team. I'd also like you to arrange an anesthesiologist."

"You're not bringing your nurse?"

"No."

"Why aren't you using one of your theaters?"

Will I emphasize the need for privacy? No, better not to say anything. "My team's on holidays. Unfortunately, my client's only available for surgery in the first week of January. I asked her to wait until my team returned, but she couldn't. Oh, she'll be with you for seven nights. In one of your private rooms, of course."

Seven nights' accommodation seemed to cheer the administrator up. "We'll see you on the third, Doctor."

When Milly knocked on Beaumont's door, she was wearing a new tracksuit and Nike gym shoes. "Hello. I walked for five miles. Over nine thousand steps. I bought a pedometer," she gushed.

"Well done. Let me explain the procedures and then you can ask questions."

Ten minutes later, she said, "I want Angelina Jolie's lips."

"I thought you would. Now I have to tell you what can go wrong," Beaumont said, reaching into his briefcase. "This is an Informed Consent that details those matters. You need to initial every clause and sign it. I'll witness your signature, which I shouldn't, but I can't think of another way to protect your privacy. Do you know anyone who you can tell about the surgery?"

"No, I told you I don't have any friends."

"You don't have a close girlfriend or boyfriend?"

"I wish I did." Milly squirmed.

"What about an old boyfriend? Someone you're still friends with."

"No," she said, turning bright red. "I don't want to talk about friends. I don't have any. I'm happy to initial and sign anything you want. You don't have to go over it with me. Nothing in the world could stop me from having the surgery."

"I can't do that. Make yourself comfortable. It's going to take half an hour."

"When they'd finished, Beaumont said, "Take your tracksuit pants off. I need to look at your thighs."

Milly didn't move.

"Milly, I'm your surgeon. You have to trust me. I want to see whether I'll have to liposculpt your thighs."

She stood up and with trembling hands slowly lowered her pants. "I've got horrible legs."

"As a matter of fact, you don't. You have hardly any fat on your thighs, and they have some definition. I'll take the fat for your lips from your stomach."

"So you don't have to do anything to my legs?"

"Calf augmentation would make them perfect, but that's something for the future."

"Calf augmentation?"

"Implants."

"Like boobs?"

"Same principle."

"My God."

Beaumont laughed. "While you've got your pants off, I'll check your butt."

"Oh, you're not going to tell me that there are butt implants?"

"If you want a butt like Jennifer Lopez's, you can have one. All it takes is implants."

"Unbelievable! Are there implants for everything? That would be so embarrassing," Milly said, quickly pulling up her tracksuit pants. "You can check my butt while I'm out cold on the operating table."

"Okay, but I need you to take your top off."

"No!" Milly cringed. After you've checked my butt, you can check my boobs. They're tiny."

"Sorry, change of plan. I'm going to do your breasts at the same time I do your face. After that, you'll only need one more operation."

"Are they going to look like my Mother's?"

"No, nothing like them. Barbara's are round; yours will be teardrops contoured to your body. No one will be able to tell that they're implants," he said, and then laughed. "Well not until you're in your forties."

"Now come on, please take your top off. I can't help you unless you do."

Milly was bright red, and looked like she was going to burst into tears as she slowly removed her T-shirt. She reached behind to unclip her bra, but Beaumont, with one deft hand unclipped it in one movement.

Jesus. They are small. It's like they never developed. "You exaggerate," he said. "You're naturally petite. They look small to you because you're carrying so much excess weight. Do you know why you love eating?"

"No."

"Because you're unhappy. By the time I finish you'll be a fox. You'll be happy, and your food cravings will disappear. You can put your top back on."

"You're very kind. I know they're tiny. These horrible boys said some terrible things when I–I–"

"Go on," Beaumont said.

"No. I better get going. Dr. Beaumont, it's so nice to have someone to talk to. Can I come around tomorrow night?"

"It's Christmas Eve."

"I know," she said. "Are you going out?"

Sonya will understand if I cancel. I'm exhausted. "No. I'll see you tomorrow night, Milly. If you like, you can call me Simon."

The following morning when Beaumont opened his emails, there was one from Milly.

Dear Simon, It's easier to express my feelings by email rather than in person. I hope you understand. I feel like I have found a soul-mate in you. I made a slip last night and thought I should explain. While I was at university, I had a sexual encounter with two boys. I don't want to go into detail, but after they had had their way, they ridiculed me. My breasts are tiny, and they let me know it. I don't want to talk about it, but I did want you to know why I quit law. I'll see you tonight. Milly.

Beaumont was pleased. Everything was going to plan. Milly was already confiding in, and becoming reliant on him.

Chapter 40

Sydney saw in the New Year with another spectacular fireworks display that lit up the bridge.

Two days later, on a humid Monday morning, Beaumont scrubbed up in the operating theater of The Paragon. A nurse helped him insert his hands into a pair of latex gloves. Milly looked up from the operating table and gave him a dopey smile. *Jeez, she's dog ugly! No one else could do what I'm about to. Only I can turn God's mistake into an object of beauty.* "See you in recovery," he said.

His favorite music, the backing to The Godfather movie, percolated through the theater. "Commencing at 7 A.M.," he said, making the first incision. Nine and a half hours later, Milly was wheeled into recovery.

Beaumont sat sipping his second cup of coffee in the cafeteria. It was quiet, and he suspected the upmarket hospital was functioning at less than fifty percent. The Boulevard was almost empty, with only one surgeon operating over the holiday period. He waited for an hour before going into recovery. Milly was propped up and looked groggy. Sleep after a rhinoplasty was always difficult and she would be upright in bed for the next three nights. He had arranged for around the clock nursing. After the nurses wheeled into her room, he quickly checked her and said, "I'll see you in the morning."

She didn't hear a word.

Beaumont spent the following morning with Milly. Her face was badly swollen, and she had two black eyes. However, she was in surprisingly good spirits and had demanded that the nurse bring her a mirror. "I love my lips," she said.

"They're not going to remain that size. They're swollen."

"Two more nights sitting up to sleep," she groaned. "If it wasn't for that the discomfort would be minimal."

"It's essential. That's why the nurses are here to prop you up if you slump. You'll be off the drip tomorrow and be able to walk around.

The swelling will peak on the third day and then you'll see rapid improvement."

"I peeked at my boobs. I think they're wonderful. I can't wait to take a proper look."

They all peek. "You'll be able to tomorrow. Ask the nurse to help."

"I'm so grateful, Simon. The nurses talk about you like you're God. They said you were angry with the anesthesiologist, though. Did he do something that he shouldn't have?"

"Yes, he lisped," Beaumont said. "Nancy boy."

"I don't understand." Milly yawned.

"You don't have to. I better let you get some sleep."

"Oh, I nearly forgot. The little Asian nurse who was looking after me this morning wants you to westernize her eyes. You've done one of her girlfriend's eyes, and she's saving so she can have the same."

"That's nice to know."

Milly was dozing off and on. Just before midday, she slipped into a deep sleep.

Beaumont spent the next five mornings with Milly. By Sunday, she could see what her new nose was going to look like and was thrilled. "I want to touch it," she said.

"You can," Beaumont said. "You have to be gentle, though. In three months, ninety percent of the swelling will have subsided."

"And I no longer have a jaw. Instead, I have a cute little chin. It's amazing what you've done to my face. I love my cheekbones. No one's going to recognize me. Oh, and I can't stop looking at my boobs."

Yes, even by my standards the transformation is amazing. From ugly duckling to beautiful swan in less than ten hours. "It's only going to get better."

"Did you check my butt?"

"We can talk about that after."

"I just wanted to know if you checked."

"You asked me to, and, yes, I did."

The first thing that Beaumont did when he returned to his surgery was to tell Mary that in the future, he only wanted to perform three procedures a day.

"That's a change," she said. "Is it one of your New Year's resolutions?"

Work will be optional soon. I might become a full-time investor. "I just want to slow down. Oh, and I only want to perform emergency procedures on Fridays. No emergencies, no surgery."

"You know you have commitments through to mid-April, with up to six procedures on some days."

"That's fine. I can cope until then."

After Mary left his office, Beaumont turned to the social pages of *The Sunday Telegraph*. A huge smile crossed his face when he saw the headline, *Banker Sues Surgeon*. The article went on to say that merchant banker, Yvonne Chapman, had issued a malpractice suit against prominent plastic surgeon, Brett Golding, and was seeking more than five million in damages.

Beaumont also knew that it wouldn't be long before he heard from an angry Andrew Houghton. He flicked to the front pages and skimmed the news items. Ten minutes later, Julie buzzed and said, "It's Dr. Houghton for you, Dr. Beaumont."

"Andrew, Happy New Year. What do I owe the pleasure of your call?"

"Don't you know? That Chapman woman you referred to me is suing Brett Golding. I've been subpoenaed."

"No! It's the first I've heard of it. She never mentioned litigation to me. She said that all she was interested in was having the surgery remedied. Would you like me to call her?"

"It's too late. Besides, her lawyers will almost certainly subpoena you too. Please don't make any more referrals."

Shit! I never thought she might drag me into the litigation. If I get subpoenaed, Brett will know who set him up. God, I hope she doesn't get me involved. Hang on, what am I worried about? After I marry Milly, I won't have a worry in the world. "I'm sorry, Andrew, I never anticipated her litigating. In the future, I'll refuse to see any of his clients."

"Unless his insurers settle, he won't have any clients. If this case gets to court, he'll never practice again," Houghton said.

How sweet it is. "It'd be a shame if his career finished on such a low note."

"Perhaps. I wonder what's wrong with him."

"I'm sorry, Andrew. If I'd known this was going to happen, I would've never asked you to help."

"It's not your fault, Simon. Shit happens. I hope I don't see you in court."

Milly was at Beaumont's house every night and each morning he'd receive one or more emails from her. Some of them were incredibly intimate and told of a bitterly, unhappy childhood. They were long, tedious and repetitive. It was like a dam wall had been torn down, and he was the receptacle for her outpourings. Perhaps it was the age difference, but he found her intellectually dull. Three weeks after the surgery she looked terrific. She was letting her lustrous, dark black hair grow, and it sat it on her shoulders.

"Dad called. He wants to visit. I'm worried sick. What am I going to tell him?"

"It's not a problem," Beaumont replied. "Call him, and say that you've had plastic surgery and that he may not recognize you. That way he'll be prepared. Tell him that you're thrilled. If he loves you, he'll be as pleased as what you are."

"Yes, that's a good idea. You're so wise. I'm lucky to have a friend like you."

Oh, I'm going to be far more than a friend. "Are you worried about your mother?"

"That bitch! I couldn't care less about what she thinks."

"I'm sure that it won't be long before she's gives me a piece of her mind."

"Let's not talk about her. When can I see your dental surgeon?"

"Not yet. I'll let you know. I don't want him undoing any of my work. How much do you weigh?"

"I've lost twenty pounds. I'm one hundred and fifty pounds."

"Come here. I want to check your tummy."

She was still shy, but she came over and stood in front of him while he lifted her T-shirt and checked. "Excellent," he said. "Now listen to me. I don't want you to lose any more than two pounds a week. If you stick to that, I'm almost certain I won't have to perform an abdominoplasty. In fifteen weeks, you'll be one hundred and twenty pounds and look sensational. After you've recovered from the subsequent procedures, you'll able to start at the gym and tone your muscles."

"I don't know whether I want to go under the knife again. I can hardly drag myself away from my mirror. I look fantastic. I went to the supermarket yesterday, and these boys were checking me out. That's never happened before." She stopped talking and rested her head in her hands. When she looked up she said, "Do you think I should have the surgery?"

Of course, you should have the surgery. Without it, my creation will be incomplete. I can't marry you with imperfections. I'll put some bait on the hook. "That's for you to decide. I can't make that decision. If you don't want Elle Macpherson's legs and Jennifer Lopez's butt, that's fine by me."

Milly's face filled with consternation. "Will there be postoperative pain?"

It's going to be easy. "With surgery, there's always postoperative pain. However, it will be less severe than you what you went through with the other procedures. You won't have to sleep upright for three nights. I won't lie, the butt surgery will be a little painful, but it's nothing you can't cope with."

"I don't know. I'm happy. I don't think I need it."

It didn't work. I better change the bait. "You're right. Your mother's going to be upset enough when she sees you. Can you imagine what she'll be like if you have the surgery, and she sees you in a tight dress and high heels? She'll go ballistic."

The look of consternation on Milly's face disappeared. "Oh hang it. I've come this far. I might as well complete the job. When can you operate?" She smiled.

Jackpot. "Early February. I'll let you know the date tomorrow night."

Hurricane Milgate hit Beaumont's surgery without warning. Barbara Milgate didn't announce herself at reception but instead charged straight into Beaumont's office. Fortunately, he wasn't seeing a client. "You bastard," she shouted. "What have you done to my little girl?"

He didn't stand up and nor did he ask Mrs. Milgate to sit down. "I made her beautiful," he said. "Do you have a problem with that?"

"You've destroyed the character in her face. She…she looks bland. Poor Joe's in a state of shock."

Don't you mean a state of euphoria? "Is Mr. Milgate unhappy?"

"You had no right. You broke the law. I'm going to complain to your Institute. You didn't get parental consent."

"I didn't need it. The age of consent in New South Wales is eighteen. I didn't break any laws. She looks fantastic. I hope you're not jealous of your daughter."

"Don't you dare talk to me like that. I'll never set foot in this surgery again and nor will my girlfriends. You won't have a practice after I get through with you."

"My practice will continue to thrive. Your girlfriends will still come to see me; they just won't tell you. When you see one of them with a superb nose job or facelift, you'll know it's me, though," Beaumont jeered. "I'm the best, and everyone wants the best. Think about that when you have your next facelift. Whatever the result, you'll know it would've been better had I performed it. Oh, and Mrs. Milgate, I'll never operate on you again. You're going regret today's little outburst. Now get out of my office and don't come back."

"When Joe gets through with you, you'll wish you'd never been born," Barbara Milgate screamed as she stormed out.

Mary looked in on Beaumont and said, "What was that about?"

"Nothing. I'll be operating on the first Friday in February. The client is Milly Milgate. She'll be in for three nights. I'll give you the details after. It's pro bono."

"Milly Milgate and it's pro bono?" Mary asked. "What are you playing at? Is that why Mrs. Milgate's furious with you?"

"Mary, enough with the questions. Just do what I tell you to."

Joe Milgate had been shocked when he first saw Milly, but after recovering, he was pleased for her. "My father had the infamous Milgate honk," he said, holding his nose. "And his father before him. I was sorry when I passed it down to you. You have the cutest nose. That damn Yank has magic in his fingers. Take it from me, what he did to your Mother is mind-blowing."

"I know what he did, Dad. We don't need to go there." Milly's eyes danced.

"Maybe he could get rid of my honk? What do you think?"

"You use your features to intimidate your opposition when you're negotiating deals. Do you think this would scare them?" Milly said, touching her nose.

"You've got a point. I'll stick with what God gave me."

"Are you upset with me?"

"Not in the slightest. You look nothing like you did a month ago, so initially it was a shock. If you're happy, I'm happy." He chuckled and rubbed his chin thoughtfully.

"What's funny?"

"I'm sorry about how your Mother reacted. She's like Cinderella's stepmother. I've never seen her so angry."

"I don't care. It's done, and there's nothing she can do about it."

"Spoken like a true Milgate. I'm glad you're happy. It warms my old heart."

"Thank you, Daddy," Milly said, hugging him.

Milly's second surgery went without a hitch, and while she complained of a sore bum for a few days, Beaumont could not have been more pleased. She was annoyed that she couldn't sit down for two weeks, but it was the calf implants that were proving problematic. He had told her to buy a pair of boots with two-inch heels to walk in. She was fine when she was walking, but at night when she took the boots off, her legs ached. Ice packs provided some relief, but had she had her time again she wouldn't have had the calf implants. "You never told me that my legs would hurt so much," she said accusingly.

"Everyone's different. I told you that you'd be wearing those boots for at least two months. If you're lucky, it'll only be six weeks. It's not long when you weigh it up against the benefits."

"I suppose so. God, I sound like my mother," she laughed. "Don't ever let me sound like her."

Chapter 41

In early April 2002, the case of *Chapman vs. Golding* got underway in the New South Wales Supreme Court. Under cross-examination, Yvonne Chapman said that Simon Beaumont had referred her to Andrew Houghton. The cat was out of the bag. That night Golding called Beaumont, and told him, no matter what the outcome of the case, his career as a plastic surgeon in Sydney was over. Beaumont mocked him, calling him yesterday's man, but when he put the phone down a sense of unease overcame him. He had been too eager to sink Golding and hadn't thought through the ramifications. Even if defense counsel hadn't found out about him from Yvonne Chapman, he would've when he cross-examined Houghton. Beaumont was annoyed. He had made a careless mistake and knew that somehow Golding would find a way to pay him back. His need to marry Milly had just intensified.

Milly had always hated gyms, but now she was torturing herself for up to an hour a day, and loving it. The weight continued to fall off and her desire to consume copious quantities of food vanished. She had been eating out of boredom and feeling sorry for herself. Now she bounded out of bed in the mornings eager to start another day. Beaumont had prepared her gym program and supervised her first week of workouts. "Do what I say," he said, "and don't listen to the clowns they employ as instructors. Half of them are queers. They haven't got a clue, and in your case, have no idea about the surgery you've been through."

"What have you got against gay men?" Milly asked.

"Nothing. It's what I call pretty boys who hang around gyms."

Milly had wanted to buy body hugging Spandex gym gear, but Beaumont had insisted that she wear an unfashionable, blue, woolen tracksuit, so that her body could breathe. Even so, she looked terrific and attracted many admiring glances. She had never experienced this before, and when she'd been wolf whistled by some construction workers, she had broken out into a huge smile.

Hollywood heartthrob, Seth Hawke, had just won his second Oscar for his portrayal of a punch drunk boxer who gets lucky and wins the world heavyweight title. When his manager called the surgery to say that Seth was taking a holiday down under and wanted a little work done, Julie and Mary were beside themselves. A little work turned out to be a facelift, platysmaplasty, upper and lower eyelid blepharoplasty, a brow lift, and laser of the forehead and the crow's feet. Hawke's manager told Beaumont that Seth would be holidaying in Queensland for six weeks after the surgery and that when he returned home, it was critical, that no one be able to tell he'd gone under the knife. Beaumont had toyed with saying, "Listen, dumbass, he's got a craggy face, and I'm about to take ten to fifteen years off his chronological age. How do you propose that I hide the change?" Instead, he said, there'll be no visible scars, to which the dumbass manager replied, "That's all I'm asking." Since Nicole Kinnane, Beaumont had operated on seven Hollywood stars and the novelty was wearing off. Had it been anyone else except Seth Hawke, he would've declined the surgery, but Hawke was Hollywood royalty.

When Beaumont looked at Milly, he was in total awe of himself. His euphoria was such that he thought that the only comparable feat was God creating Eve from Adam's rib. Milly doted on him and had told him many times that she loved him without defining love. Did she love him as her doctor, as a father figure or as the man she lusted over? He would soon find out.

Because of her looks, boobs and ass, she oozed sex appeal, but intellectually they had nothing in common. The Russian State Philharmonic Orchestra was playing at the Opera House, but when Beaumont suggested going, Milly had asked him if he was ninety. To make matters worse, she had insisted that they see Zoolander. She laughed all the way through it while Beaumont had grimaced. He thought there'd never been a sillier movie. As they left the theater, he glanced at her. She was wearing a plain white blouse, skintight, light blue jeans and platform sandals. *God, you look sensational which is just as well, because I'm never going to bed you for your intellect,* he thought.

When they got back to his house, Milly bent over the coffee table to pick up the TV guide. *Eat your heart out, Jennifer Lopez.* She had a fabulous ass, and he felt a stirring. *Now I'll find out what your definition of love is.* "Come and sit next to me," he said, patting the sofa. "I like having you in my life."

"I love having you in mine. You've given me a life I never could've imagined."

"I'm glad," he said, kissing her gently. "Beautiful lips."

"They should be. The world's best plastic surgeon made them."

He kissed her again, this time, more firmly while undoing the top two buttons of her blouse. He slipped his hand inside her bra and marveled at his genius. Her breasts were perfect. "You're a very sexy woman."

"No one's ever said that to me before."

He unclipped her bra and threw it and her blouse on the floor while lifting her legs onto the sofa. He kissed her and fondled her breasts but didn't get any response. He was doing all the touching and wondered whether she'd ever had her hand on a man's dick. After about ten minutes, he undid the top button of her jeans and felt her freeze. Before he could go any further, she sat bolt upright, and said, "I'm sorry, I have to go." There were tears in her eyes.

"What's wrong?"

"I can't talk," she said, picking up her clothes as she ran out the door.

The following morning Beaumont received a long rambling email from Milly talking about what happened to her at university without being explicit. She was like a child. She said that he too must have at least one dark secret and that she wanted him to share it with her. After that, she would tell him what had happened to her.

Chapter 42

Andrew Houghton called first thing in the morning to tell Beaumont that Yvonne Chapman had accepted an out of court settlement of four million plus costs. What he said next was staggering. Brett Golding's medical indemnity insurers had told Golding that they'd no longer provide cover, and he'd been unable to obtain insurance with any other insurer. Without medical indemnity insurance, he could not continue to practice and had resigned as president of the Institute. Houghton said that the insurers had evidently known far more than they had let on. He suspected that the Chapman settlement was not the first that they'd made on behalf of Golding, and that the Institute might have pushed him out."

"I'm not all that surprised," Beaumont said, "every successful claim adds to the premiums paid by all members. Perhaps some of the more active members said enough's enough."

"It's a sad ending to a brilliant career," Houghton said, "but it's for the best."

Yes, it is. I don't have to worry about the nasty, little prick anymore. Nor will I have to worry about a second-class imposter claiming to be the best. "You're right, Andrew. I feel for him. Poor old Brett."

Steve Levine was surprised when Beaumont called and asked if they could meet. It was three years since Beaumont had last visited Steve's offices. He had added a second level, and the place was buzzing with two harassed receptionists trying to cope with constantly ringing phones. "You've done well, Steve, and to think it was me who got you started."

"We both know that's not true, but you've been a loyal client and a good friend. We've both done well."

"I'm glad you think so. I don't. I wanted to see you because I'm adding a standalone extension to the hospital. I want to move my injectors and therapists out of the surgery and into the new facility."

"How much do you need?"

"Nothing. I have more than enough to pay for it," Beaumont said, pushing a rough plan across Steve's desk. "I want you to talk to the architects, get plans and specifications, and put it out to tender. I want it built before Christmas."

"Are you expanding the surgery? Do you need more space?"

"Steve, you know that when it comes time to sell, there's no good-will in a plastic surgeon's practice. These are the goodwill," he said, holding up his hands, "and without them there's nothing."

"I'm still not with you."

"There's plenty of goodwill in the injecting and therapy facility because anyone can do it. I want to make it easy to sell as a stand-alone business."

"Are you going back to New York?"

"Never, well certainly not to live. I'm thinking about selling every-thing and getting into a new profession."

"What?"

"I don't know."

"You're at the peak of your profession. Why would you want to sell?"

"I can't earn enough. I'm thinking about becoming a full-time investor."

"Oh no! Do you know how hard it is? For every Warren Buffet, there are a thousand losers."

"I know what I'm doing. I haven't made up my mind about selling. Should I go down that path, I want my assets in a form that makes them easy to sell."

"I can't fault that logic. On a personal note, have you been to see Debbie and Jack?"

"No."

"He's the spitting image of you. Now he's walking, there's no stop-ping him."

"Steve, let me know when you've chosen a builder. Remember, you've only got eight months," Beaumont said, pushing back his chair,

Milly was wearing a pale green, summery dress when she let herself into Beaumont's house, and called, "It's me. Are you there?"

"Where else would I be?" he said, as he came out from the kitchen and kissed her. "You get more beautiful every day."

"Thanks. Can we talk about last night?"

"Sure, let's go in the living room."

"I need you to understand. I do want to make love. It's just that when we got close last night, I had terrible flashbacks about that day. Until I tell you what happened, I'm going to keep having flashbacks."

"But you told me. I know."

"No, I didn't. It was far worse."

"Well, why don't you tell me now?" Beaumont said, sitting on the sofa.

"I can't. It's too horrible" Milly said, wringing her hands. "Have you ever done something so terrible that you've never talked to anyone about it?"

This will go on forever unless I can win her confidence. I can tell her about New York. I'm not going to have to worry about plastic surgery for much longer. Soon I'm going to be a rich, kept man. "Sure I have," Beaumont said, and related what had occurred in New York, and how he had changed his name.

"Jack Donahue," she said, "it's a strong name. I like it. Thank you for sharing. It must have been so stressful, but it's nothing compared to what happened to me."

"Tell me about it. You'll feel better after you have."

"I can't. The only way I could tell you is by email. Even then it'll be hard. I don't know whether I can do it."

"Take all the time you like. You don't have to do it today, tomorrow or next week. I don't want you to feel any pressure. Only tell me when you're comfortable."

"You're so patient with me. I'm lucky to have a friend like you. Someone I can confide in," she said, snuggling up to him.

Friend! What's going on in that brain of hers? "I'm glad you feel that way."

When Beaumont turned on his laptop the following morning, there was an email from Milly, in a format similar to a lengthy legal document. It was in point form and covered everything that had occurred on what she described as *that terrible day*. It was only near the end when expressing her hurt and degradation that she started to ramble. He read it and then read it again.

She had attended a lecture in the morning and when it was finished, two boys invited her to have a drink at the local pub. There had been the usual banter about sex, and who was hot and who wasn't. They had teased her about being a virgin, which she had denied. After a few hours, the trio decided to go back to one of the boy's homes and continue drinking because his parents were overseas. The boy, Spencer Everton, was the son of foreign minister, Winston Everton. *Why is it always the rich kids who get into trysts? It was the same when I was in college,* Beaumont thought. Everton had opened a bottle of wine, and they'd sat on the sofa drinking, one boy on either side of Milly. The teasing became more intense, and the other boy whose name was Tom had grabbed Milly's hand and shoved it inside his pants. He was rock hard, and the two boys had started laughing. Everton asked her if she'd ever had her hand around one like that before. Stupidly, she had said yes. Fearing being ridiculed, she hadn't removed her hand, but had no idea what to do with it. Everton had then unzipped his pants, stood up in front of her, and shoved this huge thing in her face and told her to suck it. She was drunk, but there was no way she was putting that monstrosity in her mouth. Not wanting to show fear she had laughed and told him to zip himself up. In the meantime, Tom had said, "Are you just going to leave it there or pull it?" A few seconds later he screamed in agony and yelled, "Spencer, she hasn't got a clue, she thinks she's choking a fucking chook. We'll have to teach her."

Everton had shouted, "I knew she was full of bullshit. She must be the oldest virgin in the state."

Again, Milly denied being a virgin, and Tom challenged her to get into bed with him. They were soon naked, but he wasn't much more experienced than her, and try as he might, he couldn't get it in. It was then that Everton had burst into the room, stark naked, with a bottle of oil in one hand, and his huge glistening thing in the other. "Is it my turn?" he said.

"I can't get it in," Tom yelled.

"Fucking hopeless," Everton said, and had jumped into bed on the other side of Milly and thrust his huge penis against her ass while groping her tits.

Milly was scared but drunk, and the boys took no notice when she said, "No, no, I don't want to do this anymore."

"Jeez, you've got little titties," Everton said, passing the bottle of oil to Tom. "Oil her up, and put some on your dick. You'll be in like Flynn."

She went on to describe how they had vaginally and anally fucked her for hours while making degrading comments about how small her tits were and how fat she was. Despite her drunkenness, she had refused to suck them off, and they had roared laughing while they'd knelt on either side of her and smacked her face with their penises.

When she arrived home, she was bleeding from the vagina and rectum.

She finished by saying, "It was horrible, Simon. That was my first and only time. When we got close, I froze. I want to have sex with you, but I'm scared."

Christ! I wonder if she knows what she wrote. There's enough there to bring the foreign minister down. Not quite Profumo, Christine Keeler, and Mandy Rice-Davies, but the media will have a field day if they ever get hold of it. Don't worry, Milly, I can help you. By the time I finish with you, you'll love sex.

Chapter 43

Beaumont had never stopped seeing Sonya. She was an attractive and enthusiastic lover who never asked or demanded anything. There were others he could have called, but there was no one quite as convenient as Sonya. The one exception was the lawyer, Samantha Armstrong, who he called regularly and was repeatedly rebuffed. That night in Melbourne had made a lasting impression, and the thought of repeating it drove him to persist.

Since Beaumont had taken an interest in Milly, he'd not only cut back on surgery but on consultations too. He was still making a fortune, which wasn't surprising given that he was charging thirty thousand for a facelift, five thousand more than any of his peers. Force of habit compelled him to flick to the social pages of *The Sunday Telegraph*. Staring at him were Joe and Barbara Milgate, and the accompanying article said that Mrs. Milgate had established a fund for children suffering in Somalia. It went on to describe how she'd cried after learning about the Somalians' plight. Joe had kicked off the fund with a five million dollar donation from Milgate Mining Limited. *Take it easy, Joe, that's my money you're spending. I don't know whether I'll call you, Joe or Dad?* A huge grin spread across Beaumont's face. *I know what I'll be calling Barbara, though. She'll be Mom.*

Mary knocked on his door and said, "What's funny. Share it with me."

"It's nothing. There's some strange stuff in the social pages. Barbara Milgate's trying to become Australia's Mother Teresa."

"There's some strange stuff on social media too. Have you upset someone?"

"Probably. Why do you ask?"

"You're being slandered. The popular plastic surgery websites that call for reviews are being inundated. You're being called everything from a butcher to a greedy money grabbing bastard. It's across all the sites."

It has to be Golding. "What can we do? Can we demand that the postings be taken down? We've got to get rid of them."

"I've contacted the administrators of the sites. They claim they're public forums, and there's nothing they can do."

"How bad is it?"

"The most clicked site is perfectoface.com. Users rank surgeons on a scale of one to five stars with one being the worst. You've got more than a hundred one star reviews and your average is less than two."

"Shit!"

"Do you have any ideas?"

"No. Keep persisting with the administrators and I'll try and think of something. Tell them I'll take defamation action if they don't pull them."

"I've already tried that. They don't care."

When Milly entered Beaumont's house, her head was down, and she looked nervous.

"Hi Milly," he said, kissing her. "Did you come straight from the gym?"

"Yes. Did you read my email?"

"I did. That was a terrible experience. What those boys did was horrific. You did nothing wrong."

"I know. I wish it'd never happened. I can't stop thinking about it. When we were going to make love a few nights back, I froze. I wanted to, but I couldn't."

I'm going to solve that problem. "Don't worry, I'm patient, and I'm going to help you. Would you like a glass of wine?"

"That's what got me into trouble last time."

"You're uptight. One wine will help you unwind. That's hardly the same as getting drunk. I'll put some music on."

"Yes, Alicia Keys' *Fallin'*. It's with my CDs, and I will have a glass of wine. Just one, though."

Who the hell is Alicia Keys? I was thinking of the three tenors or Sarah Brightman. "Sounds great," he said.

"Here, let me do it," she said, "I'll set the stacker up, so we're not changing CDs all night."

Yes, but they're going to be all your selections. "Here," he said, passing her a CD. "It's one of my favorites."

"Pavarotti? He's for oldies."

"Never mind. Here's to us," Beaumont said, clinking glasses.

They kissed and cuddled, and Beaumont said, "Do you like this?"

"I love snuggling; it's the next part that worries me," she said, sipping her wine.

Five minutes later Beaumont took her T-sheet off and asked her to raise her arms while he lifted her sports bra over her head. He was waiting for her to tense, and then he would pull back.

Instead, she said, "You're adept at removing women's clothes, aren't you?"

"It's part of being a plastic surgeon."

"I bet it is."

It's going better than I expected. "Has anyone ever told you that you have beautiful breasts?"

"They are, aren't they?" she said, as he stretched his fingers from nipple to nipple while placing his other hand on the top of her tracksuit pants. "I…I…"

"Relax, you know I'm not going to hurt you," he said, easing her pants to her ankles and pushing them off with his feet.

She picked up her glass of wine and gulped it down. "I needed that."

He was breathing heavily, and she was gasping, but he knew they were gasps of apprehension, not passion. He put his hand inside her panties. She was dry. The heavy petting had done nothing. "Relax, relax," he said, soothingly as he removed her panties and started licking her nipples. Her body was rigid, but he gradually felt it loosen. He worked his way down to her belly button and eased her legs open.

"No, no, not that."

"Relax, babe. Trust me," he said, as his tongue found her clit.

"No," she said, but she didn't sit up or push him away.

What's going on? I've been down here for over five minutes, and nothing's happening. I've never failed before. Uh oh, I feel some movement in the camp. There's some more. There's heavy breathing, and now she's starting to pelvic thrust. Suddenly he felt her hands tugging at his hair, and then she let out a huge scream. With hardly a pause, he entered her and two minutes later there were simultaneous yells of exultation. Sweat poured off him.

"I...I've never experienced anything like that."

"You haven't orgasmed before?"

"Never. I thought I had."

"What about when you masturbated?"

"I got a tingle," she said, "I thought that was an orgasm. I've always wondered why women carried on about their orgasms."

"But you must've watched porn on the net."

"Of course. Stacks," she said. "I thought the women were acting. I'll always think of you as my first lover."

"Wow. That was quick. Who else are you planning to make love with?"

"I didn't mean it that way. I meant that you've erased the memory of those terrible boys."

"Incredible what an orgasm can do." He laughed.

Chapter 44

Samantha Armstrong had changed her private number, and Beaumont wondered whether it was because of him. When reception finally put him through she said, "I give you full marks for persistence, Simon, but it has to stop."

"You've got it wrong. I need your advice on a legal problem."

"If it's not divorce or medical malpractice related, I can't help you. I can put you in touch with one of my partners."

No, it's you I want to see. I want to spread-eagle you on a desk again. "Let me bounce my problem off you. If you think another of your partners should be handling it, I'll take your advice. I promise I'm not trying to get into your pants."

"Alright. I'll get my PA to call you and make a time. Simon, I hope you're not playing around."

"I'm not."

Beaumont opened the file on Felicity Mott and smiled. She was Steve Levine's friend, the one who'd resolved never to set foot in his office again. When Julie showed her in, the first thing he noticed was that she had aged. Her face was drawn, and the ring in her lip had disappeared. "You were right," She sniffled. "I wish I had of listened to you."

"What?"

"I went to Bangkok and had the surgery. It's terrible. Mr. Levine suggested that I come and see you. I'm sorry about what I said."

"I see. What would you like me to do?"

"I need your help. Mr. Levine said you could fix it?"

"Did he? Let's see if it's as bad as what you say. Go behind the screen and take everything off except your panties."

One breast was larger than the other, and her nipples were misaligned. The partially healed incision below her bikini line was thick, weeping and ugly. "Why did you have the abdominoplasty after what the other surgeons and I told you?"

"I...I don't know. It...it seemed quicker than exercising," she said, looking down at her feet.

"At least they didn't mess up the liposuction of your thighs. They got one out of three right. Get dressed," he said.

As she sat down, she said, "Can you do anything?"

"Yes, I can, but I don't think I will. I warned you, and now here you are begging. If I was to say yes, which I probably won't, how would you pay me?"

"Mr. Levine said that he'd pay."

He didn't mention anything to me. "Did he?"

"Will you help me?"

"I don't know."

"But you're getting paid. What difference does it make to you? I'm just like any other client," she said, a trace of the old belligerence surfacing.

"No, you're not. Fixing up botch-ups is far more complex. I don't know what I'm going to find when I lift the skin away. One of the surgeons who you consulted with before meeting with me might be more receptive."

"No. I want you. Mr. Levine says that there is nothing that you can't do."

Well, he got that right. "I need to think about it. Someone will get back to you. Don't get your hopes up. It's not a surgery that I want to perform."

Tears ran down Felicity Mott's face. "You're punishing me," she said. "I didn't take your advice, and now you're punishing me."

"Ms. Mott, I couldn't care less whether you listened to me or not. It's irrelevant. I do, however, think that you've got some kind of nerve seeking my help. I have another appointment," he said, looking at his watch. "Someone will be in touch."

As she slumped out of his office, he pondered about what he was going to say to Steve.

Steve answered his cell on the second ring. "I've been waiting for your call," he said. "Don't you think you were a little harsh? Felicity could barely talk when she called."

"Why didn't you tell me she was coming in?"

"I thought you might refuse to see her. I told her to call and make an appointment, and not to mention me."

Beaumont paused before saying, "I probably wouldn't have seen her, Steve. I don't like being set up."

"Set up? What are you talking about? For years, I've heard you boasting about remedying other surgeons work. I'm not asking for mate's rates. You're going to get paid top dollar."

"You told me to cut back my workload and that's what I'm doing. I'm only doing six procedures a week. Add that to the fact that I don't like performing corrective surgery, and you'll understand why I don't want to do it."

"I know exactly how your practice runs. If one of your wealthy Point Piper socialites waltzed into tomorrow, wanting a facelift before she took off for Cannes, you'd fit her in. I'm a friend; I'm asking for a favor. What's the difference?"

"Jesus! If you don't know, you shouldn't be my manager."

"You're right. I forgot you don't put much store in friendships. I'll pay you ten thousand more than your normal fee. Money's something I know you put a lot of store in."

Again Beaumont paused before saying, "Steve, you've got all the media contacts. I want you to approach the *Woman's Day* and *Woman's Weekly,* and get one or both of them to do an exposé highlighting the dangers of going to Asia to have plastic surgery. They'll base the article on Felicity Mott's experience and will include before and after pics. Arrange that and I'll do the surgery for my normal fee. You get to keep your ten grand."

"She won't show her dad or me the surgery, but you want her to tell the whole country. She's hurting, and you want to put her through a media scrum."

"I want to send a message to those contemplating going down the same path. She's going to be the billboard that spells out the dangers."

"You told me that Brett Golding used to use a similar tactic when he wanted to bury some poor dermatologist who'd encroached on his ground. The difference was that he didn't blackmail the victim."

"Steve, there are plenty of other surgeons she can go to. Those are my conditions. Call me when she and you are agreeable. If I don't hear from you, I'll know you've gone elsewhere."

Milly idolized Beaumont, knowing that he'd surgically enhanced her beyond her wildest dreams. After their night of passion, she was rapt. Her appetite for sex quickly grew, and she would say, "I never knew what I was missing," and then she would ask him to *do that thing.*"

He would smirk knowing that she wanted him to go down on her and respond, "What? I don't understand? You'll have to tell me exactly what you want."

She loved it, but when he tried to coax her into reciprocating, she wouldn't. She said the thought of putting his dick in her mouth made her ill and blamed it on that day. When he rolled her on top of him, she'd say, "What am I meant to do?" and then, "I don't like it."

After they'd had sex, she'd lay face down, naked on top of the sheets, using her elbows as support and talk to him. She weighed one hundred and twelve pounds, and her body was taut and toned. He would lay on his back, hands behind his head and marvel at his creation. Perfect legs. Perfect ass. Perfect tits. A flawless face, button nose, pronounced cheekbones and voluptuous lips. Despite this, he still found her boring, and his mind often drifted to Samantha or Sonya while he was on top of her. They'd had no compunction about giving him head or riding him. He knew what the problem was. He was more than twenty years older than Milly, and they had few common interests. When he had those thoughts, he reminded himself, that he wasn't with her because of her intellect or the sex.

As he had planned, she had become totally beholden and did little without asking him. When he'd asked her to move in with him, she hadn't hesitated. It would only be a few more months before he landed his prize, and joined the ranks of the super-wealthy.

Chapter 45

Milly's father had suggested that she give something back to the community by getting involved in raising funds for good causes. Beaumont was supportive, and Milly embraced the idea. One night when she was drawing up invitations for a function, she said, "Can we go to your surgery? I have to do some photocopying?"

"Not tonight," he replied, "I want to watch the rugby. It's state of origin."

"But I have to have the copies for the morning," she moaned.

"There's a spare set of keys in the top drawer of my desk. If you want to drive there, be my guest. There's a security touchpad on the right as you enter. The code is 1981."

"The year I was born," Milly said, getting up from the sofa. "That's romantic. I won't be long."

If she gets immersed in charity work, I'll get some peace, Beaumont thought.

Samantha Armstrong asked Beaumont to take a seat at the coffee table adjacent to her desk. She was all business and made no mention of their Melbourne tryst. "Some asshole's defaming me on the internet," he said. "I want you to stop him."

"I told you that my areas of expertise are divorce and medical malpractice," she said. "Luckily for you, I do have some experience related to internet defamation. This firm was subject to some unhelpful comments on the net that we were successful in having removed. Do you have any idea who's attacking you?"

Yes. That bastard, Brett Golding, but if I tell you, you won't act for me. Oh, and I really want you to act for me, Beaumont thought, undressing her with his eyes. "No, I have no idea."

"That may or may not be a problem depending on how sophisticated your troll is. If he's clever or based overseas, you won't be able to do anything. You won't be able to locate him, and the websites won't remove the defamatory material."

"What are you suggesting?"

"We used a firm of private detectives specializing in computer fraud. A couple of brilliant, young IT guys. They tracked the source from where the comments were emanating, and once we had a name and address, we didn't need them anymore."

"What did you do?"

"He was a disgruntled former employee. Once he knew we were on to him, he removed the offending comments."

"What else did you do?"

"I'm not with you," Samantha said, crossing her ankles.

Great legs. "Did you sue him? Seek damages? You know, do those nasty things that lawyers are trained to do?"

"We wanted the defamatory comments removed. Isn't that what you want?"

"Yes, but I want to send a message too. If we find him, I'm going to sue."

"What if he doesn't have a cent to his name? What will you do?"

Oh, he's got plenty. It's Golding, and I want to bring him down. "I'll worry about that when you find him."

"If," Samantha said. "Email me the websites and I'll get our guys on to it. Is there anything else?"

"No, that's it. I don't suppose you get down to Melbourne much these days?"

"Give it up, Simon. It's not going to happen."

"I don't understand? You had a good time. You're in an open relationship. What's stopping you?"

"That's none of your business. Email me those websites. I'll be in touch."

As the elevator whisked Beaumont to the underground parking garage, he checked his messages. Milly sounded distressed and had asked him to call as soon as he could. "What's up, babe?"

"It's Daddy," She sniffled. "He's in hospital. He's been diagnosed with lung cancer."

That's what happens when you smoke sixty cigarettes a day. "Hey, don't fret. They can work wonders these days. If they've caught it earlier enough, he's going to be okay. Where are you?"

"I'm at Langton Private Hospital. I have to go. The oncologists are seeing Daddy now, and I want to hear what they say."

"Tell Joe that I'm thinking of him, and that he can beat this thing. Keep your chin up, babe."

Hang on, Joe, hang on. I don't want you to cark it yet. At least have the decency to wait until I've married your daughter. What a bummer. It's ended the possibility of a lavish wedding with hundreds of guests. I'm going to have to move fast.

Chapter 46

Milly was a little more upbeat when Beaumont got home. He cuddled her and told her how sorry he was.

"What a pity it's Daddy and not the witch," she said. "He has a black spot on the lung. The oncologists said that one positive is that it hasn't metastasized. He's going to have radiotherapy and chemo. Poor thing."

"It makes you realize how fragile life is. Your dad's a tough cookie, though. If anyone can beat it, he will."

"That's what he said. They took his cigarettes, and he was like a bear with a sore head. He said that if he was going to go, he wanted to be doing something he enjoyed. That's when I lost it."

"You've had a rough day. You need a nice glass of wine," Beaumont said, taking a bottle of Chardonnay from the fridge, and putting his arm around her. "Let's have it in the living room."

"I was shocked when I got the call. I thought Daddy was indestructible."

"Life is tenuous. After hearing the stress in your voice today, I thought that if anything ever happened to you, I'd die. I know it's selfish, but I want to marry you."

"Oh, Simon, that's not selfish. It's beautiful. I feel the same, and I'd love to spend the rest of my life with you."

So far, so good. "I thought about a grand wedding and hundreds of guests, but that's so unfair to your father. The last thing he needs in his condition is stress and excitement. How do you feel about doing something daring?"

"I'm not with you."

"I thought we'd elope. Get a flight to Vegas on Friday week, get married on Sunday and come back the following week as Mr. and Mrs. Beaumont. If you want to have a big, lavish wedding later, we can do that after your father recovers. I think it'll lift his spirits when he finds out that I'm looking after his little girl."

"I don't know. It's only seven days. It's awfully fast and isn't Las Vegas sleazy? Why can't we get married here?"

"We'll get married in one of the Chapels at the Bellagio. It's very classy, and there are some great shows in Vegas. We could go see Whitney Houston, Cher, Bruce Springsteen and other headliners. You'll love it. If we get married here, we'll have to wait thirty days for a license. I can't wait that long."

"Oh, that's so romantic. I just don't know. It's so rushed."

Now I'll close the deal. "Yes, you're right," Beaumont said, sipping his wine. "I didn't think. You say you don't like your mom, but I know that deep down you love her. She'd be so upset if we eloped. She'd be angry because you married me, or because she couldn't arrange Sydney's biggest wedding and invite all her posh friends. Either way, she'd be very unhappy. I'm happy to wait. You're worth it."

"When can we buy the rings?" Milly asked.

Deal closed. "Tomorrow, but you can't wear the engagement ring until we're on the plane. You can't breathe a word to anyone."

"Let's do it. Are you going to wear a wedding ring?"

There's no way I'm going to broadcast that I'm married. "It's inconvenient for surgeons to wear rings. I'm working in a sterile environment. I'd like to, but I can't."

"It's not important. I know you love me."

On Monday morning, Beaumont told Mary that something urgent had arisen and that he had to go back to the U.S. on Friday. "I'll be gone a week. Cancel all surgery and consultations. Apologize and rebook the surgeries for the following two Fridays."

"What happened?"

"I can't say. I'll tell you when I get back."

Mary looked puzzled but didn't persist. "Felicity Mott and the people from the *Woman's Weekly* are in reception. Will I show them in?"

"Thanks, Mary."

There were two journalists and a photographer with Felicity. Beaumont backgrounded the surgery that she'd had in Bangkok and what had gone wrong. Then, in great detail, he went into the dangers of having surgery performed in Asia. One of the journalists said, "Didn't Felicity see you before she went to Bangkok?"

"She did, and I warned her what could go wrong."

"Why did you ignore the doctor's warnings, Felicity?" the journalist asked.

"I was desperate to have the surgery. The hospital looked on the up and up and the doctors were supposedly board certified. The biggest attraction was cost. Their fees were less than half what they were here."

"Doctor, are the fees charged by plastic surgeons in Sydney exorbitant?"

"We're not talking about cancer research. This is elective surgery. It's a competitive market and we have to comply with rigorous standards. Compliance is expensive but worth every cent as Felicity's experience proves."

"Don't they have standards in Asia?"

"I think they might have problems with enforcement," Beaumont said.

"Can you tell us more about the shortcomings in Felicity's surgery so that we can put captions to the photos?"

"I can do better," he said, pushing a drawing of the female torso across the desk. The breasts were different sizes, and the nipples were asymmetric. The line across the abdomen was thick and jagged. There were arrows, letters, and extensive notes. "Everything you need to know is there. Is there anything else?"

"Doctor," Felicity whimpered. "When are you going to operate?"

"Three weeks. Mary will contact you with a date and time."

"Thanks for your time, Doctor," the senior journalist said.

When Beaumont got home on Wednesday night, Milly was nervous and found it hard to look him in the eye. "I'm sorry," she said, "I took Daddy to the hospital today for his chemo. I'm so excited about Friday that I just had to tell him."

That's the last thing I wanted. "How did he react?"

"He was happy for me." She paused. "But...but..."

"But what, babe? Spit it out. I won't bite."

"He called his lawyers and asked them to prepare a prenup

agreement," she said, reaching out and picking up an envelope off the coffee table. "He said I should get it signed before we get married. I'm sorry. It wasn't my idea."

Fuck! I knew it. If only she'd kept her mouth shut. Still it won't make any difference. Silly old bastard. With luck, he'll cark it the day after we're married. "I'm happy to sign, but I'm not sure why," He said. "I've got thirty million, and as far as I know you've got nothing."

"Yes, but Daddy said that you would know that I was a beneficiary of his estate. He also said that if you didn't object, it would prove that you loved me. I'm glad you didn't," Milly said, kissing him.

"I do love you," Beaumont said. "We'll need to find a witness. Let's go to the service station and get it signed and witnessed."

"And I love you, Simon. I can't wait to be Mrs. Beaumont."

Chapter 47

For all her family's money, Milly wasn't very worldly. She flaunted the engagement ring that had set Beaumont back two hundred large at every opportunity. The attractions that captivated her in Las Vegas were the rides on the main drag. She carted him off to the MGM Grand for a day at the theme park. The following day she took him to the other end of the strip, and they rode the roller coaster on top of the Stratosphere. On the way back to the Bellagio, they stopped at The Venetian, where she insisted they take a gondola ride. The day before they were due to return to Sydney they took a two-hour helicopter tour of The Grand Canyon.

"Can we stay another week?" she had pleaded.

"I can't. I have surgery. I can't leave my patients in a lurch."

She had pouted, but it had no effect. By the time they boarded the plane for the short flight to Los Angeles, Beaumont had had enough of Las Vegas to last him a lifetime. When he settled into 1A on the Qantas flight to Sydney, he breathed a massive sigh of relief. The flight attendant took his jacket, and brought him an OJ. He smiled, mission completed.

Barbara Milgate was furious. Not because she hadn't been able to put on a society wedding, but because Beaumont had married her daughter. She was jealous. Milly was the sole beneficiary of her father's will. Then, as if to add salt to the wound, the man her daughter was sharing a bed with, had turned her from an ugly duckling into a fox. Worse, there was no sign that she'd had surgery. Even her damn tits looked natural. If she got a wrinkle or two in years to come or became a little saggy, she only had to tap Beaumont on the shoulder, and her youth would be restored. When journalists emailed Milly in Vegas and asked for photographs of the wedding, she'd been only too pleased to provide them. *The Daily Telegraph* had devoted two pages usually set aside for social gossip to show them. Barbara Milgate had been incandescent with rage.

Joe Milgate was mid-way through his treatment and looking the worse for wear. He was pleased for his daughter. He'd had his doubts about Beaumont, but when he'd signed the prenup without so much as a peep, Joe thought that perhaps he'd misjudged him. In his mind, Beaumont was a freak. What he'd done with Barbara's tits had given him endless pleasure and salvaged his marriage. What he'd done with Milly defied belief. Only a year ago she'd been ugly and lacking self-assurance. Now she was vibrant, gorgeous and exuded confidence. Joe envied Beaumont his skills.

Once he was cured he would throw them a huge wedding, the likes of which Sydney had never seen before. Milly would turn twenty-one in six weeks and receive her first distribution of nearly one hundred million from the trust. She knew about the trust, but had no idea how it had grown. Her distributions would be a fixed percentage of the trust's income. When Joe established the trust, he never thought that its assets would become so valuable. He had tried to have the provisions of the trust deed amended, not to cheat Milly, but to protect her. He knew that great wealth was not easy to cope with, and often led to stress and unhappiness. The lawyers had advised that because the trust's settlor, the person who legally created the trust, was dead, amendments to the deed were problematic.

Beaumont was in the OR at 6:30 A.M. on Monday performing his least favored surgery on a woman in her early fifties. She'd had a gastric band fitted twelve months earlier and had lost more than seventy pounds. There was no way exercise, sit-ups and walking were going to remove the mass of loose skin around her stomach. Only an abdominoplasty would do that. Usually, this procedure took two hours, but because of the large amount of skin to be removed, and the contouring of her hips and thighs, he had allowed four hours. The next procedure was a rhinoplasty on a recently retired rugby player, and he finished the day's surgery with a breast reduction on a nineteen-year-old girl.

At 4:30 P.M. he made the short walk to his office and started reading the correspondence that had piled up in his absence. There was little that Mary had not told him, or that hadn't been emailed to him. She greeted him with a big smile and said, "Congratulations. She's a beautiful girl."

Yes, and you look like the cat who swallowed the canary because you know that I created her. "Thanks."

"Do you need me for anything?"

"Let me finish getting through this," he said, nodding at the pile of papers on his desk. "We'll talk in the morning."

After he'd finished reviewing his correspondence he opened his emails. One that caught his eye was from Samantha Armstrong. There were two attachments to it. The first a letter from Mordant & Hewitt signed by Samantha to Luke Cotchin demanding that he remove all defamatory internet postings relating to Dr. Simon Beaumont and that if he did not, litigation would commence forthwith. The second attachment was from a firm of lawyers acting for Cotchin, denying the postings were defamatory, but stating that their client had removed such postings as a gesture of goodwill. The lawyers concluded by saying, "We trust this matter is now resolved."

In the body of her email, Samantha said that Cotchin was in his early twenties, suffering from Asperger's, and had little in the way of assets. He was a troll who wiled away the day by attacking prominent surgeons, actuaries, accountants, architects and other professionals. Samantha thanked Beaumont for his instructions and sought his consent to closing the file.

That's not going to happen! This prick seriously defamed me, and withdrawing the postings hasn't compensated me for the damage done to my reputation by those who've already read them. He was annoyed that Brett Golding wasn't the defamer, and instead, it was some bored idiot with nothing better to do with his time. The receptionist put him straight through to Samantha, and he said, "I've just read your email. I need to see you."

"How are you?" she said sarcastically. "Are you having a nice day?"

"Sam, I'm busy. When can you see me? It's urgent."

"You sound flustered. I can fit you in for fifteen minutes just before midday tomorrow. Not a minute more."

After Beaumont put the phone down, he thought, *I'm not going to let that prick get away with a slap on the knuckles. He hasn't apologized and hasn't even admitted that the postings were defamatory. Fuck that!*

He could have gone home, but ten days alone with Milly had sapped him. She was unbelievably tedious. He dragged his laptop closer to him and googled *superyachts for sale.* There was a one hundred thirty-five foot Benetti in Monaco for thirty million euros that captured his attention. After ten minutes looking at boats, he typed in Boeing and went searching for jets. On the way back from LA, he had been thinking about doing more traveling. Naturally his mind had turned to private jets. When he shut the computer down, he was disappointed. Amazingly, a hundred million didn't go far. With luck, Joe Milgate would cark it soon, and he'd have three billion to spend on toys.

The last thing Beaumont did before leaving the office was to skim the social pages of *The Daily Telegraph*. Debbie Stenson's smiling face stared at him. She was the keynote speaker at a fund-raiser for battered women being held at the Pinnacle-Regency next week. Tables of ten were selling for five thousand dollars and the Premier's wife was hosting the event.

Beaumont stopped on the way home and picked up pizzas. As they ate, Milly told him how busy her day had been.

She had gone to the gym, then taken a long walk before having her hair cut and styled. After that, she had taken her father to the hospital for radiotherapy and then she'd had coffee while he'd had water. He had lost all taste and couldn't even drink beer.

When they'd finished their pizzas, Beaumont said, "I'm going to watch *Four Corners.* It's about the Mafia's influence on the 1960 election and the assassination of John Kennedy."

"Oh no. I want to watch *Sex and the City.*"

"That's okay; I'll watch *Four Corners* in the bedroom."

"No, I want to spend time with you. Why do you have to watch something that happened in 1960? It's not like you can change it. I want you to watch *Sex and the City* with me. It's fun. You'll like it. We can cuddle. Please."

Can this get any worse? "Okay," he said, picking up his wine.

Five minutes later Milly was snuggled up next to him, and giggling over Carrie and Mr. Big. During the first ad break, she said, "Daddy's arranged a table at a function to raise money for battered wives. Keep next Tuesday night free."

Shit! It just got worse. Far worse. "I can't go," he said, "I'm having a meeting with Steve Levine and the architects about the extension to the hospital."

"You'll have to make it for another time. Daddy wants us there."

"You go. I can't. My meeting is critical."

"I can't go by myself. It'll look terrible. I want to show off my hand-some husband. Please, Simon."

"I'm not going. How many times do I have to fucking tell you?"

Milly jumped. "You don't have to shout. You scared me," She sniffled.

"I'm tired," he said, "I'm going to bed."

"Poor darling. I'll come with you. We'll watch the last of *Sex and the City* and then we'll play around. That'll relax you."

There's nothing wrong with your sexual appetite. If only you'd participate. Wrap your legs around me or grab my ass. You like receiving, but don't like giving. Perhaps it's because you're young or maybe it's because you're just a lazy fuck.

Joe Milgate's health was rapidly deteriorating. He picked at his food while the waiters in the Hyatt's dining room hovered around his table hoping for a big tip. "Milly, I wanted to see you by yourself. I know you're aware of the trust that I created for you when you were born."

"Daddy, I don't want to talk about money. I just want you to get well."

"Hear me out. It grew far faster than I anticipated. The trustees will be making a deposit into your account of nearly one hundred million on Monday."

Milly gasped. "I don't know what to say."

"You don't have to say anything," he said, sipping his beer. "Shit, that bloody chemo ruins the taste of everything. Even beer tastes like piss. It's important that you don't blow it. You see those dopey pricks who win the lottery and two years later they're broke. It's because they've never handled big money before. You're in the same shoes as them but with a lot more cash. If I knew I was going to live forever I'd tell you to buy shares in Milgate Mining, but we both know I don't have much more time, and you don't know anything about running mining companies."

"Don't say that! You're going to beat this cancer."

"Listen to me. Put half into government bonds, invest thirty mil in the banks and put twenty in a term deposit. Don't make the mistake of wasting it."

"I'll have Simon to help me."

"Yeah, he seems okay but sometimes money does funny things to people. That's why I made you get the prenup."

"Simon has his own money. He loves me. How could he have married me for my money? He didn't know I had any."

Milgate grimaced and his voice rasped. "What Simon has is chump change or as some of my rough mates would say, stripper money. I'm not saying he knew, but he would've known that you were a beneficiary of my estate. He just wouldn't have known that you were the sole beneficiary, or how much you were going to get. That type of money changes people. I hope it doesn't change him."

"Daddy, you're going to be around for years, and money won't change Simon. He's not the type."

"I hope you're right. There are two other things you need to know about my will. I made your mother sign a prenup before we got married, but if she gets nothing, she'll contest the will. I've left her more than enough to live in luxury for the rest of her life as well as a poison pill should she get too greedy. There's a provision to the effect that she loses her inheritance should she contest the will," he said. "I've also left Harry Cusack a hundred million. I got him out of a fix when he was a wild young man. He would've been imprisoned for ten years. That was thirty years ago. Best decision I ever made and I couldn't have asked for a more loyal lieutenant. If you have any problems after I'm gone, talk to Harry."

"I wish you wouldn't keep talking that way."

Samantha Armstrong showed Beaumont into her office and before she could speak he said, "I want you to sue that prick for every cent he's got."

"He's autistic and without any money. I told you that. He'd be lucky to have fifty thousand to his name. It's pointless suing him."

"He didn't even admit he defamed me."

"Don't give me that. You know enough about the law to know that his lawyers can't admit liability. It's standard legal procedure. You'll gain nothing by suing him. We'll win the case and won't even recover costs. You'll win, but you'll lose. I spoke to his lawyer. He's been a silly young man, but he's been punished enough."

"In your opinion. I don't care about the money. I want to send a message to internet trolls that if they defame me, they'll live to regret it. I want you to sue him, Sam, and when he can't pay, you can bankrupt him."

"Our guys were able to track him down because he wasn't sophisticated. If you stir up a hornet's nest, you might find yourself under severe attack, and next time, our guys mightn't be able to locate the culprit. I'm advising you not to sue."

"How about you try and persuade me over dinner?"

"What? What did you say? You've been married all of two weeks. You're all class."

"Don't get sanctimonious with me. Have you thought that I might be in an open relationship too?"

"I saw the photos of your wife. She's gorgeous and you're already hitting on other women."

"Not other women, Sam. Just you."

"You're such a liar. Why don't you give me your wife's number? If she says it's okay, I'll have dinner with you. How does that sound?"

Beaumont crossed his arms. "That's not going to happen. By the way, thanks for your advice, but I want you to sue that bastard."

"Time's up, Simon," Samantha said, looking at her watch. "Thank you for your instructions, but this firm declines to act for you on this or any other matter. Let us know who your new lawyers are, and we'll forward your files. Goodbye."

What a bitch. "Have it your way, Sam. It's your loss."

When Milly told Beaumont about the hundred million, he was

suitably stunned and claimed that he'd had no idea that her father was so wealthy. When he asked her what she was going to do with the money, she told him what her father had said, and asked him what he thought.

"Your father's a clever man, so I'd heed what he says. My only reservation is that you're very young. Do you want to be like Warren Buffet? Have all that money and spend nothing on fun things? Or do you want to be like Donald Trump? Have planes, yachts, helicopters and golf courses? Live life to its fullest."

"It's a hundred million. It's nothing like their wealth. I don't think I want to live like either of them."

When your father carks it in the next few months, you'll have more than Trump. "All I'm saying is that it's not much fun having money unless you spend it. My Lamborghini is an indulgence. I could drive a Ford and have a lot more money, but I want to enjoy my success. Do you understand?"

"Yes, of course."

"Why don't we think about it? Put it on deposit with the Commonwealth Bank while we make up our minds. At least, we'll know it'll be safe. If the bank goes broke, Australia will go broke."

"Are you taking me out on Monday?"

"I was going to throw you a surprise party, but I thought it'd be unfair to Joe. I've booked a quiet restaurant in Double Bay. I know it's not much of a twenty-first."

"That's so thoughtful and all I want," Milly said.

Beaumont could have spent the hundred million and more, but knew he had to play his cards carefully if he was to get a share of Joe Milgate's estate. After much consideration, he suggested to Milly that they invest fifty million and use the other fifty million to buy and fit out a Boeing 737. Not only could they use the plane for pleasure, but they could fly his patients in from Asia and other far-flung places.

Chapter 48

Beaumont worked late on Tuesday night, not leaving to go home until after nine o'clock. He was sipping wine and watching the news when Milly got home.

"How was the fundraiser?" he asked.

"Fine."

"Did you get a lot done with Steve and the architects?"

"Yes, it went well."

"Liar!" she shouted. "Steve was at the function. He didn't know anything about the meeting. He tried to cover for you, but it was too late. Where did you go?"

"I had a stack of paperwork to get through. I stayed back at the office."

"Please, please stop the lying. I know why you didn't go. I met your ex-partner. Is it true that you've never seen your son?"

"I don't want to talk about it."

"Didn't it ever cross your mind to tell me that you had a son before we got married? What other secrets are you keeping from me?"

"I was worried that you might have rejected me."

"I love you, Simon. I'd never reject you because you had a child from a previous relationship."

"How was I to know that?"

"I hadn't finished," Milly said, stamping her foot. "If I'd known you had a son who you refuse to see, I would've had second thoughts. What type of man doesn't want to care for his own son? How can you be that cold?"

"I had a deal with Debbie. No kids. She went off the pill. She broke my trust."

"Oh, I know all about deals. I was meant to be Milton, not Mildred. What a horrible name. I listened to my parents fight most of my life over their deal. Was it my fault that they got me instead of a boy? No! They made my life a misery."

"It's not the same."

"Yes, it is. Is it little Jack's fault that you and Debbie had a deal? No! Is it his fault that Debbie broke the deal? No! Don't you have a heart?"

"Jack and Debbie, is it? You must have had quite a conversation."

"We did. She said that deep down you're a good man, but misguided with some strange ideas."

"Really. What else did she say?"

"She said you hate gays, but I already knew that."

"Did she tell you why?"

"She said that you'd say it was because you were worried about contracting hepatitis or HIV, but that was just a smokescreen for your homophobia. It's 2002. What year are you living in?"

"I'm going to bed."

"Why didn't you tell me the real reason you didn't want to go? Why did you lie to me?"

"Because it's none of your damn business. I'll sleep in the spare room."

BOOK 3

2003 FABULOUS WEALTH
– OH SO CLOSE BUT OH SO FAR

Chapter 49

When Milly spoke to her father about what Beaumont had done, he seemed unconcerned. "A lot of men have secrets they hope will remain hidden forever. I wouldn't be too upset. He sounds like his anger stems from the woman's betrayal of trust. I can understand that."

"What about his hatred of gays?"

"He's no different to a lot of my friends." Her father laughed, and then grasped his side in pain. "Shit, it even hurts to laugh."

"Are you alright?" Milly asked, taking his hand.

"Don't worry about me. I'm okay."

"Daddy, your friends are yesterday's men. They're all over sixty."

"That's not true," her father said. "Harry's only fifty-eight, but I know what you mean. Milly, what difference does it make to you if your husband's homophobic? How does it hurt you?"

"It doesn't. I'm just surprised that he's so old fashioned. I wish I knew him better."

"You should have thought of that before you married him."

"But I love him so much. He changed my life."

"Then you have to support him, even if you don't like his views. That's what wives do."

"Used to do in your time," Milly scoffed.

"Have it your way. Let's talk about something I do know about. Simon's crazy suggestion about buying a Boeing 737. Here are the numbers. You'll forgo interest of three million, depreciation will be five million, then you've got maintenance, the crew, fuel, landing fees and God knows what else. Conservatively twelve million per annum. Your husband will need to do two hundred forty thousand a week in fees, every week of the year just to pay for the plane. Only fools own planes."

"I don't think Simon's a fool."

"He's brilliant at what he does, but that doesn't mean he understands money, or maybe he does and saw you as an easy way to get his hands on billions. A plane is just a fool's toy. I'm glad we got him to sign that prenup."

"You're wrong, Daddy," Milly said defensively.

Beaumont raged when Milly told him what her father had said, and insisted that Joe didn't understand the big picture. Despite Beaumont's pleading and cajoling, Milly wouldn't relent. "I can't go against Daddy. He knows far more about investing and finance than you. He said that we can fly first-class to any destination in the world and that we don't need to pay fifty million to do it."

I just have to keep calm. Joe will be dead within three months, and we'll have three billion. I'll have the plane, a superyacht, and a Sikorsky. That's the least I deserve for putting up with Milly's crap. "I was going to use it for my practice, babe, but if that's the way you feel, I'll have to live with it," he said.

"I feel terrible. I could talk to Daddy again. You could come with me."

"That's alright. The last thing I want to do is put pressure on him while he's undergoing treatment."

"That's so considerate."

If only you knew. "It's the least I can do."

Milly soon found herself on Sydney's charity circuit. She was attractive, wealthy, connected and had plenty of time. Her mornings were spent at the gym, walking, and taking her father to the hospital. In the afternoons and at night she attended meetings with other women like herself, devoted to raising monies for the less fortunate. Beaumont encouraged her involvement, knowing that the more time she spent raising funds, the less time he had to spend with her. It wasn't long before she was spending at least two nights a week at fundraisers or arranging functions. Beaumont, sexually unfulfilled and bored took these opportunities to meet with Sonya at his surgery. She was sexy, totally uninhibited and there wasn't a sexual act that she wasn't up for. The antithesis of Milly.

Chapter 50

In February 2004, Joe Milgate was admitted to Langton Private Hospital. Milly was in denial and lived in hope that her father would miraculously recover. Beaumont knew better. The doctors tried to make Joe comfortable by administering large doses of morphine. He drifted in and out of coherence as the fateful day drew closer.

Milly visited every day, but her father had wasted away and his throat was dry. She held his bony hand and wiped his brow with a cool cloth. In a rare moment of clarity, he pulled her toward him and whispered, "He's no good. He married you for your money. I'm sorry. I've asked Harry to look after you after I've gone."

Joe had been babbling for weeks, and Milly paid no heed to what he had said. "Poor Daddy," she said, stroking his face.

On a stifling Sydney day with the temperature hovering around 45 degrees C, 113 degrees in terminology Beaumont understood, Joe Milgate lost his battle. Milly was beside herself with grief. Harry Cusack was the only non-family member at Joe's bedside, and he broke down and wept uncontrollably. Barbara Milgate dabbed at her eyes with a white handkerchief, but they were crocodile tears.

Beaumont put his arm around Milly and helped her down the hospital steps to the sidewalk. "He was only sixty-six." She sniffled. "That's too young."

Yes, but he'd smoked three packets of cigarettes a day for fifty of those years. "He's not suffering anymore. He's at peace."

That night Beaumont made Milly take two Temazepam. After she'd fallen asleep, he went to his study and turned his computer on. He stayed up late, googling superyachts, jets, and helicopters. All his hard work was about to pay off.

The following morning *The Daily Telegraph* devoted page three to the life and achievements of the late Joe Milgate. The stock of Milgate

Mining Limited plummeted at the open as the market panicked about the loss of its founder. Later in the day, professional traders pushed the stock higher as vultures, looking for a stake in an undervalued takeover target, started to circle.

Only family and close friends attended the funeral. It was another sweltering, humid morning and a huge storm was brewing. As the casket was lowered into the ground, there was a tremendous clap of thunder followed by flashes of lighting that lit up the sky. Joe Milgate wasn't going without a fight. As the first warm spots of rain hit, mourners shuffled past Joe's grave dropping red roses on the casket. Beaumont caught the eye of Barbara Milgate. Her face was flawless, and there wasn't a wrinkle to be seen, but it was hard. She dabbed her eyes but there was no redness, nor were they filled with tears. Milly had held up well until Harry Cusack let out an ungodly scream as he dropped his rose on the casket. "Why?" he shouted. "Why?"

With that, Milly lost control and started sobbing. The two of them stood above the grave, and Harry put his arm around her. "I promised your father I'd look after you. Anything you need, and I mean anything," he gasped, "I'll be there for you."

Barbara Milgate stared at them, contempt written all over her face.

Beaumont took Milly's hand and said, "Come on, babe, keep your chin up. You're doing great. Once the wake is over you can put this horrible day behind you."

"I'm not going. Let's go home."

"Are you sure that's what you want?" Beaumont said, wiping a tear from Milly's cheek and squeezing her hand.

"Yes. Harry and his friends will want to reminisce about the wild times and good old days. They won't want me there when they're telling their colorful stories. I told Harry. He understands."

"What about your mother?"

"She knows Harry won't let her into his house. She won't go. Did you see her teary performance? No academy award there," she said bitterly. "She's such a fake."

Two months later, Milly, Barbara, Harry, and Beaumont sat in the meeting room of Freemonts, Joe's lawyers, and listened as his will was read. He may have projected himself as a simple man, but his affairs were incredibly complex. He had controlled domestic and international private corporations, trusts and charitable institutions. His lawyers briefly explained that he had wanted to minimize his taxation liabilities and protect his assets.

The first bequest was to Harry for one hundred million dollars. Beaumont watched as the heavyset tough, tattoos decorating his hands and arms, burst into tears. Milly gripped Beaumont's arm tightly, and he hoped she wouldn't turn on the waterworks.

The next bequest was to Barbara for fifty million and the house. Her face dropped, and she stared at Harry as if to say, 'how dare he leave you more than me?' The lawyer then droned on for another five minutes about what would occur, should she decide to challenge the will. When he finished, she asked, "Can I have a copy of the will to show my lawyers?"

Beaumont put his hand to his mouth and smiled. *Barbara, you're forty-five. You have a house worth close to fifty mil and another fifty mil in cash. Do you want to run the risk of losing your inheritance? I don't think so.*

The last bequest was to Milly for the remainder of Joe's estate. The trust from which she was receiving one hundred million per annum vested on Joe's death. All of the trust assets, including a controlling interest in Milgate Mining Limited, were hers.

Barbara Milgate grasped the arms of her chair and stared daggers at Milly.

The lawyer concluded the meeting by saying, "If you don't mind, Mrs. Beaumont, we'd like to spend a little time with you. Your late father's affairs are complicated, and you'll need our guidance before realizing the assets."

"And my husband," Milly said. "I want Simon to hear what you have to say."

After Harry and Barbara had left the lawyer said, "The value of the estate and trust assets aggregate just over four billion dollars. As you are aware, the vast bulk of the value is the controlling interest in Milgate Mining Limited.

I'm on third base, and there are no outs, Beaumont thought. *Can it get any better? A billion more than what I'd expected. I'm rolling in it!*

Chapter 51

Unfortunately for Beaumont, Milly had inherited her late father's rat cunning, and most of his ability with numbers. Merchant bankers and stockbrokers hardly gave her a minute's peace in their pursuit of her controlling interest in Milgate Mining. She rejected staggering offers only to receive even larger ones a few days later. When she bounced them off Beaumont, he was keen to accept, saying that cash would give them flexibility and freedom.

After two months of haggling, Milly terminated negotiations, deciding to retain the stock. Because of the size of her holding, she was offered two seats on Milgate Mining's board. She accepted one for herself and the other for her accountant.

Beaumont was furious when he heard that she was keeping her stock, and incandescent with rage when told that she'd given the second board seat to her accountant.

"I'm your husband," he shouted. "Why didn't you nominate me?"

"What do you know about mining companies?" Besides, you're far too busy with your practice. There's a lot more to being a public company director than attending monthly meetings. Please, don't shout."

"Who told you that?" he sarcastically replied.

"Don't be like that, Simon. I asked the accountants and lawyers about the plane and they're doing a cost-benefit analysis to see if the company can justify it. We'll be able to use it when it's free."

It's getting worse. It won't be fitted out like the Playboy *jet, that's for sure, and we'll only get to use it when corporate executives aren't. What a bummer.* "I don't understand you, Milly. We could be having fun, and instead, you're making work for yourself."

"If it's that important, let's buy a Learjet. They're nowhere near as expensive. You could learn to fly."

I don't want a toy. I want a Gulfstream or a Boeing, and why would I want to waste my time learning to fly? "I'll think about it."

When Beaumont raised buying a superyacht, Milly said that they already had his cabin cruiser, and there was no point in buying another boat. He knew it would be pointless raising the helicopter. She was so mean that she used the photocopier at his surgery at the weekends, rather than buying one. The only spending that Milly did was to acquire the most expensive mansion in Wolseley Road for fifty-five million. Spread over four levels, it had twenty bedrooms and six kitchens. Beaumont knew why she had bought it. She couldn't stand the thought of her mother living in a grander house. When he asked her if she needed him to sign any papers on the acquisition of the house, she said, "You don't need to, we're buying it in the name of a corporation that will act as trustee of a discretionary trust. We move in on the seventh of January."

Beaumont sold his house for twelve million with settlement in the second week of January. His profit before costs was seven million. Most folk would've been elated. He wasn't. It was peanuts compared to what Milly had inherited.

"You're turning into your father," he said. "Have a listen to yourself."

"Don't be angry with me. I love you. Without you, I'd be nothing."

That's true. "You have a funny way of showing it. Actions speak louder than words."

Milly infuriated him when she used words like *we're* and *ours* when talking about what she called their assets. On the plus side, she was so busy that she was hardly ever home. If it wasn't a board or committee meeting, it was a fundraiser. Three years ago she hadn't had a girlfriend; now she had many. Most of them had absentee executive husbands and were bored. Raising money for charities helped them cope with their empty lives.

Milly and Beaumont were still active in bed, and she enjoyed sex, but wouldn't participate in ways that satisfied him. He told her that it turned him on when she was on top, and he could see her gorgeous face and beautiful boobs. It made no difference, and she refused to mount him, saying that she didn't like it. At first, he'd thought it was because of her inhibitions, but now he knew it was because she was lazy. When he rolled her from her back to her side and then on top, she got angry and refused to move. As far as fellatio went, he had given up. In that area, she was totally inhibited and still claimed that it was because she had been degraded at university. Fortunately, Sonya wasn't inhibited in the slightest, and his clandestine meetings with her were all that kept him stimulated.

Beaumont was sick of Milly. She was far too young and selfish with her money and herself. It didn't worry him as he'd never planned for their marriage to be until *death do us part*. What he had hoped for was that he would get his toys while they were together. It was time to have a conversation with her about divorce and the division of their assets.

From reading the newspapers, Beaumont had learned that Linton Avery of the boutique legal firm of Quist & Avery was the divorce lawyer used by the A-listers. Avery had agreed to see him at short notice, and Beaumont had been impressed by the young lawyer when he'd spelled out his rights. More importantly, by meeting with him, Beaumont had made it impossible for Milly to use his services.

Beaumont was watching television when Milly kissed him on the cheek. "Don't wait up," she said. "I'm going to be late."

As if I'd wait up for you. "What is it tonight? Unmarried mothers, battered wives or are you saving the starving kids in Ethiopia?"

"I find it hard to say no when I'm asked to help. Do you think I enjoy going out every night?"

You find it easy to say no to me? "They don't want you. They want your money. Do you think these would-be Sydney socialites would be seeking your help if you were broke? They wouldn't want to know you."

"I don't want to argue."

"You never do. Did you ask your lawyers and accountants if you could go out tonight?"

"Of course not. You're being silly."

"You seem to ask them everything else about our private lives."

"I'm going. I hope your mood's improved by the time I get home."

As Beaumont heard Milly's car pulling out of the driveway, he picked up his cell phone. "Meet me at the surgery in an hour."

Chapter 52

Beaumont sat in one of the client chairs in his office reading the latest copy of *Lancet* when he heard Sonya say, "Simon."

"In here," he replied. "Lock the door."

She was wearing a white cotton dress and sandals. They embraced and kissed.

"Would you like coke, orange juice or mineral water," he asked.

"Mineral water please," she said. "What's wrong? You're not yourself."

"I'm okay. I just need to talk to an adult. I'm going through hell."

"I don't understand. You tell me the same story every time we meet. Have you thought about seeing a marriage counselor?"

She's mean with her money, just like her father was. "No, and I never will. I know what the problem is. The age difference. She's immature." Beaumont laughed.

"She's a beautiful woman."

"Yes, one hundred percent manufactured by me. When God made her, he did a lousy job," Beaumont said, stretching out his legs and pushing himself back in his chair. "I corrected his work."

"Have you told her that you're unhappy? Is she unhappy?"

"No, she's happy and oblivious to how I feel. She's selfish. She enjoys sex, but she's not prepared to do anything to spice it up."

"Not like me." Sonya joked.

"That's for sure," Beaumont said, rubbing his forehead with his hand.

"I've never seen you like this. You're tense and stressed. Why don't I see if I can help you unwind?" Sonya said, pulling her chair closer to his.

She reached over and started to undo his belt. "Just lay back and enjoy," she said, as she unzipped his fly, slowly stroking him with one hand while pulling his pants and jocks down with the other.

"That's good," he moaned.

"Just relax. Let the tension wash away," she said, dropping to her knees. Her tongue began flicking up and down his shaft.

He sat up and put his hands behind her head, trying to force her to envelop him.

"You'll spoil it," she said, pulling back. "Lie back and let yourself float away. Don't move."

He felt her take him in her mouth and started thrusting. "Relax," she said, putting one hand on his stomach and pushing him back into his chair.

Beaumont's groaning filled the office, and they didn't hear the slight click.

"No, no," Milly screamed, as the papers in her hand spilled to the floor.

Sonya jerked her head away and jumped to her feet. Beaumont sat up, his erection on full display.

They heard the front door slam and Sonya said, "Oh shit, that's done it."

"I'm not worried. Hey, get down here and finish what you started."

"Are you stupid? I can't. I feel terrible. I'm going."

In all the years, I've known you, you've never raised your voice to me. If I want to keep you on the side I'd better express some regret. "I'm sorry. You're right that was a stupid thing to say. I'll see if I can catch Milly and smooth things over."

"Good luck with that." Sonya frowned. "I wouldn't want to be in your shoes."

Beaumont didn't drive with any urgency. He was calm. He had been going to orchestrate a fight with Milly. Getting caught with Sonya saved the need to contrive anything. His one regret was that Sonya hadn't finished before Milly burst in.

The house was lit up like a beacon and the front door was wide open. He could hear Milly in the bedroom. There were two half packed suitcases on the bed. Her eyes were red, and her cheeks stained with mascara. "You low life bastard," she said. "If I hadn't of wanted to use the photocopier, I'd have never found out."

"Did you see what she was doing? If you'd have done it, I wouldn't have had to look elsewhere," he lied. "She loves being on top too. Don't blame me. You were about as exciting as a statue in bed."

"How long has it been going on?"

"How long ago was it that you first refused to give me head?"

"I hate you. Daddy was right. When you did my surgery for nothing, he told me that he didn't trust you. I said you'd done it because you loved me. You were my soulmate. I'm glad he insisted that I get a prenup. Ever since he died, all you've wanted to do is spend his money. You'll get nothing from me."

"We'll see about that. I deserve plenty after putting up with you for the past few years. You know you should be ashamed of yourself, forcing me to look elsewhere for something that most couples enjoy. Bitch!"

He was leaning up against the door when she barged past him with a suitcase in either hand.

"Can I help?" He mocked.

"You're the last person I'd ask for help. Harry will pick up the rest of my stuff tomorrow."

"I'm changing the locks in the morning. Send someone over tomorrow night. Not that thug, Cusack. I won't let him in."

"You're scared of Harry. He's never liked you. When he and Daddy were talking, he used to call you pretty boy. He said there was something about you that didn't ring true."

"How much did Cusack have to do with you when you were as ugly as sin? Nothing. Oh, and were you ugly! You made Quasimodo look handsome. You owe me, and you're going to pay."

At the front door, Milly turned around. "I've never hated anyone as much as I hate you. I'd like to see you dead. You try anything, and you'll regret it."

"Goodbye, Milly. Have a nice life. Oh, and before you marry some other poor bastard be sure to tell him, that you're in an inert object in bed."

Chapter 53

For Beaumont, it was a quiet day with only a few appointments. He gave little thought to what had occurred the night before. He was positive that Milly would make the next move, and by midday, his feelings proved to be correct. When he opened the hand delivered letter from Freemonts he smiled. It demanded that he disclose each and every asset that he owned anywhere in the world. *What a cheek. She's going to make a claim for a share of my assets.* Freemonts thoughtfully pointed out that if he tried to conceal any of his assets, he would be guilty of contempt of court, and could be fined or imprisoned or both. Like most western countries, Australia had legislated 'no fault' divorce and twelve months separation was all that was required to dissolve a marriage. It had taken much of the acrimony out of the process, and ninety-five percent of divorces required little more than the completion of a standard set of forms. However, custody and property disputes were as bitter and acrimonious as ever. The penultimate paragraph of the letter said that he was not to contact Milly and that all communications were to be through them. The final paragraph said that two members of their staff would be at his home at 7 P.M. tonight, to pick up the remainder of Milly's belongings. If this was inconvenient, he was to contact them.

Beaumont called Linton Avery at Quist & Avery and told him what had occurred and that he was emailing him a copy of Freemonts letter. He knew that Avery would demand the same information from Milly and that Freemonts would point out that he had executed a prenuptial agreement. As far as Beaumont was concerned it was all part of the game.

Early in the afternoon, Beaumont was contacted by lawyers, Braithwaite & Grantham, who were acting for a severely disfigured plaintiff in a malpractice case. They were clever and had emailed him photos of the plaintiff before asking him if he would appear as an expert witness. Having never seen worse surgery, he accepted without hesitation. He had appeared at a number of trials as an expert witness and developed a reputation for being precise, yet eloquent. The defendant, a dermatologist, had performed a facelift and brow lift on the plaintiff, with disastrous consequences. Beaumont studied the photos on his desk and was appalled.

He insisted on examining the plaintiff, a thirty-eight-year-old female advertising executive who was too embarrassed to go back to work. He told the lawyers that she should use the second entrance when she came to see him. Just before 5 P.M, Julie buzzed to say Anita Bartlett was in reception. It was one of those rare times when a patient's photos did not accurately portray the level of disfigurement. Ms. Bartlett also brought photos of herself before the surgery when she had been an attractive, raven-haired, vibrant, young woman. She told Beaumont that she had been feeling run down and looking tired. When she mentioned this to her dermatologist, he had told her that he could restore the vitality to her face, and she had believed him. Naturally, she asked Beaumont what he could do for her, and for one of the few times in his life, he was guarded with his response.

At precisely 7 P.M. Beaumont heard the front door buzzer and opened the door to see a nervous young man and woman, each holding two suitcases. The young man said, "We're from Freemonts. We're here to pick up Ms. Milgate's belongings."

Beaumont showed them into the master bedroom. He had piled her clothes, linen, towels, toiletries, and makeup on top of the bedspread. "Everything you can see is hers," he said. "When you've finished in here, the utensils on the kitchen table are hers. That's it. Can you hurry? I'm going out, and you're holding me up."

After they'd left, Beaumont turned his laptop on and copied one of Milly's early emails to a disk. He threw his ski jacket on and pulled the hood up before driving to a discreet internet café in Canterbury, about six miles from Sydney. He parked on a dark side street and walked back to the café. He quickly opened a Hotmail account in a false name and copied the email on the disk to a new email. He deleted the email addresses and names from the copy, inserted Milly's email address and hit send.

Steve Levine had been insistent and secretive about meeting when he called, and Beaumont had agreed to see him at his surgery on Friday night.

"I'm sorry to hear about you and Milly," Steve said.

"Don't be. I'm not. Can I get you something to drink?"

"No thanks. I want to say what I have to say and leave."

"You sound edgy. What's wrong? What's upset you?"

"Debbie and I are getting married. I'm going to be bringing up your son, Jack, as if he was mine. I need to know how you feel about it."

"So that's why you're so jumpy. Congratulations, and as I've told you many times before, I don't have a son. If you're looking for my blessing, you've got it." Beaumont grinned.

"Debbie thinks there's some good in you. She's wrong. You're a heartless, arrogant sonofabitch. Only a bastard would've made Felicity Mott tell the whole country that she'd made a mistake, just to prove a point."

"Is she unhappy with the surgery?"

"She thinks that you're a superb surgeon, but as a man, you're an asshole."

"Steve, where's this going?"

"I don't want to act for you anymore."

"Did Debbie tell you to dump me?"

"No. She said there was no reason I shouldn't continue to represent you. I don't want to, though. I used to like you. I don't anymore. You better find yourself another manager."

"Why would I do that?" Beaumont said. "I don't need a manager. I've been throwing you a few scraps out of misguided loyalty, but you don't seriously think I need you. If you've said all you've come to say, you can get out."

"One question before I go, Simon. Do you have any friends?"

"Get out!"

Beaumont was surprised that he hadn't heard from Milly. He copied another of her more revealing emails and repeated the exercise of a few nights earlier. This time at an internet café in Bankstown, about ten miles from the city.

Chapter 54

When Beaumont entered the courtroom, he was surprised to see that every seat was taken. Surprisingly, there were three reporters sitting in the front row.

He had been a witness in the New South Wales Supreme Court many times before, and his demeanor was relaxed and confident. Anita Bartlett's counsel took him through his qualifications, background, and experience. After establishing that he was indeed an expert witness, counsel went over the specific surgery that the dermatologist had performed. Beaumont's testimony was damning, and he savaged the dermatologist saying that he had never seen worse surgery. When asked if it was possible to remedy the surgery he had answered that it could be corrected, but only by an extremely skilled surgeon. "Someone like yourself?" counsel asked.

There is no one like me, but I better humor this lawyer. "Yes."

Counsel finished his examination and Beaumont stretched and looked around the court. After his testimony, he was positive that the dermatologist's insurers would be eager to settle and that he wouldn't be cross-examined. He rarely was.

The judge looked at the defendant's counsel and said, "Your witness."

"Thank you, your Honor," a young man in his early thirties replied.

Beaumont looked at the confident face below the horse hair wig, and a little tremble went through him. He had seen that look before when he looked in the mirror, and he knew what it meant.

Defense counsel's early questions were somewhere between exaggeratedly respectful and condescending. Beaumont knew the smartass was taking the piss out of him, and concealing it by being overly polite.

"Are you single or married?"

"Separated."

"Separated. That's a shame. Do you have any children?"

248

"No."

"Doctor, I remind you, you're under oath. Do you have any children?"

Counsel for the plaintiff jumped to his feet. "I object. Relevance?"

"It goes to the character of the witness, your Honor."

"I'll allow it. You may answer, doctor," the judge said.

Bastard! I know where this is going. "I have a child from a previous relationship. I thought you were asking if there'd been any children from my marriage."

"Of course, of course you did," Defense counsel said. "A boy or a girl?"

"Boy."

"How old is he?"

"Four."

"When was the last time you saw him?"

"I haven't."

An audible gasp went around the courtroom.

"Sorry, doctor, I didn't hear you."

"I haven't."

"You haven't? Ever?"

"I just said that."

"Yes, you did. How have you supported your son?"

"I don't understand."

"How much have you paid for his upkeep and welfare?"

"I haven't. Look, our arrangement was–"

"Just answer the question, Doctor. How much have you contributed to supporting your son?"

"Nothing."

Cries of "no, no," came from the gallery.

"Nothing? How much did you earn from all sources last year?"

"I'm not sure. Eight million, I think."

"Eight million, and yet you're not contributing anything to your son's upkeep. Doctor, on another tack, who is responsible for what occurs in the operating room?"

"The lead surgeon."

"Not the interns, residents, nurses or the anesthesiologist?"

"No. The lead surgeon."

"Tell me, who is Valerie Fielding?"

Which one of them tipped this smartass off? Debbie, Milly or Golding? "She was a patient of mine in New York."

"What procedure or procedures did you perform?"

"Breast augmentation."

"What was the outcome?"

"The surgery was perfect."

"So Ms. Fielding was pleased with the outcome."

"I don't know."

"Why?"

"She couldn't speak."

"Why?"

"She was brain damaged."

"Brain damaged in the operating room that you were responsible for?"

Another gasp came from the gallery.

"Yes, but–"

"Just a yes or no, doctor. There's no need to embellish your answers."

"Did Ms. Fielding sue you?"

"Yes, but not only–"

"How much did the court award her?"

"Twenty million dollars, but that–"

"Twenty million. Twenty million. It's a enormous sum. Doctor, who is Jack Donahue?"

"I was. I changed my name to Simon Beaumont."

"Why?"

"I wanted a fresh start."

"You didn't want the Valerie Fielding court decision hanging over you?"

"No, I didn't."

"Doctor, do you think if a person makes a mistake, they should be able to conceal it by changing their name?"

"I didn't make a–"

"Just answer the question, doctor."

"No. Yes, I mean no."

"Yet you did. Where did you reside in the U.S?"

"New York."

"Where was your name change processed?"

"Anchorage."

"Forgive my geographical ignorance." Defense counsel smiled. "How far is Anchorage from New York?"

"Four thousand miles."

"Four thousand miles! Why did you want your name change processed in some outpost?"

"I don't recall."

"Oh, I think you do. Wasn't it because you thought that it would be harder to trace you back to Valerie Fielding?"

"I can't remember."

"That was when the internet was in its infancy. I'm sure that if you'd realized then, that filing the forms in Anchorage would make no difference, you would've filed them in New York. That's right, isn't it?"

"I told you. I don't recall."

"One last question. You hold yourself out as an expert witness. Do you think you're a fit and proper person to appear in this court?" Defense counsel asked before pausing. "I'll withdraw the question, your Honor."

"I want to answer that," Beaumont said.

"There's nothing to answer, doctor," the judge said. "You're excused."

Beaumont was fuming. Being discredited by that smartass lawyer would have no effect on the size of the damages award that Anita Bartlett would receive. Clearly, the purpose of the cross-examination had been all about making him look as bad as possible. That's why the reporters had been there. By tomorrow morning, everyone would know about Valerie Fielding and his change of name. He wasn't worried about the disclosures adversely impacting him. After all, he was going to be very wealthy soon. Besides, he was rightfully recognized as the finest and most expensive plastic surgeon in Sydney. That wouldn't change, and whoever had maliciously set him up would've known that. Whoever had leaked details to that lawyer, had done so purely out of spite.

Debbie was lots of things, but she wasn't spiteful and malicious. Steve had told him that he didn't like him, but he was far too professional to leak confidential information. That left Brett Golding and Milly. Golding hadn't been seen or heard of in months. *You're as nasty and devious as your late father, Milly. Well, I've got a few surprises in store for you.*

Chapter 55

Beaumont chuckled when Linton Avery called to say that Freemonts had refused to provide a schedule of Milly's assets. Instead, they had forwarded Avery a copy of the executed prenuptial agreement, and insisted, that Beaumont provide a schedule of his assets within seven days.

Milly finally called Beaumont and demanded to know what he was playing at by sending her copies of her emails.

"I can't talk to you," he said. "Your lawyers have said that all communications have to go through them."

"Don't be stupid. What are you playing at?"

"I could ask you the same. Did you get off on telling those blood-suckers about what happened in New York? That smartass lawyer made a fool of me in court. Spiteful bitch!"

There was a long pause. "I don't know what you're talking about. I saw that stuff about you in the newspapers this morning. It wasn't me."

"You're a poor liar, Milly. You must have loved those articles."

"You're right. I did. They made my day, but I didn't breathe a word about you to anyone. Now answer my question. Why are you sending me those emails?"

"It wasn't me. Perhaps someone else has got hold of them."

"Don't play games with me. You're the only one who has them. No one else has seen those emails."

"Do you remember when they got personal and intimate? When you couldn't even talk to me about them?"

"Yes," she said, the aggression disappearing from her voice.

"You know if they were to find their way into the media, they'd probably bring the foreign minister down. Can you imagine the scandal? I wonder what your new snooty friends would think after they've read them."

"You bastard! You can't show them to anyone. I sent them to you as my doctor. You make them public, and I'll see you never practice medicine again."

"I don't think the authorities would see it that way, especially after they read the emails you sent me after we first had sex. They're not the type of emails you send to your doctor."

"What do you want?"

"Your bloodsuckers are trying to steal half my assets."

"I can stop that."

"You didn't let me finish, my darling. I put up with you for nearly three years. I deserve something for that. I want five hundred million."

An audible gasp emanated from the earpiece. "Don't call me darling, you bastard. You're not getting one cent of my money."

"My lawyer disagrees. You lived in my house and never contributed anything. Then there's the surgery I did for nothing because I loved you. The courts regularly set aside prenuptial agreements when they're unfair to one party. If we go to court, I'll be asking for two billion. Not only that, I'll instruct my lawyers to find a way of getting your emails admitted into evidence. If they can't, I'll leak them over the internet. That's why I never objected to signing that prenup agreement your stupid old man wanted. Do you want to run the risk of going to court?"

"You never loved me."

"You got that right, but I won't be admitting it in court." Beaumont laughed.

"You're blackmailing me."

"No, I'm not. I'm telling you what I'm going to do if we can't reach an agreement that I'm happy with."

It was dusk when Beaumont locked the back door of his surgery. He could see the glow of a cigarette and a man standing next to the Lamborghini.

"Hello, Simon."

"What do you want, Harry? How did you get in?"

"Never mind. I'm here to offer you some friendly advice. Drop the blackmail threat and your stupid claim. Do it, and Milly will drop her claim for half your assets. You can both get on with your lives and forget about trying to hurt each other."

"And if I don't?"

"You don't want to know. You're not going to get anything from Milly. Walk away while you still can."

"That sounds like a threat to me."

"Put whatever spin you like on it. I'm just trying to help you."

"I bet you are, Harry. If anything happens to me, my lawyers are safeguarding two envelopes that they'll mail immediately. One to *The Daily Telegraph* with copies of the emails, and the other to the New South Wales Police Department. You figure heavily in the second letter."

"Stupid, Simon. Stupid," Cusack said, stubbing his cigarette under his heel.

Chapter 56

Milly had taken a suite in the Hilton pending the settlement of her Point Piper mansion. She was sipping a latte in the bustling lobby coffee shop, Caffe Cino, on Friday night when Harry Cusack joined her. "What did he say?" she asked.

"He's not gonna to back off. He's awfully confident that you're gonna pay. Do you want to tell me what's in those emails?"

"No."

"Well, we need to come up with a plan to stop him. Tell me what his weaknesses are."

"I can't think of any," Milly said, finishing her latte. "He's conceited and thinks he knows everything, but I don't see how we can use that."

"What or who does he love?" Cusack asked, beckoning a waiter. "What's precious to him?"

"Other than himself, I can't think of anything. Oh, he loves his hands. He thinks there's magic in them. He's not wrong."

Cusack shifted his chair closer to Milly. "Maybe if I took a hammer to his hands, he might see reason."

"No, that'd be the worst thing you could do. Then he'd have nothing to lose. All he'd want was revenge, and I wouldn't put anything past him. He might even try to kill me."

"Yeah, and killing him is out of the question. I dunno whether he's bullshitting about those envelopes, but we can't take the risk."

"If it wasn't for the envelopes, could you have him killed?"

"Yeah, no problems. You'd just have to say the word."

"Harry, that's something that's never going to happen. I'm not a murderer."

"I thought you hated him."

"I do, but if it wasn't for him—"

"I understand," Harry said, "but you're making it hard. He's got no weaknesses, doesn't love anything or anyone, and you don't want to touch his hands. Does he hate anyone?"

Milly raised her eyebrows and said, "How does that help?"

Harry held his hands out, palms up. "I'm just looking for an angle. Some leverage."

"Besides me, he hates Brett Golding, but I can't see what good that does. Oh, he'd never admit it, but he's homophobic. Well selectively homophobic. Gay women don't worry him, but gay men make him sick. He won't even operate on them."

"I can understand that." Harry frowned.

"And I can understand why you feel that way, Harry. You're from my father's generation, and God rest his soul, he used to call them poofters. Fortunately, those days are long gone. Why shouldn't two people who love each other be together? Simon is meant to be a man of the times, but he's in a time warp, and would fit right in with yours and Daddy's generation."

Harry closed his eyes and tapped his fingers on the table. "I've got an idea. Hear me out."

For the next ten minutes, Harry outlined his plan.

"I don't like it," Milly said. "It's disgusting."

"It'd solve your problem."

"How are you going to get hold of those pills? What did you call them?"

"Rohypnol. Roofies is their street name. They're the perfect date rape drug. Your father left me a hundred million. There's nothing I can't get my hands on."

"How dangerous are they? If things went wrong, could they kill him?"

"Nah. They're like Valium, but about ten times as potent. The pills can easily be ground into powder, and dissolved without a trace when used to spike a drink. It's tasteless, odorless and takes effect quickly. But here's the great part. It erases memory, brings on amnesia and all traces of the drug disappear within twenty-four hours. It's perfect for our purposes. That's if you've got the courage."

Milly clapped her hands, and said, "Yes, yes, we'll do it, but we won't do it."

"What?" Harry asked, looking puzzled.

Beaumont wasn't surprised when Milly called. "Let's meet and sort the settlement out. I don't want to fight you."

"I'm glad you've come to your senses. I'm not asking that much. Will I come to the Hilton?"

"No. I want to go somewhere quiet where we won't be disturbed. I want to get this over with and never set eyes on you again."

Beaumont remembered Bar 77, the bar that he'd gone to with Samantha Armstrong. It was out of the way and quiet. ""That's easily fixed," Beaumont said, "write this address down. I'll see you there at eight o'clock tonight. Bring your checkbook."

"No, I have a meeting to attend. It'll have to be Friday night."

"Who are you saving tonight? The endangered Tasmanian wombats?"

"You make me sick."

Chapter 57

It was just after eight o'clock when Milly pulled into the ill-lit parking lot of Bar 77. "He's here," she said, nodding toward the yellow Lamborghini parked away from the other cars. The parking lot was half full, and she reversed her Merc into a dark space three spaces from the Lamborghini.

"Of course he's here," Harry said. "Remember what I told you. Don't take any tollways or freeways when you drive the car back to his house. We don't want your gorgeous face appearing on CCTV or being snapped by a camera. Don't speed or do anything to draw attention to yourself. Oh, and make sure you leave fifteen minutes after you've spiked his drink. If you leave it any longer, he won't be able to walk."

"Harry, I don't need any last minute instructions. We've been over it a hundred times."

"Okay, get in there and get it done."

Beaumont was sitting at a table, illuminated by a small lamp. His jacket was hanging over the back of his chair, and he was sipping white wine. "You're late," he said, beckoning the waiter. "Would you like a drink?"

"What are you drinking?"

"Semillon."

"I'll have the same."

"I'm glad you came to your senses," he said. "Five hundred million is nothing for you, and those emails will go viral if they ever see the light of day. Winston Everton's days as foreign minister will be over, and your old boyfriend, Spencer, might find himself in trouble."

"He was never my boyfriend. Do you think I care about him? He's like you. A user. I shared my most intimate thoughts and feelings with you, and then you go and do this. You're worse than him."

Beaumont cast his eyes around the room before staring at Milly. "You're stunningly beautiful. Guys have been ogling you ever since you arrived, and their girlfriends and wives wish you weren't here. Contrast that with three years ago."

"When you've finished complimenting yourself," Milly said, "let's get down to business. I'm prepared to drop my claim for half your assets and pay you fifty million. That's it."

"You're bluffing," Beaumont said. "Cough up the five hundred and you can forget about those emails ever surfacing. Anything less, and who knows? I could take the fifty, but in a few months, I might come back for more. Pay me the five hundred and that will never happen."

"How do you know I'm not recording this?"

"Easy. You know the minute the police knock on my door, those emails are out there. I know you. You'd never run that risk."

Other than his quick glance around the bar, Beaumont had never lost focus, and Milly had had no chance to spike his drink. "You think you hold all the cards," she said. "You might like to know that a friend of mine offered to kill you. You ever come back for another bite; he will."

The smirk that Beaumont had etched on his face disappeared. "You keep that thug, Cusack, away from me." Then he grinned. "Another bite? I knew you'd pay."

"God, I hate you," Milly shouted, waving her hands wildly. The lamp crashed to the floor, and the table was in semi-darkness. As the waiter came over to clean up, Milly tipped the powder into her glass and gently shook it.

"There's glass everywhere. Why don't you take that table?" the waiter said, nodding toward a corner table.

Milly picked up the wine glasses, and they resettled themselves.

"You have my bank account details. Make the transfer on Monday morning. You shouldn't think badly about it. Look at what you were and what your life was like compared to what it is now," Beaumont said, taking a long sip of his wine.

"Bastard! What choice do I have?"

"None if you want to keep your private life private."

Milly drained her glass. "I'm going," she said.

"Me too," Beaumont said, standing up. He felt strange and a little woozy. Nothing a breath of fresh air won't fix, he thought, as he lurched out the door.

Milly stood at the entrance watching Beaumont stagger across the parking lot. He got halfway to his car and turned around. "You drugged me, you bitch!" Then he felt the strong arms of Harry Cusack guiding him into the back of the Merc.

Harry threw the keys of the Lamborghini to Milly. "I'll be right behind you. Remember, stay on the back streets and keep your foot off the accelerator."

Half an hour later, Milly climbed into the front passenger's seat of the Merc. "How's he been?"

"He hasn't moved. I'll drop you at the Hilton and see you tomorrow night."

"Harry, make sure the real thing doesn't happen. Create the illusion and get the photos. I want you to stay with him the whole time."

"You don't hate him. If you did, you'd unleash these guys."

"You don't understand."

Chapter 58

At nine o'clock on Saturday night a dark brown Ford pulled up at the front of The Royal Sydney Hospital. Two men wearing black hoodies lifted a semi-conscious man from the back seat and left him lying on the steps. The men quickly jumped back in the car, and it screeched off down the driveway.

Nurses placed the man on a gurney and wheeled him to emergency, where he was surrounded by other patients. A fourth-year resident was treating a woman lying on the gurney next to the man, when the resident shouted, "Nurse, nurse, it's Dr. Beaumont. Wheel him into one of the consulting rooms. I'll be there in a minute."

"Dr. Beaumont, Dr. Beaumont," the resident said, "can you hear me?"

Beaumont muttered something incoherent.

"Jesus, he doesn't half stink, does he? He smells like he's been drenched in aftershave, and there's oil all over him. What's he been up to?" one of the nurses asked.

"Rapid breathing, rapid pulse rate and dilated pupils," the resident said.

"Where, where am I?" Beaumont slurred.

"You're in The Royal Sydney Hospital, Doctor. You're safe. What happened to you?"

"Hospital? What? What am I doing in hospital?"

"Doctor, think. Where have you been? What were you doing? Who were you with?"

"I can't remember. Can't remember anything. What day is it?"

"It's Saturday night. Tell me, what you did today?" the resident asked.

"I don't know."

"What's the last thing you remember doing?"

"I was in my office yesterday. I can't remember leaving to go home. Maybe I was robbed."

The resident reached out and picked up a small metal box. "You had your cell phone, keys, and wallet. Is there anything missing from your wallet? Cash or credit cards?"

Beaumont flicked through his wallet. "No, nothing. I think we can rule robbery out."

"Why do I smell?" Beaumont asked. "And what's that greasy stuff on my body and hands?"

"I thought you might have gone a bit heavy with the aftershave," the resident said.

"It's horrible. I'd never wear anything like that."

"Do you want us to call the police? Security's just examined the CCTV footage and you were dropped off by two men in a brown Ford. Does that ring any bells?"

"No, don't get the police involved. I have nothing that I can tell them. I don't know why I was in that car," Beaumont said, putting his knuckles to his temples in a vain attempt to remember.

"I'm going to run a few tests to see if we can find out what happened to you," the resident said.

"No, you're not," Beaumont said, swinging his legs off the gurney. "I'm feeling better. I'm getting out of here."

"Let's at least do your bloods."

"No, get someone to arrange a taxi for me. I need to get home and shower."

Beaumont sat in the back of the taxi and closed his eyes. He knew that the more he tried to remember, the more frustrated he would become. If he relaxed, the answers would come. As the taxi pulled into his driveway, he could see the Lamborghini pulled up to the garage door. He knew that he'd never subject it to the elements over-night. He always parked it in the garage. Did he park it there or did someone else? He was tired. Perhaps after a good night's sleep, the answers would come to him.

On Sunday morning, Beaumont awoke refreshed and remembered meeting with Milly to talk about the settlement. He also recollected her accidentally smashing a lamp and the waiter showing them to a new table. He could not recall leaving the bar, getting into his car or driving home.

The only way he would find out what happened at the bar was by talking to Milly. When he called her, he went straight through to her voicemail, and he left a short message. When he hadn't heard from her by midday, he called again but again went through to her voicemail. His luck didn't improve when he called the Hilton later that afternoon and was told that Ms. Milgate was not in her suite. Beaumont made his last call at 10 P.M., but Milly still didn't answer. He went to bed, frustrated and angry, knowing that he was operating in the morning.

Chapter 59

The nurses knew there was something wrong when Beaumont told them not to worry about the music; that he preferred to operate in silence. They were used to his temper outbursts. However, they had never seen him quite as fixated before, and his level of intensity was extreme. He operated at a fanatical tempo, and while the surgery was up to his incredibly high standards, there was something different about him.

"Are you alright, Doctor?" one of the nurses asked.

"Why wouldn't I be?" he snapped.

At 2 P.M. he sewed sutures in the upper eyelids of a forty-five-year-old, male, advertising executive.

Then he walked briskly from the hospital to his surgery. "Did Milly call, Julie?" he asked.

"No, but Mr. Golding's called three times and wants you to call him as soon as you can."

"When I get time."

The day's mail was open in his in-tray. Sitting on the bottom was a large, unopened envelope marked *Private & Confidential, Simon Beaumont*. He was about to open it when Julie buzzed to ask whether she should put Mr. Golding through. Beaumont hesitated before accepting the call. "Hello, Brett. What can I do for you?"

"What can you do for me?" Golding laughed. "Nothing. Absolutely nothing. I was in court when you appeared as an expert witness for Anita Bartlett. I guess you won't be appearing again anytime soon."

"It was you, you bastard! You fed that information about me to that slimy bloodsucker. Those documents I submitted to the Institute were confidential. You breached that confidentiality. I ought to sue you," Beaumont said, tearing the large envelope open.

"Be my guest," Golding said, in a mocking tone. "A juicy court case will keep your checkered background in front of the media. I'd enjoy that."

"No," Beaumont shrieked, and dropped the phone.

"God, there's no need to overreact, you nearly blew my eardrums out. Simon, Simon, are you there?"

Julie and Mary raced into Beaumont's office. "What's wrong?" Mary asked. "You're as white as a ghost."

"Nothing," Beaumont said, dropping the phone in its cradle with one hand while shooing the women out with the other.

There were two glossy photographs in the envelope. In the first, he was naked, spread-eagled and lying face down on a bed. He had a dopey smile on his face. Three naked, aroused men, their bodies glistening with oil, stood around the bed. Their faces were blacked out. In the second photograph, he had a sick smile on his face and was lying on his side facing away from the camera. A heavily tattooed, naked man, with an enormous erection lay on the other side of the bed, his arm around Beaumont's shoulders. The man's face was blacked out. Beaumont put the photos in his bottom desk drawer and buried them in files before charging to the toilet. He hadn't eaten since breakfast, and he dry retched violently. His eyes watered, and he was unsteady on his feet. He now knew what had happened. As he rinsed his face with cold water, he trembled uncontrollably. He couldn't face anyone like this, so he sat in a cubicle and tried to regain his composure. Tears ran down his cheeks. How could Milly have done that to him? Thirty minutes later, he made his way back to his office. "

No calls. I don't want to be disturbed," he shouted, as he closed the door.

He was still shaking when he picked up the phone and punched in Milly's number. Unlike Sunday, she answered on the first ring. "I've been waiting for your call," she said. "How are you feeling?"

"You bitch! I feel sick. I can hardly think."

"And you've only seen the tame photos."

"How could you do it? How could you?"

"I had five hundred million reasons."

"If I went to the police, you and that thug, Cusack, would go to jail for a long time. I should."

"You're probably right." Milly laughed. "I can see the photos being entered into evidence. You've always wanted to become world famous."

"What are you going to do with them?"

"Nothing. Providing no one ever sees my emails, no one will ever see them. If my emails are published, those photos and many more will find their way to the internet. Do you understand?"

"I'm not a fool. I still don't how you could've done it. I would've never done that to you. Never."

"Daddy never trusted you. He suspected that you did my surgery for nothing so you could get to his money. He was right, wasn't he?"

"That's a joke. You were as ugly as sin, and I turned you into an oil painting. Now you're bitching. No matter how much I hated you, I could've never done what you did to me. Every time I think about it I want to vomit."

"Maybe I didn't."

"What's that supposed to mean?"

"I just needed the photos. I didn't need to have you raped."

"You mean I didn't get–"

"You'll never know," Milly interrupted. "Goodbye, Simon."

The End